TURNING West

—— THE PERSIAN PRINCE BOOK III ——

JACK A. TAYLOR

TURNING West

THE PERSIAN PRINCE BOOK III

Scripture quotations taken from The Holy Bible, New International Version®, NIV®. Copyright © 1973, 1978, 1984, 2011 by Biblica, Inc. Used with permission of Zondervan. All rights reserved worldwide. www.zondervan.com

Soft cover ISBN: 978-1-4866-2739-4
Hard cover ISBN: 978-1-4866-2741-7
eBook ISBN: 978-1-4866-2740-0

Word Alive Press
119 De Baets Street Winnipeg, MB R2J 3R9
www.wordalivepress.ca

WORD ALIVE
—P R E S S—

Cataloguing in Publication information can be obtained from Library and Archives Canada.

One

The wind off the Persian Gulf carried the stench of brine and ashes as Ardeshir Ben Nabonidus, prince of Persia, paced before the crumbling mud walls of his hut. This land had once shimmered with rows of pomegranate trees heavy with ruby fruit, wheat fields swaying like a golden sea, and corrals filled with wild horses. Now the farm lay in ruin, a blistered plain littered with blackened stalls, drifting ash, and charred stumps.

The air was thick with the acrid bite of burned reeds from a nearby swamp, the sour tang of stagnant irrigation ditches, and the faint scent of dates clinging to a lone surviving palm. Above him, the sun blistered the landscape, its molten light catching the jagged bones of his shattered homestead.

His shadow fell against the planks of the doorway as he cocked his head, listening. He looked up at the red pennant hanging limply from a post marking the entrance to the former farm. The sound of his son's cries arose from the hut, defying the vengeance of the angry Han general who had placed that pennant as a declaration of his emperor's displeasure. Ardeshir had, after all, escaped the Han and taken the emperor's own daughter as his wife.

He continued to look about. The knee-deep snow, flowing down from the Zagros mountains, topped the charred timbers of ransacked barns, residences, and the once thriving banquet hall. An illusion of peace settled over this land still whimpering from war.

As a black raven swooped around the hut and across the yard, taking refuge in the swaths of forest surrounding the former sanctuary, Ardeshir set his back against the door and entered the hut's darkened interior. He scooped up the wailing child and ferried his son to the waiting breast of Lu Hou, his bride.

"Artabanas," he whispered, puffing out his chest as he smiled at his son. "This Persian prince of ashes seems to demand an audience!"

The young father watched the infant attack his mother's nipple with the ferociousness of a young lion. The boy suckled and sighed as the room swallowed up the last echoes of his demands.

As Ardeshir knelt, wrapping a newly crafted blanket around mother and son, a knock at the door reverberated in the quiet.

"Shalom," a female voice called out. "It is me, Farzana."

Lu Hou nodded and Ardeshir rose to answer.

The young Armenian woman he encountered at the door unfastened a bundle from her back and revealed a squirming child.

"Shalom, Prince," Farzana greeted him, placing her child in Ardeshir's arms. "There's more snow here than I've ever seen this low off the mountains. Watch this boy. Davit has the lion strength of his father." She kicked off her boots. "Every time I think of the violent way he was conceived three years ago, it makes me shudder. But then I let him nurse and he becomes the lamb which Sanjay and I agreed to raise. How is your little one?"

"He might be a twin to your own son," Ardeshir said. "Lu Hou could use the encouragement of a mother like you, though. Is there any word about my sister, Yas, or any of her men?"

Farzana shook her head. "Sanjay should be back soon from the market and the Temple of Fire in Susa, where he's been inquiring."

The woman lowered herself onto a cushioned pillow and watched Lu Hou tend to the baby.

"When the Han emperor's warlord attacked us here at the farm, Sanjay and I were in the city, getting supplies. When we returned, Sanjay buried everyone in the paddock where the wild horses were kept. It took him weeks… but as you know, your sister wasn't among the dead."

"I can't imagine the trauma of seeing your home and family destroyed like that," Lu Hou spoke up. She switched the baby to her other breast. "My home in the emperor's garden was so peaceful… apart from General Ban Chao and his leopard. After our long journey here, three moon cycles, when I saw that my new husband had brought me from that palace to a field of ashes, I was not happy. I thought I had married a prince who would be honored by his people."

"It wasn't my people who dishonored me in this place," Ardeshir said. "I think we all grow up with the idea that our home is the only place we can truly be happy."

Without shame, Farzana began to nurse her boy. As Ardeshir took a step back, the two women broke into motherly conversation.

Ardeshir bundled himself in a fleece-lined sheepskin jacket and deerskin cape before stepping outside. For three weeks, he and Lu Hou had hidden in the tunnels under the old barn as he scavenged for suitable boards to build a home for his new family. He had overturned a cart at the tunnel entrance and covered it with blankets to block the wind and snow he knew would soon come.

That's when Sanjay, his young farmhand, found him hauling wood and lent a hand. For two months, they had moved to more comfortable surroundings in nearby Susa while the shack and horse barn were finished. Despite Lu Hou's pleas for them to wait until the snows had passed, however, he had moved her into this mud-plastered hovel after the birth of their son.

Sanjay unhitched a cart from his horse and unloaded the supplies he and Farzana had brought from the market.

"Still no word on your sister from those in Susa." Sanjay led the stallion toward the horse barn. "One survivor said that everyone was either killed or captured. He hid in a tree outside the fence until it was all over."

The horse sauntered into the shelter and Sanjay closed the door after it. Turning back toward the cart, he helped Ardeshir unload a heavy crate of fruits and vegetables.

"The witness was hardly old enough to be a man," Sanjay continued. "He said hundreds of warriors charged in before anyone even arose. The only reason he lived is that he was off the property looking for his dog, which had chased after a rabbit at first light. He used to curse that dog. Now he blesses it."

"It's the mercy of the Almighty that spared you," Ardeshir said. "Every blister and callous on your hands is a sacred scar of love for those who perished. I would promise vengeance against the emperor's warlord, but my army is gone and my zest for life has withered. I can only offer to help you rebuild this farm until my people restore my honor."

"According to the rumors, the emperor's warlord killed you and your wife. A trader told me that the emperor's daughter played a flute and the warlord's men killed a girl with a bone flute not far from here. They didn't find you, so they burned the farm and killed everyone." Sanjay gestured to the red pennant hanging limply from the post at the former farm's main entrance. "That pennant is their warning that no one escapes the hand of the emperor."

Ardeshir spat on the ground. "I should remove that cursed symbol of death."

"Do I have your permission to take it down?" Sanjay asked. "Even when I was stolen by raiders from my village in Hindustan, I didn't have to witness such devastation. I can't imagine what you endured to snatch the emperor's daughter

3

from his palace. I told Farzana that we have the prince of Persia and the princess of the Han Empire living together like paupers." He stretched out his hands and pivoted in a slow circle. "You're rulers of all this and only have one family of orphans for your subjects. What purpose will you find to regain your rightful place?"

"My father taught me to seek peace and pursue it. I'll first pursue peace by finding out what happened to my family. My father was taken by pirates toward the south of the Great Sea, and my aunt is a dying queen on her throne in the north. My sister has disappeared, and perhaps she's been captured by the emperor's warlord in the east. For now I'll turn to the west and find those who can help me in my quests."

Sanjay nodded gravely. "I can watch over your family while you're gone. Farzana and the princess will enjoy raising their sons together. We can relocate to Susa where the followers of the Way have a shelter for people like us. I'll find laborers and rebuild this place to its former glory."

"Let's not share this with our wives yet," Ardeshir said. "The princess has hardly gotten used to the idea that this is my kingdom for now."

Just as they looked up, a rider with the bearing of a cataphract warrior trotted into view atop the hill.

"There's a rider watching us," Sanjay pointed out. "Not sure if I recognize who it is. Should we move these crates inside in case there are more warriors on the way?"

"Yes!" Ardeshir prompted. "I'll help you with the largest two and then you can take the rest in while I arrange the weapons. Move as if you're in no hurry. I hope you remember how to fight."

"Does this mean the winter is past?" Sanjay asked. "The worst thing about the coming new year and spring is that every warlord gets itchy to stretch their legs and prove themselves in some conquest. Maybe they'll think we are poor squatters taking advantage of this empty land. If there's more than one of them, I won't be able to do much to help."

Ardeshir squinted up at the hill. "I don't see the rider any longer. Let's hurry, in case there are any bandits around who may want to take our supplies. I'm sure they must have seen your wagon and followed you. And we should probably move the women into the tunnels."

"Maybe the best thing we can do is to hide the supplies under the snow. If they check the house or barn, they won't find anything to steal."

Ardeshir agreed, and soon Sanjay got busy shoveling snow off a patch of ground large enough to store all the supplies from the wagon. He would cover it with blankets and settle snow overtop everything once it was secure.

Meanwhile, Ardeshir returned to the hut, inhaling deeply of the cold air.

When he entered, he found Lu Hou and Farzana so comfortable by the fire that it took some persuasion to move them away.

"We haven't got much time if there are soldiers moving our way," Ardeshir insisted. "I hope this will be nothing. Wrap the boys up warm. Yourselves too. It's cool in those tunnels and we won't be able to light a fire until we're sure it's safe."

"I cannot believe that people live like this," Lu Hou grumbled. "Where are the gardens? Where is the peace? Where is the music?"

Farzana smiled as she bundled up her boy. "It will all be here soon enough. We only have to survive until then."

Yas shook the bars of her cage as the cart rumbled through the farthest reaches of Hindustan.

"You're my prize for the emperor's fighting games," sneered the warlord from a safe distance. He wore a vest of lacquered rawhide, hardened leather, bronze, and iron. His rawhide helmet was supplemented with a layer of metal lamellar. His shield hung loosely off his shoulder along with his crossbow. A javelin fit into a notch on the side of his saddle. Various daggers and throwing stars were secured across his vest.

His protection was primitive compared to a Persian cataphract or Roman legionnaire, but his skill on a horse was unmatched. Yas had witnessed this in person during the attack on the farm, not to mention during several more recent raids by adventurers trying to intercept the war party returning east.

Her mind replayed the events of that terrible day of the attack on the farm. Although she had fought her way through a swath of warriors, her sword and javelin bringing death to all who dared confront her, a group of six martial artists had snuck up and managed to capture her in a net, sweeping her off her horse. At least she'd managed to kill two of them before being secured in her mobile prison.

"If I escape, I'll take three of your men for every man you took of mine," she yelled towards her captor.

The warlord smiled and shrugged. "No speak Persian," he said in Persian. "You will show your fighting skills to the emperor. He may allow you to live and look after our three hundred thousand horses. We have thirty thousand slaves like you to care for them. We're breeding the horses for war, and soon we will erase the Persian Empire from the memories of men."

She settled back in the cage and seethed.

Rumbling through the villages of Hindustan was a humiliation. Common folk often stood at the edge of the road and threw rotting vegetation and dirt at her. Other cages were crammed with prisoners too, all of them huddling for warmth. But she was kept alone and cold throughout their journey into the mountains. It was enough to test the limits of her endurance.

Now she snarled at anyone who dared mock her, the result of her forced helplessness. General Ban Chou was the worst of them all.

At least she began to realize that her grasp of Cantonese was starting to return.

Another horseman, Colonel Zhang Wei, rode up beside her. She recognized him from her last trip to the emperor's gardens.

Instead of snarling, she tried a different tactic.

"What did you do with my brother and the emperor's daughter?" Yas asked as gently and calmly as she could in broken Cantonese. "They were supposed to be back in Susa a year ago."

"The council fed them to the lions," the colonel said. "Your brother was a disgrace to your country. His truth was of no use to our people and his wisdom no match for the emperor or the council of twelve. He was weak and needed to use magic to overcome his enemies."

"What kind of magic?" Yas persisted.

"Knowledge like that is not permitted for a man like me. I am told what I need to know. And that is not one of the things I need to know."

"You remember the emperor's Persian chef, don't you?" Yas asked.

"You mean the man you set your heart on marrying?" Wei replied.

"What happened to him? How many of us did you capture?"

"We have thirty-eight of your people," the soldier reported. "As for the chef you speak of, he's in the front carriage. He will be given the opportunity to return to his position, since his replacement was not satisfactory. The others will die in the fighting games, in the park of wild things. Or they'll be used as slaves—that is, if they have any special skills we can learn from."

Yas groaned. "Why didn't you kill us all?"

"We are a people of mercy. We destroy those who deserve justice and those who try to oppose us. Your brother and the princess faced justice. The men at your farm tried to oppose us."

"You didn't ride all this way to capture one chef," Yas said. "You were here for another reason." The truth slowly fell into place. "You came all this way for my brother, didn't you? You said that he used magic. He escaped, didn't he?"

The soldier looked away and stared straight ahead up the road. Suddenly, he heeled his horse forward without responding.

As Yas watched him go, she wondered. Could Ardeshir truly be alive? The small flicker of hope heightened her determination to survive. For now she just needed to conserve her energy and spend her time observing the strengths and weaknesses of these warriors.

For one thing, all of the men bowed and catered to the general. All except one; it soon became clear that Wei would be her target to form an alliance.

The border of the Han Empire was so obvious that a line may as well have been drawn in the sand. The emperor had secured his territory by assigning his favored warriors farms after their military service, and these farms tended to run along the empire's frontier. These warriors were thus given responsibility for guarding the heart of the empire. As each generation of soldiers completed their service, another swath of land was added. In this way, the empire encroached inexorably on its neighbors, who felt helpless against the slow creep.

Once inside the borders of the empire, the mocking Yas endured from children and villagers grew more intense. They no longer just threw vegetation but stones, sticks, and even human refuse. The warlord seemed to relish this treatment and he slowed the procession during the worst of these displays to prolong his prisoners' agony.

Once a village had been traversed, he himself made a round of the prisoners, mocking them one by one.

"Where is your Persian pride, now?" he called to Yas. "You stink so bad, even the lions won't want to eat you. When we reach the gardens, we'll take your stinking clothes away and let people see how worthless you are without your flimsy protections. A woman like you? In leadership? It only shows how weak your armies are."

There was no refuge from this torment. Her clothes did reek of filth, rot, and sweat. And when the cooks at last resorted to throwing the rice through the bars so it landed in the muck oozing between her toes, she stopped even trying to scramble for it.

On the third day after entering the empire, while the warlord was far to the front of the caravan, the colonel stopped by her cage with a small gourd of water.

"Wash yourself," he said. "Clean your cage. We are a people of mercy. I will bring you something to eat after dark."

The water was hardly enough to clean her face and arms, but at least it helped raise her sense of dignity and hope. The man's gesture seemed to affirm her judgment of his character.

So when the sun slid away that evening and the emperor's soldiers huddled around their fires laughing, she waited.

The quietest step behind the cage alerted her to company.

"I am here," Wei said. "I have more water. Some food. You must stay strong for what is yet to come."

Her hands shook from the chill, but she snatched these offerings through the bars and gorged on bread, rice, and fruit. She drank deeply of the water and later felt grateful for the darkness when it came time to relieve herself in the corner of her enclosure.

Every few nights, Wei returned. His visits became a fixture of her imprisonment and helped her endure the daylight humiliations.

When the caravan passed rushing streams, overflowing from the spring thaws, she longed for a chance to plunge into their turbulent currents to be swept away, wash, or drink her fill.

It was the flowers bursting with color on the side of the road that let her know spring had come to the emperor's land. But she felt no hope. Hope had curled up in the corner, subsumed by the reek of her own vomit and refuse.

The colonel soon stopped coming, for she grew too despondent to reach out for what he had to offer. Death would be a welcome friend.

It seemed at first that their efforts to bury the supplies under the snow and snuggle away in the tunnels would be wasted, for the spring sun threatened to melt the white covering and expose their rations. Ardeshir moved the horse into the forest and built a small corral with plenty of feed that he refilled each morning. He and Sanjay then alternated guard duty.

But no more horsemen arrived. There was no imminent attack.

On the fifth day of their watch, Sanjay suggested that they move back to the shack—and that's when the militia arrived in force.

The attacking horsemen didn't even dismount. They charged into the farm-yard and shot flaming arrows into the shack, waited a few moments, then raced away when no signs of life emerged.

At dusk, Ardeshir crept out of the tunnels and secured his horse. He over-turned the cart and filled it with the supplies from under the snow. He and San-jay helped the women and babies into the back, then set out toward Susa.

"We'll have to raise an army of our own before we can start trying to reclaim my royal rights," Ardeshir said once they were underway. "We'll track down the friends of the Way and consider what the Almighty has for us after that."

He remembered his father telling him about the fish symbols drawn in unusual places. Those symbols would guide him to a hidden refuge.

It took most of the afternoon to locate the first fish symbol near the market. Ardeshir would have missed it as nothing more significant than scratches on a post if he hadn't been searching so intently.

They located seven fish before finding the place.

An old woman, hunched over a gnarly cane, shuffled to the entrance of the shelter at the end of the trail, greeting the two families. After explaining his situ-ation, the hostess welcomed them while a servant brought them tea.

"I am Adrina, caretaker of this home," she said in a husky whisper. "I knew your father and mother before they even came to this country. We shared many adventures before discovering that this is where the Almighty wanted us to come. I was sad to lose your mother... and now I hear we may have lost your father."

"How did you meet my parents?" Ardeshir asked.

Adrina took time to sip her tea. "My sister and I travelled west with our grandfather. Thugs killed him and sold us to the Temple of Artemis in Ephe-sus. Your mother was a priestess there before she escaped with the help of your father." She paused, as if remembering something. Her lips twisted in a grimace and her brows furrowed. "It's a long story, but your father was a gladiator. He even became the emperor's champion. We'd all become followers of the Way and the followers of Artemis tried to destroy us in the forum. Your father fought to save us. We travelled to Susa ahead of him... and I'm happy to say I met you when you were first born."

"Did you know my aunt?" Ardeshir asked.

"Oh, yes. She has been a queen most of her adult life, although we only met later." She paused for another sip of tea. "I hear she's dying. If it weren't for you, the royal line may have died out by now. I also hear that the Magi's militia is working hard to find you."

She nodded toward a young girl who was serving the assembled group, passing a fruit platter around the circle of guests. Ardeshir reached for a handful of dates.

"Your aunt was so distraught when your father was taken by those pirates," Adrina added. "She still believes he may be alive, waiting for someone to rescue him."

Ardeshir popped a date into his mouth and smiled. "Knowing my father, he'll find his own way out of his problems. One day I may go west and see what's happened for myself."

Just then, Lu Hou placed a delicate hand on his forearm. "Husband, don't you think you have taken me far enough west? Some in my village believe the sun falls into the sea not far from here. I'd like to stay in one place and raise our little Prince Artabanas."

She rocked the boy, who stared up at her until his eyes closed and his body went limp.

Two

The tickling sensation was like a feather brushing across her cheek. Yas opened one eye and strained to focus through the blur. A brilliant red tulip hovered over her face before she watched it descend for another brush against her skin. She breathed in and noted the distinct scent, so different from all the crud around her in the cage.

"Wake up!" a child's voice urged in Cantonese. "Wake up! Your flower is waiting."

The light rain from the night before left her soaked, but discomfort had been her way of life for months. She groaned and the flower vanished.

Something poked her in the back.

"Wake up, sleeping bear!" another voice said. "You stink!"

When the poking persisted, she reached behind her to grab the source of irritation—but the poker was too quick.

Yas rolled onto one elbow and focused on three wide-eyed girls. One held up the red tulip, one a handful of wisteria and bamboo, and the last a fistful of peonies.

"Leave me alone," she growled in Persian.

The child with the tulip stepped forward and dropped her flower through the bars. It fell into a blob of mud the size of her head and deflated. The girl with the bamboo and wisteria deposited her gift atop the tulip. The last girl tossed her peonies through the bars. Some of them made it onto the pile.

Yas glared at the trio, then picked up the tulip and shoved it into her mouth. She chewed several times and spat it out through the bars. The giver of the flower looked on with dismay and pouted. The other two wrapped their arms around their friend to console her.

One of the comforters looked up and shook her finger at Yas. "Ungrateful bear!"

At that moment, Colonel Wei emerged from behind a hedge and scowled. The girls scurried away and Yas focused on the man she still hoped might become an ally.

"We have arrived," the colonel said. "It is time to wash and prepare you for presentation. Take off your clothes and someone will throw water on you."

"I'm not taking off my clothes," Yas said. "If the emperor wants to see me, he can smell what General Ban Chou has done to me. Not even your animals suffer like I have."

Wei pivoted and walked away without a further word. He returned in minutes with a group of soldiers and four women. His orders were clear.

"Wash. Clean."

The soldiers began by throwing buckets of water into the cage. Yas held onto the bars and growled.

After a deluge of water had been tossed at her, one of the soldiers unlocked the cage. Yas attempted to leap past them but only succeeded in having them rip off her tunic and tackle her to the ground. The scrawny, filthy bag of bones she had become had no strength to resist.

The men held her down while the women scrubbed her clean. She ceased to struggle and allowed her mind to ride free on her stallion across the plains of Persia. At least Ardeshir wasn't here to witness her humiliation.

Ardeshir and Sanjay huddled around six candles and cups of tea with four other members of the Way as they discussed what to do next. In the past month, the group had returned to the farm and resurrected several of its buildings. There had been no other incursions by the cataphracts, but Lu Hou and Farzana still didn't feel safe to take their sons back, especially with Ardeshir continuing to speak of heading west to find his father.

Adrina hovered nearby, ensuring that their clay mugs were filled. "Now, don't you worry about your wife and son," she said to Ardeshir. "Farzana and I will take good care of them while you're away. Of course you must find your father while you can."

One of the clay lamps began to flicker and Ardeshir took it into the food preparation room and refilled it with olive oil. The wick sputtered back into full flame as he returned to the gathering, adding its warmth to the other three lamps sitting in alcoves on the wall.

"I'll be looking for the thespian assassins in Caesarea," he announced. "They'll know where I need to go next. I'll take a horse and leave right after the sabbath. Or maybe I'll use a chariot."

"Your last trip there didn't go so well," Sanjay reminded him. "Are you sure you don't want to take the Royal Road? You could take a convoy by road all the way to Ephesus. King Darius the Great built that road so our couriers could get from Susa to Sardis in nine days. It would take three full moon cycles to walk that far. And a horse or a chariot isn't safe along some of that stretch."

Ardeshir shook his head. "I'd never last that long in the saddle, not at that speed. And it's unrealistic to think I can keep up with the Persian couriers. I'll be fortunate to get to Caesarea in one moon cycle without wearing myself out—or the horse. A trading caravan does seem like a good idea, though. But it seems like such a long time to be away, chasing a fading possibility, while my wife and son wait for me here."

Lu Hou placed a hand on her husband's shoulder. "He's asleep," she said. "If you don't search for your father, you'll always wonder. Your soul will remain restless until you die. Your mind will always be searching, and I will lose you. I believe we are safe from the emperor's men for now, and your sister can take care of herself."

Ardeshir took her in his arms and let her rest her head against his chest. "I feel great shame for not going after my sister. She travelled half the world for me. Going after her would be the right thing to do."

"Your sister came to my father with an army and a caravan of gifts." Lu Hou gazed up into his eyes. "What do you have to offer the emperor? How would you even hope to get through Hindustan in your condition?"

He pulled her close again. "As usual, you see with the eye of truth. If I can rescue my father, perhaps there will be a later opportunity to raise an army and find Yas. We'll entrust her into the hands of the Almighty."

Yas was propped up by two sentries as she stood before the emperor in the palace. They forced her head to look down and she noted the red silk gown sagging off her bony body like a shapeless sack. Incense filled the room and stung her eyes.

Water had been poured down her throat, but her mouth felt raspy and dry. Her tongue felt swollen and unresponsive.

"So this is the mighty warrior who fascinated our war council." The emperor turned to her. "What might do you bring this time? Where is your brother and his wife?"

So her instincts had been right. It seemed that her brother had escaped.

She turned her palms up, the sign for seeking permission to speak.

"Speak truth!" the emperor said.

What did the sovereign of truth want from her? She rolled her tongue around her mouth, grasping for words. They came out in a whisper.

"The last thing I heard was that my brother and the princess were here," she ventured. "That you fed them to the lions."

One of the guardians boxed her ears and her knees buckled. These brutes clearly weren't happy with that answer. She shook her head as the soldiers attempted to pull her back to her feet.

"There is no princess," the emperor said. "If you mention her again, we will cut out your tongue and feed it to the wild things."

She stifled a smile. "I know nothing else."

The guardians dragged her from the room and dumped her outside the door of the palace. The hospitality was certainly different this time when compared to her previous visit!

Two other soldiers laid her on a stretcher board and carried her past the koi pond to a dark, dank space. Although she was waist high off the ground, they flipped the board and let her fall to the hard floor. She gasped for breath.

Within the hour, a young woman arrived with a torch and set it into an alcove. She brought in a small bowl half-filled with rice and another half-filled with a broth of some kind.

"Eat to live," the woman said before bowing and leaving.

Yas looked around and realized they had deposited her in a small cavern, apparently carved out of the granite. Rivulets of water dripped down one rock-face to form a pool the size of her hand; it was shallower than the length of her index finger. A rat sat transfixed at the edge of the darkness, its nose quivering. Nothing else was visible.

She crawled toward the bowls, keeping an eye on the rat. The blue rice bowl had fine etchings of a dragon and a unicorn. The red broth bowl had etchings of a serpent, a fish, and a leopard. She sipped the broth and savored the rice a few grains at a time.

She hadn't been brought all this way to die. Feeling renewed determination, she left a few grains for the rat. It nibbled them greedily.

The last thing she wanted was to fall asleep and give that rodent the chance to nibble off her toes. Of course, if the situation got really bad, she could eat the rat too...

She tucked her feet under her red silk robe, cross-legged, and leaned against the wall near the entrance. The rat responded by moving back to its corner. The torch wouldn't last forever, though.

A week after his last embrace with Lu Hou and Artabanas, Ardeshir swung up into his saddle to resume his journey after having taken a much-needed pause at a rest stop. The fusion of color across the landscape, accompanied by a heady array of perfumes, heightened his senses to the wonder of creation. Gentle spring streams had transformed into rushing rivers, demanding creative efforts to pass through the waters.

Hakob, the Armenian caravan leader he had paid to accompany him, was a seasoned veteran of the journey along the Royal Road and had recruited sufficient mercenaries to secure protection through the dangerous hinterlands as they moved through Armenia toward Syria.

The two men had bonded quickly when Ardeshir explained that he was travelling west to find his father, who had been the emperor's champion in Ephesus. Hakob's uncle had been a gladiator in Damascus but hadn't lasted long enough to become a champion. Hakob now pledged to show Ardeshir some of the combat techniques he had learned to defend himself on the road.

One of the most amazing parts of the journey so far had come during a side trip to explore a tunnel under the Euphrates River at Babylon.

"This tunnel was built hundreds of years ago by Queen Semiramis to connect her two palaces," Hakob had explained. "You can see that these arches are plastered with bitumen. The walls are twenty bricks thick and the tunnel is twice my height... and more than that across. You could drive a chariot through here if you want."

"How in the world did she build a passage under a river?" Ardeshir asked.

Hakob chuckled. "She diverted the river into four temporary lakes so the stream could dry out. It took one hundred sixty days to dig a channel whose roof was even with the riverbed. After the tunnel was pitched tight, she used the water of the Euphrates to seal the top and make it hard as stone."

Shivers had raced up his spine and down his arms. What if the roof caved in? Standing inside the tunnel, knowing that the river rushed by overhead, gave him an eerie feeling. He much preferred the carefully constructed stone bridges built by the Persians and Romans. Their only problem was that the crossings attracted bandits.

At one Euphrates crossing in northern Syria, the caravan camped out for three days in preparation for just such a crossing. Four other caravans were ahead of them and three further caravans crossed from the other side.

On the third night, the fires flickered low sometime after midnight. That's when the first screams of terror shattered the night.

This is what Hakob and his men had prepared for. Horsemen charged through the camp hurling firebrands onto tents, tarps, and carriage coverings. The flames spread quickly and panic drove traders, passengers, and soldiers into their carefully rehearsed formation.

Ardeshir raced to the riverbank and dipped in the four buckets he had been assigned. He then rushed back, spilling half his water, but doused the flames on the cook's wagon. Others were right beside him throwing their water on other hotspots.

The soldiers formed a circle around the encampment and a small band chased after the ambushers. Once several of the mercenaries had been drawn away to the pursuit, another group of bandits stormed the enclosure for the horses, camels, and donkeys. An elite troop lay in wait; their crossbows took out most of the raiders.

By sunrise, there was little evidence of the ambush. Dead raiders had been dumped in the bush for recovery by their compatriots, and the destroyed tarps and coverings had been replaced.

The soldiers were mounted and wary. Hakob organized the group and completed the river crossing without further incident. Afterward he took the time to dismiss his mercenaries and pay them for their services.

Ardeshir breathed in relief as they crossed into Roman-occupied territory. The rest of the trip would depend on Roman oversight. Indeed, the first legionnaires they encountered were impressive towers of strength, their armor glistening in the sun.

Standing by Ardeshir, Hakob pointed to a road crew of Gauls digging a new route to the north.

"The Romans have more than a hundred provinces like this one connected by over three hundred roads," said Hakob. "They mark them in miles and have more than two hundred fifty thousand miles spreading out in patterns like a spiderweb. They're built to last and will make it so much easier for us to travel quickly."

"I'll leave you at Damascus," Ardeshir told him. "My contacts are in Caesarea."

Hakob waved. "If you're in Damascus in two moon cycles from today, I'll be loading up to head back. If you find your father, congratulate him for me. I'm a great fan of the games and pay homage to the great gladiators of our day."

It took less than a day for Ardeshir to find a caravan heading to Caesarea. The donkey carts contained apples, olives, figs, and dates bound for Rome. The camels carried spices and silk and handcrafted pottery from the Orient.

The three-day journey passed quickly, despite the nagging backache Ardeshir suffered from being in the saddle so long. Without Hakob to distract him now, he had many matters to wonder about. Would he be able to find the thespian assassins? Was his father still alive? Had the members of the Magi's militia or the emperor's brigade found Lu Hou and Artabanas? Did Yas still live?

His prayers focused on finding either Arsama or Tertullian. Arsama was the tall, broad-chested Persian convert to the Way who had alerted him on his last trip about his father's plans toward Ephesus. The man had defended Ardeshir after being attacked by a gang of sailors. Tertullian, the crafty leader of the thespian assassins, had rescued them when the situation became overwhelming; he liked to disguise himself as an old man bent over his cane, despite the fact that he was a head taller than any other man Ardeshir knew.

From a rise overlooking the Great Sea, Ardeshir watched a flotilla of Roman warships glide into the harbor. These majestic weapons of death were meant to guard the trading vessels that held together life in the empire. Antlike men scurried up and down the warships' masts pulling in the sails as four levels of rowers maneuvered toward the dock. They avoided the dilapidated buildings on the south side of the bay, as well as the aging dock surrounded by old fishing vessels.

Both the new and old wharfs were piled high with crates, fish nets, and baskets of fruit. Ardeshir even noticed a band of slaves tied together. The tang of sea air, kelp, sewage, fish, and the smoke of fires along the shore hit strongly with a gust of wind. As usual, a cloud of gulls hovered overhead.

Ardeshir checked his horse into a stable near the inn where he decided to quarter. The inn's whitewashed exterior showed the dirt of decades of exposure to the elements. Vines grew over the red tiled roof.

An ancient Hebrew man dozed behind his desk, his mouth gaping to reveal two missing teeth. He wore a blue-patterned robe topped with a red silky turban that looked so worn Ardeshir doubted he ever took it off.

As Ardeshir waited, a muscular Brit with a scimitar nudged the old man.

He awoke with a smile of recognition.

"Ah, the Perthan," said the innkeeper. "Back to give us more trouble, I thee. Are you truly a printh?"

"I'm here looking for my friend," Ardeshir said, ignoring the question. "Do you know Arsama? Or perhaps a man named Tertullian?"

"How many nights do you need? As you might remember, we are always very full."

"Perhaps three or five. I trust the baths are still free."

"Yeth, with a mattage."

Ardeshir paid in advance for three nights, enjoyed his bath and massage, then settled in to enjoy the dinner of lamb shank, rice, flatbread, and tomatoes accompanied by a wine from Gaul.

As he wiped his fingers off on the towel provided, a familiar figure slipped through the curtain over the door of the room.

"Shalom, stranger," the voice boomed.

It was Arsama.

"Shalom to you, friend," Ardeshir replied. "What is the news of your heart and your home?"

Arsama slumped to the floor with his back against the wall. The bent of his nose reminded Ardeshir of the last time they'd seen each other, battling sailors on the city docks. "My heart has been captured by the finest of women and my first son crawls around my feet. You will understand that my time with you will be limited."

A servant arrived to clear the plates and leftovers.

Ardeshir snatched a date and tossed it to Arsama. "I too have a son, and perhaps it would have been wise to stay home with my wife and son, but I felt an urgency to locate my father. I won't trouble you except for any news you may have heard."

Arsama nodded. "I remain in contact with Tertullian. I even hired him to trace where your father may have gone, but so far there is little news. Our group only knows that your father was captured by brigands and taken towards Alexandria." He chewed the date while furrowing his brow. "I heard a rumor that the brigands were seized by a Roman galley and the pirate ship burned. No word of survivors, and no confirmation whether it was the ship your father might have been on."

The same servant returned with two clay lamps, their wicks flickering. He placed them in alcoves set into the wall. He was in and out quickly without a word.

Ardeshir rose and checked the curtain to see whether anyone was listening.

"I thought you told me last time that some of my father's old enemies had given him some trouble," he said to Arsama. "I thought you said he was intent on re-establishing the church in Ephesus with the apostle. How do I know what to believe? How should I even begin my search? I don't have much time."

"Do you have time to personally visit every port along the Great Sea?" Arsama asked. "Sometimes you have to place the right amount of money in the right palms to reap the best rewards. If you can wait, take advantage of the eyes and ears that travel for you."

Ardeshir leaned back against the wall and shrugged. "I don't have the resources."

"So you are the pauper prince of Persia." Arsama smiled. "Welcome. You've claimed a faith that believes in the power of prayer to the One who sees all and knows all. Instead of spinning like a whirling dervish, focus on the One who gives peace and ask him to give you the news you need."

"I see you have become as wise as the Magi," Ardeshir said. "I'll join you at your next dawn meeting after the sabbath."

But until then, he began making plans to explore the city.

Three

The air inside the Han emperor's great judgment arena was thick with incense and the metallic tang of bronze. The scent of burned sandalwood coiled upward in pale ribbons toward the carved rafters high above. Twelve councilors sat in a perfect crescent, their lacquered chairs gleaming like pools of black water; each man was draped in layered silk robes embroidered with dragons and cloud-scrolls that shimmered in the shifting torchlight. The polished marble floor beneath them mirrored the scene in fractured reflections, broken only by the faint tremor of distant drums.

Outside the arc of judgment, Yas had passed guards in crested helmets who stood like stone statues, spears upright, their eyes fixed forward. Beyond them, the gathered crowd had pressed in, their murmurs muffled as if swallowed by the weight of the Emperor's unseen presence.

As she now waited for a decision, the council of twelve sat on the dais before her, evenly divided on what to do with her. The white-bearded, blue-robed elders perched on their seats behind the long oak table carved with symbols of dragons, snakes, oxen, monkeys, and other signs of the zodiac.

She focused on the seven white stones and seven black stones arranged in a straight line across the front of the table facing her. The white stones rested in the box of truth, signifying the possibility of life and freedom. The black stones represented lifelong slavery, or maybe even death.

The red silk gown still hung off of Yas's bony frame like an old sack, but the life and energy inside her had resurfaced. Her eyes radiated intensity and a keen awareness of everything happening around her.

General Ban Chou stood erect behind her, having just finished letting loose a diatribe over what a rebellious, uncooperative prisoner she had proved to be.

Next she turned to her right and studied Liu, the palace gardener and a friend of Ardeshir's. When she'd been given the opportunity to choose an advocate, she had chosen him.

"Honorable guardians of truth," Liu began when it was his turn to mount a defence. "What right have we to stand before your judgment? The dirt under your feet sheds more light than the tongue of those with darkened minds. What hope have we if not for your mercy?"

He then stood silently, waiting for the guardians to answer.

"Speak your claims and we will decide," the oldest of the guardians spoke.

Liu cleared his throat. "In a previous time, this prisoner came as a humble champion of Persia, defending the sacred honor of the emperor by defeating three terrorists in combat at the koi pond. Her prowess among our select warriors was seen in our war games. Our troops learned many things from the skills she willingly shared. She fought against the general as one defending her homeland, her family, and her people, not as one seeking to overthrow our beloved emperor." He knelt in the sand of the arena. "We petition you for mercy, asking that you assign her to the lowest of duties as a slave of the one who knows all. If she has any worth at all, allow her to prove herself with her gifts to our empire. We await your answer, which will be life itself."

The lead guardian stood. "We have heard your plea. We have one last question." The old man looked to the left and right, peering along the line of his fellow guardians. "Where is the brother?"

Liu put his face to the ground and spread his palms upward.

"Speak truth!" the guardian ordered.

Liu sat back on his haunches and drew a deep breath. "The truth is that the last we have seen of the brother is when he was thrown into the den of lions, along with his consort. None of us has heard or seen from him since. We must assume that the judgment of the council was carried out and that what happened to the brother will not have any impact on what must now happen with the sister."

The guardian raised his hand. "Leave us! Back to the cave."

As Yas was led out of the arena, she smiled to herself. She had won her battle against the rat; at least it would not be waiting for her return to that dank cavern.

It took until the sun was at its zenith before Ardeshir found what he was looking for. The first time he had stumbled onto this well, on his previous excursion, he had been running for his life after finding his aunt, the queen, at the governor's mansion. Today the stench of rotting sewage, unwashed humanity, and human waste still hung like a putrid blanket over the surrounding mudbrick homes. Beggars, zealots, vendors, and crippled sailors lounged along the alleyways. The dogs still scavenged among the garbage.

No one was at the well and he found himself filled with disappointment. What had he expected? The girl he had met last time, Mariam, was likely married by now or busy elsewhere. Besides, he was happily married to Lu Hou. His encounter with Mariam had been brief and heady at a time when he'd been desperate for help.

Still, he waited. Most of the women would come in the later afternoon, he deduced, when the heat had lessened.

The first woman who showed up for water was elderly. Her frayed robe dragged in the dirt and had several holes near the hem. She carried a single gourd and dragged her left foot as she moved. Ardeshir's offer to help was gladly received and she took back her filled gourd and sat on a stone bench nearby.

"Are you waiting for someone?" Ardeshir asked.

The women eyed him closely. "Why would a stranger want to know something like that?"

"I'm waiting for a friend named Mariam and wondered if you might know her."

"Do you mean the weaver's daughter?"

"I don't know much about her," Ardeshir admitted. "Her mother gave me hospitality the last time I was here and I wanted to greet them again."

"So you must be the Persian who abandoned her." The woman contorted her lips. "Pretending to be her brother's friend. She told us how you charmed her and made all forms of promises but left her with nothing. I'm not sure you are welcome here."

Ardeshir sat next to the woman on the bench. "It wasn't like that at all. She offered me water and I fed their chickens and chopped their wood in exchange for a meal. There was nothing promised."

The woman smiled. "Mariam always did have a good story to tell. But if you're back to claim her, you're too late. Some other Persian married her and she has her own son now."

A mix of relief and disappointment arose within him. "So she has moved on from here?"

"Oh, she'll be here. She may even bring her little one. I'm warning you not to expect anything."

Three other women arrived, filled their gourds, and added their commentary on his shameful neglect of Mariam. He sat patiently, trying to assure them of his integrity and honor.

A short time later, Mariam appeared, looking far different than the last time he'd met her. Back then, she hadn't been much more than a child herself, dressed in a simple tunic and tattered shawl. Now she was a woman in form and manner. She strolled confidently into the square with an infant on her back and two gourds in her hands. Her dress was stylish and new. Her scarf, colorful.

Seeing Ardeshir, she stopped and stared, her mouth forming a perfect "o."

"If it isn't the running man… Ardie, if that was your true name." She jutted her chin over her shoulder, indicating the child on her back. "You didn't forget me, it seems. But as you can see, you're a little late. I couldn't wait for you."

Ardeshir smiled. "I told you that you were unforgettable, and I couldn't wait either. I also have a son. I came only to greet you and thank you again for your hospitality."

Mariam unwrapped her son and held him out to Ardeshir while she lowered the bucket for water. "My ima died with a smile on her face, imagining all the places you told us about. The emperor's garden and the palace in Persia. Such a fantasy, thinking you might be the prince of Persia marrying the princess of the Han Empire."

"That's exactly what happened," Ardeshir said, rocking the boy. "I am the prince of Persia and I married the princess."

Mariam eyed him with skepticism as she poured water into the two gourds. "So you now live in a palace with hundreds of servants carrying out your every wish? Where are your bodyguards? Why are you here?"

"Brigands kidnapped my father, the Han emperor burned my estate, and I am here to rescue my father while my wife and son go into hiding." He held the boy up and rotated him gently, awaiting his response.

She smiled. "You are a good storyteller and it's clear you know how to handle a child. Never mind. I married a real Persian who doesn't have to pretend to be anything other than he is."

"What is the name of your true Persian?"

"Arsama," she said. "Why? Do you think he's one of your lost subjects? He's a follower of the Way and provides for us well."

"I can see that."

The news struck like a sledgehammer to his heart. What was this feeling? Betrayal? Jealousy? Yes, he'd married Lu Hou, but the attachment to Mariam had been strong.

At least she had married well.

"Tell me, did your husband leave you to visit someone last night?" Ardeshir asked.

She stepped back from him, her brow furrowed. "How did you know?"

"He came to see me," he replied. "He's working with me to help me find my father. You can ask him when you get home. He can tell you who I truly am."

The first woman who had come to the well rose from the stone bench and stretched. "Well, we've had our entertainment for today. The charlatan who abandoned our Mariam is a storyteller who chases fantasies and lonely women. The next time you come back, young man, I'll tell you about my life as the queen of Sheba."

The other women laughed and dispersed.

"If you truly know Arsama, I guess it is safe to invite you home," Mariam said. "We're living in a better part of the city now, but I still come to this well to meet with the ladies. I've told them so many stories about you that I don't even know what to believe anymore."

They began to walk, Ardeshir following a step behind her.

"And how is your brother?" he asked as they emerged from the stench of the shanties and passed into a neighborhood of solid basalt and limestone homes. "He must be so proud of his nephew."

Mariam winced. "My mother and brother died from a fever last year. I myself was sick, but Arsama nursed me to health with the help of some friends of his. They dress strangely and seem almost invisible when they come and go."

"Yes, the thespian assassins. They helped save us both when I was here last. Has Arsama told you how he got that broken nose defending me?"

"He told me that he was ambushed on the wharf by sailors as he walked with a friend," she said. "I always assumed it was some woman he fought to defend. If half of what you tell me is true, my whole world will have to be reimagined…"

As the door to her cell in the cavern rattled, Yas snuggled deeper into the blanket Liu had smuggled in for her. She didn't want to escape the cave's warmth to face the cool morning air. The torch from the night before had long ago sputtered to extinction, but the faintest fingers of light were now spreading over the stone floor.

"Good morning to the rat eater," a voice called. The door squeaked open. "Today we have rice and chicken feet for your morning meal."

A young woman Yas didn't recognize stepped into the cell and laid down a bowl. She wore a green linen gown with yellow fish sewn into the pattern.

"I wasn't able to wash the feet," she added, almost in apology, "but perhaps you can lick them clean. I will bring you water."

The girl then shut the door and left—only to return in a few moments to relight the torch.

The three dirty chicken feet made Yas regret that she had killed the rat. It seemed that the rat would have appreciated this treat. She laid the toenailed appendages in the dirt by the door and savored the half-filled bowl of white rice.

"Where does this food come from?" Yas asked.

The girl hung close to the cell door. "We save it from the pigs. But don't worry. These are the royal pigs. We keep them fattened with the scraps from nobles. Maybe one day, when you prove yourself, you will get to taste the pig's feet soup."

"And where do you live?"

"I live with my family near the teahouse by the village shops. I was chosen by the great General Ban Chao, the unicorn himself, to serve the emperor. My family was pleased to sell me into his service so they may eat without worry. My only task is to do what I'm told."

Yas peered up at her through the dim light. "Do you ever wish you might be free to tell yourself what to do?"

"I don't understand what you're saying," the girl said. "We live to please and so we live."

"How would you like to please me?"

"I live to please the great general. If he is pleased to have me please you, I shall do that. First I will ask him what is his pleasure."

"Don't ask him," Yas said. "My request is too small to bother such a great man. I only wanted some slippers to keep my feet warm. Perhaps your mother can spare a pair she wishes to throw in the garbage."

The girl frowned. "I don't understand this idea of throwing something in the garbage. Nothing is thrown away in our gardens. We pass it on to the next in line."

"Perhaps you can find two rags to wrap around my feet then. It is cold at night and the warmth would help me as I await my judgment. You can have the rags back when I don't need them anymore."

Nodding, the girl backed out of the door and shut it behind her.

Yas settled back under her blanket. There was no guarantee her request would result in anything, but she needed allies. And it seemed that she'd lost access to Colonel Wei.

In the meantime, all she could do was await the council. They appeared to be delaying their decision. Was it too much to hope that a slow judgment might mean some small chance of survival?

A knock at the door broke her out of a daydream focusing on life at her adopted family's farm with a thousand horses. The sun shone off their hides. Their snorts sounded so strong in her ears that she almost missed the knock.

Without waiting for any response from her, the door swung open.

Liu stood framed by the light, holding a pair of slippers. "The girl said you needed something to warm your feet. I hope these will do. They belonged to my sister before she was eaten by the leopard. There was no one next in line to receive them."

Yas knelt in place and opened her hands to receive the treasures. They were like gold.

She felt a small splash on her wrists and glanced down in surprise. Tears were trickling down her cheeks!

"May the One who is the Way see your act of kindness," she said. "How did that girl know to come see you?"

Kneeling in front of her, Liu also shed tears. "She is my niece. She knows my story. She also knows your brother."

"I can't stay here much longer," Yas said. "I feel like my mind is losing touch with reality. I dream so much that I forget to sleep. I run and ride and chase enemies and neglect to eat…"

He held out his hand and waited for her to reach out to him. When she did, he gently squeezed her fingers.

"I am your reality for now," he said. "Trust the Way. Wait quietly. The time is short and truth must have its day."

Tertullian, the giant thespian assassin, bent over an abandoned fishing net by the warehouse at the old wharf. Dawn had broken on the morning after the sabbath and Ardeshir recognized the man's bulky frame despite his best efforts to disguise himself as a beggar.

Ardeshir sauntered toward him. "What's an old man like you doing in dangerous parts like these?"

Tertullian turned towards his voice, then shifted sideways to ogle a trio of Roman galleons hoisting their sails in preparation for departure.

"I'm looking for a Persian prince, but all I get is pretenders," Tertullian said, chuckling. "What brings you back to this forsaken pit of Hades?"

"I'm hungry for news of my father," he said. "Where is he? Who has him?"

Tertullian sighed. "What are you offering?"

"Let's start with a Persian meal. Herbal rice with vegetables and lamb. Flatbread flavored with milk, sugar, and herbs. A hearty goat stew. Enough to fill you up." Ardeshir reached into his tunic, withdrew his change purse, and flipped Tertullian a coin. "The rice will have almonds, pistachios, lentils, carrots, onions, saffron, and more lamb. I can get you pumpkin, eggplant, spinach, beans, grapes, pomegranates, oranges, dates... whatever you want."

Tertullian nodded and shuffled into the nearby warehouse. Ardeshir followed him inside.

Once they were away from prying eyes, the giant man straightened up to his full height.

"Throw in a bottle of wine from Tuscany and I might almost believe that you are a prince," Tertullian mumbled. "How do you convince good men like Arsama to fall into these empty schemes of yours? We do have news of your father, as it happens. But it may not be what you want to hear."

Ardeshir sat on a crate and waited.

Tertullian found his own crate and set his foot upon it. He bent forward, resting his elbow on his leg. "The pirates did grab your father and the Romans did rescue him. An Ephesian cult then purchased him from a slave market. I hear that they are demanding that he represent them in the arena." The man straightened back up and began to pace the uneven floor of the warehouse. "He is old now. He nearly drowned at sea. Then he got hit on the head hard enough to make him forget much of who he is. He will be nothing more than a meal for the lions at the next games."

Jumping to his feet, Ardeshir fell into step with Tertullian. "Why can't you rescue him? He's a warrior deserving honor, a prince among his people. He was the emperor's champion!"

Tertullian stopped and placed a hand on Ardeshir's shoulder. "We've almost lost several men trying to get to him. He's locked away in the Temple of Artemis.

Now that the cultists know he is sought-after, he is guarded too well. We would need to wait until the games to make our move."

"When are the games?"

"Four sabbaths from now. You and I can team up to rescue your father from the lions, but until then you'll need to learn the secret arts… the fighting skills that will keep you alive in the arena."

"I have a wife and son waiting for me."

"You also have a father," Tertullian said. "You're going to have to choose between them. Do you want to be there for the old prince or the young prince? How do you want to be remembered?"

How could a choice like this be made? Would he dishonor the past by ignoring his father, or would he risk the future by ignoring his son? And who would remember him?

Four

Three days after Liu brought the slippers, Yas was given the chance to take a walk in the sunshine. Her legs were so weak that she had to lean on Liu for support as she hobbled to a stone bench. The pair of trumpeter swans on the emperor's pond glided silently by. A blue-tailed bee-eater flitted by on its way to the willow tree. A hawk circled high overhead under the powder white clouds. A dog barked in the distance.

Despite her nightmare, it seemed that life had gone on for everyone and everything else.

There had been no further council meetings, although she was given more freedom to roam the gardens—always in Liu's company, of course. Her freedom was limited and she still had far too much time alone to ponder the deeper questions that plagued her dreams. What had happened to her brother? Had either her adopted father or aunt survived the winter? Was the chef to whom she had given her heart still active in the emperor's kitchen? Why hadn't she heard from him?

As if reading her mind, Liu motioned toward a hedge from whence his niece stepped out with a package wrapped in leaves. She bowed low and laid it on the bench beside Yas.

"From the honorable chef to help your stomach adjust," said the girl.

Yas furrowed her brows and squinted toward Liu. "What does this mean?"

"The council remains deadlocked with six black stones and six white stones," Liu answered. "They are unable to choose death, but neither can they choose life. The emperor must break the tie, but so far he has been ill and unwilling to participate in the decision. Until something changes, you are freed under my guardianship." He smiled and handed her the package. "You must chew these roots to help your body get used to eating something more than rice. Your teeth are weak and so is your system. We must use this time to build you up for what is ahead."

Yas peeled back the leaves to reveal the roots. "What are you saying? Is something worse ahead of us?"

"Nothing is better or worse," Liu said. "It is life. We embrace each day and sift the truth from each event. We welcome the strength that comes from challenges and we welcome the joy that comes from blessings. I do not think we have such teaching in the Tao, but I learned much from your brother about the Way."

"Where do you keep the horses?" Yas asked.

"The horses?" Liu glanced at his niece and jutted out his chin for her to go. His niece bowed and left. "The emperor's horses are kept far from here but there are many, many horses at the soldiers' village. When you are stronger, we can walk there. For now, you need to grow the power in your legs, like a little bird learning to use its wings. You're weaker than you think."

"I want to see the chef," Yas said.

"Guard your desires." Liu glanced over his shoulder. "The chef is under careful observation. We don't want either of you moving so quickly that your choices come under suspicion. Allow me to arrange a chance meeting by the koi pond where you can pass each other freely."

Four more days passed, during which time she noticed that her food became more diverse and plentiful. The hunger pangs she had allowed herself to forget now seized her anew. Her walks with Liu had also gotten longer and she leaned on him less as they maneuvered up and down the terrain of the garden paths.

"There are few strangers who are permitted within these grounds," Liu said as he meandered. "It still surprises me that the council is debating whether you should die while the emperor allows you into his most sacred space. I think this has something to do with the impression you and your brother made on him the last time you were here. His grasp of what is true and noble is above the rest of us."

"I think it probably has more to do with his daughter, the princess," Yas noted. "Despite his decree to feed her to the lions, I believe he hopes she lives and that I can help him connect with her."

She reached the arched bridge over the koi pond, her eyes falling on Liu's niece. She gave a surreptitious nod.

That was the signal.

"Where is the chef?" Yas asked, her heartrate increasing in excitement. She looked back and forth, searching the garden.

Liu nudged her elbow and moved her closer onto the bridge. "We will sit on the bridge, dangling our feet over the edge. In a few moments the chef will walk this way. He will stand for a moment looking the other way. That's all the time you'll have to say what you need to say."

"But I have so much to say—"

"Choose your words carefully. If you choose wrong, you may never have another opportunity."

At last she saw him coming in her peripheral vision. He was carrying something large—a basket. She set her face forward and awaited the sense of his presence.

When it came, she blurted out, "Nothing has changed. But I need to know your name—"

"Orotes," he answered. "What's happened to you?"

"I'm okay. No word on my brother. How are you?"

"Work is hard," Orotes replied. "I'll send better. No more news."

And he was gone.

Yas grasped Liu by the wrist. "Can we do this again tomorrow?"

"Maybe when the moon turns from half to full," Liu answered. "It's time to go before the observers grow curious about our delay."

The visit to the home shared by Arsama and Mariam was less awkward than Ardeshir had feared. Mariam remained playful throughout the visit, calling him Prince Ardie and stretching out the story of his previous visit.

She turned to her husband and smiled coyly. "He was enough of a Persian that he gave me the hunger for a real man—and that's when you came along. It's a good thing he left or I would have been the queen of Persia by now."

Ardeshir handed over their child, whom he'd been rocking on his knee. "Tell me, how did this scoundrel ever find you and convince you to settle for someone like him?"

Mariam smiled again. "I'll give you the short version. Two days after you left, when I was feeling alone and abandoned, this poor man showed up with a broken face. He sat at our well and scared off all the ladies." She laughed as Arsama covered his face with his hands. "That's exactly what he was doing. Hiding his face behind his hands. I walked up to speak to him and he lowered his hands. I saw that face and found myself at a loss for words."

"It's the last time I've heard her quiet," Arsama said. "The truth is that she saw my face and immediately brought me some water to care for me. She took me home for her mother to fix up with some creams… and I never got around to leaving. By the time my face was healed well enough, she was used to me and agreed to be my wife."

"Yes, I did. But it was also during that time that my brother and mother became sick with the fever." She turned to Ardeshir with compassion in her eyes. "Arsama stayed to help me care for them. He caught the fever too… and I threatened him. If he died and left me to take care of the others on my own, I would never speak to him again."

"So what could I do?" Arsama sighed over the memory. "I lived. They died. There was no other choice but for us to take care of each other."

Ardeshir arose from the chair in which he'd been sitting for the last half-hour and stretched. "When I see the three of you so happy, after all that trouble, it makes me miss my wife and son even more. I need to find my father and get back home."

He stepped into his sandals and headed for the door. "May HaShem bless this home and all who live in it," he added. "May you be as fruitful as Leah and stay as beautiful as Rachel. May you find peace when all around you is turmoil and trouble."

With that, Ardeshir waved and walked out into the night.

When he returned to the inn, he encountered Tertullian waiting at the door. "You should tell me where and when you'll be while you're in the city," Tertullian said. "We have news of your father. He's fallen ill with fever and the games master thinks they'll put him on a cross instead of allowing him to fight. We may have to adjust our plans. Either way, we'll have to get on the next ship for Ephesus and prepare ourselves for whatever is to come."

"But I haven't finished my training," Ardeshir objected. "How will I help you if I can't even help myself?"

Sunrises and sunsets blended into a blur of waiting. Liu taught Yas the basics of Cantonese and she trained him in some of the finer elements of war. She adopted a routine of walking, lifting, and mastering controlled, measured movements. The art of the empire seemed to be one of adjusting her personal life to the rhythms and flow of nature.

"Flow through your day like a stream within its banks," Liu coached. "Drift through your thoughts like the clouds across the sky. Breathe in and out slowly, like the sun rising and falling. Forget your hurry. Forget your worry."

It was all easier said than done. The damage done to her sense of identity had suffocated her soul, exposing the lie of her invincibility. Her skills and training had proved futile, her faith and morality useless in changing her situation. The favor of the Almighty seemed to be no favor at all; when she grasped for faith, all she found was a bottomless well of darkness.

Liu sat beside Yas on the koi pond bridge as they dangled their feet in the water. The trumpeter swans circled a stone's throw away, eyeing the pair.

The chef, Orotes, had just come and gone.

"Keep faith," he had said. "Food coming. Emperor dying."

That last phrase had left Yas speechless. If the Emperor was dying, what did that mean for her judgment? And by the time she had formulated a reply, Orotes had already gotten out of hearing range.

"What's going to happen to me now?" Yas asked Liu. "The emperor is the only one keeping me alive."

"You and I know there is One power higher than the emperor," Liu said. "Your brother worked hard to show me that this One exists. The Way is the way. You must know this after growing up in your family."

"What I know in my head is not what I feel right now. I feel alone. I'm not sure if any of my family is alive. I already lost the family I was born into and now I've lost the family who chose me. Sometimes it doesn't feel fair."

The swans glided to within an arm's length and halted.

"I've got nothing for you," Yas said to the birds. "Go have some babies and add life to this pond."

She kicked a small spray of water in their direction. The swans darted away.

"Next time I'll try to save you something," she called after them. "Even the emperor's swans need attention."

Just then, General Ban Chao marched out of the maze, appearing near the residences. He came right for the bridge.

"Keep your eyes focused on the birds," Liu warned Yas. "If he speaks, answer. If not, say nothing."

His footsteps sounded on the bridge and stopped right behind her. Yas hunched her shoulders and waited.

Something poked her in the back of her shoulder.

"Where is the respect?" Ban Chao asked.

"You are too worthy of respect for me to glance at your face," Yas said, desperate to find the right words in Cantonese.

The general hesitated. "Why is the grand council waiting so long to announce your sentence? Have you found a way to blind them with magic, like your brother? If you're still alive after the next full moon, I shall insist that you participate in our war games. It's not right that you are being given food that could be used to fatten the pigs for our next banquet."

"As your men proved to you," Yas said. "I'm not able to prove myself in your war games. I leave my life in the hands of the emperor, who is the guide and guardian of all truth."

"One way or another, the next full moon will be the last you see," Ban Chao snarled.

The general poked Yas hard and turned away. His footsteps faded before she looked up again.

Liu swung his feet up and stood on the bridge. "I don't think that man likes you," he said.

Yas also swung her feet up and got onto her knees, reaching for the rail.

"Stay where you are," Liu said, putting a hand on her shoulder. "Colonel Wei is coming."

Yas leaned forward, her eyes at rail level, as they heard another set of footsteps on the planks of the bridge.

"What kept you from kneeling like this when we were on our way here from the West?" Wei stepped up to the railing beside her and set his hands on the rail. "I tried to help you. You were arrogant and wild. I put my life at risk and you chose to betray me."

"I almost died out there," Yas said. "I was treated worse than an animal. If you tried to help me, it wasn't enough. The general has already sentenced me to death."

"I've arranged for a new room. A woman will come and lead you there. You can bathe and find a mat for sleeping. You must become stronger if you will survive."

"If General Ban Chao is right, I don't have long to survive," Yas said.

"There's less time than you think."

The storm struck halfway through the night while Ardeshir was kneeling and heaving into a bucket in his cabin belowdecks. One moment there was a predictable stomach-churning roll and the next moment the ship had pitched almost sideways. The bucket and its contents escaped his grasp as his spine contacted a peg embedded in the wall. The pain caused him to cry out. His arms flailed and he tried to secure himself in place. A deafening roar preceded the next giant wave.

Tertullian had warned him that they might encounter a storm. Ardeshir's only previous venture upon the sea had been a daytime excursion under fair skies.

"Always be prepared for a change in weather," Tertullian had instructed before they'd boarded the ship. "If you're on deck, you'll have to tie yourself to a mast so you don't get washed overboard and eaten by sharks."

The man had pointed at the train of men hauling heavy bags of grain, timber, salt, and other goods to be stored belowdecks.

"That's good," he added. "A heavy ship will keep us safer. It's less likely to breach. If the cargo is stored correctly, the weight in the hull will counteract the force of the winds. If we hit a storm, the crew will turn us into the wind so the prow can take the brunt of it." Tertullian had lifted his nose and breathed in the salty air. "Nothing like a sea voyage to humble a man. I don't think this ship has storm sails, from the looks of it, so we'd be at the mercy of the wind and waves. A good storm could even delay us a few days if we don't make harbor."

As the ship pitched and rolled around him, Ardeshir thought it was no wonder the pirates who had captured his father might have been crippled in a storm, finding themselves at the mercy of the Romans. A broken mast or shredded sail could leave a crew helpless.

He anchored his feet against the side of a storage cabinet and hung onto the edge of his cabin's doorway.

In moments, Tertullian squeezed himself into the room. The thespian assassin ignored the vomit now coating the wall.

"Good, you're okay," Tertullian said. "The captain says the storm could last the rest of the night, so hang on. I'll check on the others and get back to you." He smiled. "Good thing I told the captain you were a prince. Only reason you got this room all to yourself!"

The next few hours felt more like days. The creaking and cracking left little comfort that the ship would remain seaworthy. Ankle-deep water found its way into his room and Ardeshir could see no way of removing it.

"Yeshua, ruler of wind and wave," he cried out. "Speak your power and peace into this storm. Your way is the Way and I rest in that."

The prayer didn't have any immediate effect, but the intensity did die down within a reasonable amount of time. Could it be that the Almighty was listening? The thought gave seed to other prayers.

"Guard Yas, if she lives. Heal Aunt Laleh. Help us find Abba. Watch over Lu Hou and Artabanas." He stretched his memory, recalling more faces. "Also watch over Sanjay and Farzana and their son. Keep Liu and his family in the Way. Encourage Arsama and Mariam and their boy. Encourage Adrina. Help Tertullian survive so we can finish this rescue."

When the ship settled enough, Ardeshir used the water and a bucket to clean the walls. Then he ventured into the passageway, intending to bail what he could over the rail from the deck.

The passageway was crowded with passengers who shared the same thought.

Afterward he returned to the stool in the corner of his cabin, folded his arms, and attempted to snatch a little nap. When Tertullian dropped by for another check-in some time later, Ardeshir nodded and assured the big man that he was fine.

The storm ended up delaying the trip by less than a day so it was a huge relief when the shoreline for Ephesus broke the horizon. Ardeshir stood next to Tertullian at the rail as they whispered their plans to each other.

"There are six of our number hidden among the merchants at the harbor marketplace," Tertullian said. "I'll make contact. Then we can discuss how we can work together. They'll have seen everyone who has come or gone from the city."

"What do you know about Ephesus?" Ardeshir asked. "It looks huge."

"Some say the city was founded by a tribe of female warriors called Amazons. Ephesia was their queen. Anyway, the city has always been known for treating men and women with the same rights and opportunities."

"I know my father had to deal with the priests from the Temple of Artemis," Ardeshir said. "Where is the temple?"

"It's inland about a mile," Tertullian replied. "Artemis is the goddess of the hunt, childbirth, chastity, wild animals, and the wilderness. And the Temple is about four times the size of the Parthenon. In fact, it's one of the seven wonders of the world. People from every nation come here to trade and live. Only Rome is bigger."

Ardeshir lowered his head. "How will we find my father in such a big city?"

"Give me some time to circulate amongst the shadows and I'll let you know." Tertullian bent over and began to apply his old man disguise.

"Shadows? I'm not sure what you mean."

Tertullian glanced over his shoulder. "Others call us thespian assassins, but we call ourselves shadows. You see, we try to act in such a way that people will remember nothing about us."

"Don't look now," Ardeshir said, "but I think I see a shadow watching us."

As the ship neared the harbor, Ardeshir made eye contact with a merchant grasping a fishing net in his hands. The man just glared back.

"If you've seen someone watching us, he isn't a shadow." Tertullian dropped a coin and bent down to retrieve it. He scooped it up in one motion and glanced at the sky. "Anyway, I know that man. His name's Marcus and he's the lookout for the local silversmiths. They often have cargo coming off ships like this one. They're also on the lookout for young girls or women they can snatch for use in the temple rituals."

"Won't he report us?" Ardeshir asked.

"Don't worry. I've given the signal. The others will take care of him before we disembark."

Ardeshir glanced toward the spot where the merchant named Marcus had just been standing. No one was there now.

He shuddered involuntarily. Who were these men he was depending on?

Five

The six warriors facing Yas appeared to be little more than large boys. Their leather armor was oversized, their grip on their spears and daggers awkward, and their discomfort level high. Each of them, though, had determined glares, clenched jaws, and a solid build.

General Ban Chao had arrived at dawn, walking into her room and pulling her out of bed.

"Today you fight," he'd announced. "Dress quick."

He had remained in place as Yas considered how to change with him standing right there in her space. The small room lined with bamboo strips was a big step up from the cave she had shared with the rat.

"Hurry! Now! Now!"

She pulled her fighting robe over her shoulders and turned her back to the man. There was no time or space to prepare herself for what lay ahead.

"I need a few minutes to wash and prepare," she said, finally. "I haven't had anything to eat or drink."

"No need," Ban Chao declared. "You may die anyway."

She finished changing, turned to bow, and followed the warrior out the door. She wasn't surprised when she realized he was leading her to the arena.

The wooden gates groaned open and Yas stepped into the blinding glare of the Han emperor's arena, the sand beneath her sandals hot from the morning sun. The scent of dust, sweat, and faint incense from the high terraces mingled in her nostrils, grounding her in the grim reality of what was to come.

The walls around the oval battleground were painted with sprawling murals of glorious scenes of Han victories—armored riders thundering through clouds of arrows, banners snapping in painted wind, and enemies falling beneath curved blades. Each image was meant to proclaim invincibility, a silent reminder of where she stood and what fate awaited most who entered.

Above, the din of the crowd swelled—cheers, jeers, and the clang of gongs—like a tide determined to crush her resolve. She felt the dryness in her mouth, the weight of her curved sword in her hand, and the burn of her heartbeat in her ears.

Fear coiled low in her stomach, but it was the sharp, tingly kind—tempered by pride, by the knowledge that if she must die she would die as the daughter of Persia's warriors: unbroken, unbowed, and burning with defiance.

Images of hulking martial artists, armed to the teeth, filled her mind as she took a final breath and looked up. She was surprised by the sight of her multiple opponents.

"Which one will I fight?" she asked.

"All of them," the general said.

"One at a time?"

"All together. Choose a weapon. We will begin after sacrifices."

The sacrifice involved the slaughter and burning of a lamb, the playing of a dirge, and the dance of a dozen women outfitted with colorful clothing and fans. Colonel Wei and a dozen officers stood stiffly to one side, watching the proceedings.

Yas began by examining the stash of weapons provided and chose a trident with an accompanying net. The trident was covered in cobwebs, but she'd seen her adopted father model its use shortly before his departure. But she'd never handled the trident and net together before. She set aside the curved sword she had arrived with.

"Foolish choice," the general declared as she stepped onto the sandy surface of the arena to face her foes. "Six warriors will be coming at you with spears. You cannot stop them all at once with this weapon."

Yas bowed to his assessment, dropped the weapons and returned to the armory table. This time she picked up a crossbow and the quiver of arrows next to it.

"I will use these," she announced, gliding like a phantom back toward the spot where she'd dropped the trident.

Ban Chao nodded and held out his arms to the six young warriors. "Today you will prove yourself. If you live, you will join me as I destroy the Persian Empire. If you don't survive, we will feed your parents to the wild things." He turned to Yas. "You have one choice: live or die."

The six spread out, facing her and flexing their spears.

Yas knelt and bowed her head as if in prayer. "Be honorable," she said, as much to herself as anyone.

The men flanked her on all sides, approaching so that even the furthest was only a few strides away and closing. She kicked the trident aside, notched her first arrow with lightning speed, and embedded it in the chest of the man immediately to her right.

The others halted as the warrior fell, writhing.

Before she could notch another arrow, the warrior on her left hurled his spear. She rolled away, deflecting the shaft of the spear with her forearm. Without hesitation she snatched up the spear and threw it back. The young warrior jumped to escape but the blade dug into his thigh. He pulled it out and stepped toward Yas. Before he could get close, his leg gave way and he crumpled to the ground. She dispatched him with an arrow to the neck.

Two of the four remaining soldiers circled behind her. One unleashed a dagger which nicked her right shoulder as she rolled aside. When she picked up the net and trident, the two closest warriors plunged their spears at her. One grazed her thigh. She kicked the back of their knees and speared them with the trident.

The remaining two looked toward Ban Chao. Their families would die if they failed.

With a nod to each other, they both charged with their spears lowered. Yas threw the net at their feet, forcing them to trip and sprawl onto the sand in front of her.

The dagger finished them off.

"I guess it's you and me now," she said to the General. She retrieved the net and trident. "These weapons are more effective than I realized. Maybe you should be the one to face the wild things." She moved toward him as he backed away. "Next time you should train your boys better."

As she raised the trident to strike, a platoon of heavily armored warriors charged into the arena and formed a circle around the general, shielding him.

"Drop your weapons and you shall live to fight another day," Ban Chao called.

Without options, she dropped the trident and net. Several of the soldiers wrestled her to the ground, tied her hands and feet, and dragged her from the arena. The blood from her wounds left a red streak behind her, but at least she had survived her first test.

The wharf at Caesarea shimmered in the late afternoon heat, the scent of brine and tar mingling with the sharp tang of fish guts spilled from the morning's catch. Gulls shrieked overhead, wheeling against a sky the color of hammered bronze, while the waves slapped lazily against barnacle-crusted pilings.

Mooring ropes creaked and the hulls of ships groaned like tired beasts at rest. Ardeshir hobbled along towards the entrance to an alley, averting his gaze from everyone in the vicinity.

Including those six sailors lounging near a stack of amphorae at the end of the alley, wearing tunics stained with salt and sweat. Their laughter was loud and crude as they mocked a stooped figure hobbling toward them—a giant of a man, six-foot-six and draped in a weathered cloak, leaning heavily on a carved cane.

A familiar giant.

Tertullian seemed to be struggling to ignore their taunts, his shadow falling long across the planks. His disguise made him seem ancient and broken.

And then he could take no more. With a sudden, almost imperceptible shift, his back straightened like a mast in the wind. In one swift motion, his cane came up and cracked hard across the jaw of the nearest heckler. The sound rendered a sharp report against the hum of the harbor.

Another blow caught a second sailor in the ribs, folding him with a wheeze. A third strike split the lip of a man mid-laugh. The fourth staggered back, clutching his temple.

The last two stood frozen, their eyes wide while the gulls circled and jeered, as if echoing the old Roman's unspoken warning: some ships aren't worth boarding.

After that burst of action, Tertullian bent over, breathing hard.

"Don't you think there's far too much violence in the world?" he asked, finally turning his attention to Ardeshir.

"If my eyes are popping out of my head, it's because of what I'm sure I saw you do," Ardeshir replied as he leaned his back against the wall. "You could have warned them. Did you walk us into this alley on purpose? I'm sure that blind man had his mouth hanging open. But of course he wasn't really blind."

The supposedly blind man had been huddled in an alcove, easy to miss, with his clay mug extended for alms. And now he was nowhere to be found.

"Drag those four bodies into that warehouse," Tertullian instructed. "I'll take care of the rest."

"And what about the 'blind' man?" Ardeshir asked. "He's probably an informant who will tell someone what happened here."

Tertullian glanced toward the entrance to the alley and smiled. The so-called blind man was long gone.

"He is an informant, but one of ours. He warned me we would be set upon by nine men. If there were any more, I might have needed your help." Tertullian grabbed a pair of arms and began dragging the bodies out of sight.

Ardeshir followed, hauling a body of his own.

"Hurry!" Tertullian urged. "Two of them got away and will be back with reinforcements. We need to get to the agora by the well, the one near the governor's mansion. If we get separated on the way, meet me there."

A few minutes later, after Ardeshir had deposited his fourth body in the warehouse, he looked around for Tertullian. The giant was nowhere in sight.

At the sound of loud voices echoing from the alley, he slid back into the shadows of the warehouse.

Two men suddenly burst into the space.

"Where are you, you maggot-hearted assassins?" one of them shouted. "On Caesar's grave, you will not survive this day."

The men spread out, shouting and stabbing into the darkness with their swords and daggers. Their eyes hadn't adjusted yet, so Ardeshir was able to take advantage of the opportunity and slip out a back window.

Too late, he realized that the window opened over water. He hung in space, grasping the ledge above him.

"Bring a torch!" a man called from inside. No doubt he'd discovered one of the bodies. "They've got to be here somewhere."

Taking a deep breath, Ardeshir released his hold and plunged into the icy water. His robe rose up over his head, restricting his arm movement. He swam for the surface, tearing off his robe in the process. All his coins were in the change purse sewn into the lining of the robe, so he yanked it up with him.

He was sure that his gasp at the surface could be heard throughout Ephesus, but he couldn't do anything about that. He kicked hard to float under the dock and out of sight.

Above him, he heard the men.

"He jumped. I heard him."

"He's under the dock. Hurry!"

Ardeshir kicked again, pushing himself towards a nearby ship, but the robe was slowing him down. He ripped out the change purse and draped the robe over one of the dock's supporting logs. Now his only coverings were a silk undertunic and loincloth. He dove under the keel of the boat and surfaced on the far side.

"He's down there somewhere."

"Keep watching. The rest of you, get down under there before he escapes."

"There were five of them, I think. One was a giant."

"Search the warehouses!"

With the men waiting directly overhead and more of them working their way under the dock at that very moment, he had nowhere to go. Loud splashes sounded nearby and Ardeshir pressed up hard against the boat.

"What was that?"

"It's our men! Necks are broken. They're up on the wharf."

"After them!"

Ardeshir scrambled up onto the deck of the boat and through the first door he saw. He scrounged around the empty cabin until he found a pair of fishermen's gear. He donned it and added a raggedy headwrap for effect.

As he exited the cabin, a gruff voice shouted at him in Aramaic. "You there! Fisherman! Have you seen any strangers down under the wharf?"

Ardeshir shrugged. "I saw two drop dead over the edge. There's an abandoned tunic on a log. No one else."

"Move your boat and stay out of the way," the man shouted. "These men are killers."

Ardeshir waved and untied the vessel from its mooring. It drifted on the receding tide as he attempted to maneuver it with a single oar. Behind him, the men's voices continued to shout. He just kept moving toward the far side of the harbor.

He had almost convinced himself that he had survived the ordeal when a new voice broke through: "Hey! That's my boat. What are you doing?"

Ardeshir glanced at the wharf, where a fisherman was rushing alongside the boat. He immediately realized this must be the boat's owner.

"Someone got murdered and those men asked me to move it to a safer berth." Ardeshir gestured toward the searchers behind him. "You can get it up ahead. I assure you, everything's right where you left it."

"You're a thief," the fisherman insisted. "You've taken my tunic and my boat."

"I assure you I'm not. I just needed something dry to wear while I moved the boat. Come, follow me and you'll get all that's yours. I'll even pay you for the use of your tunic."

A significant crowd had already gathered at the dock when Ardeshir pulled in.

"There are dangerous men around here," Ardeshir said to the fisherman as the man caught up to him. "I was protecting your boat for you." He pulled out a silver coin. "This should cover any trouble that's been caused."

The man took the coin and jumped onto his boat. "It looks like everything is okay," he said, searching around. "Keep the tunic. I can buy a hundred with this." He held it up to the crowd. "Look what he gave me!"

While the sailors, beggars, dockworkers, and riffraff pressed closer to get a look, Ardeshir slipped through the crowd and hurried away.

As he ambled down an alley, head down, three men rushed by.

"He escaped on that boat. I saw him."

"The owner said he was a thief."

"Hurry! We can catch him before he gets away."

Halfway down the alley, though, an arm reached out and grabbed hold of him, dragging him into a dark room. A hand over his mouth cut off any sound he tried to make.

Liu grinned as Yas rolled around on the floor, trying to untie herself.

"You live!" he exclaimed in Persian. "You live. Too much blood on floor. Hard to clean." He knelt down and worked to release her bonds. "General see that you not lose your skill. We rest now and prepare for greater challenge. I heal your wounds." He removed the rag from her mouth. "Speak now. What you think?"

"I think I'm hungry and would like something special to eat," she said. "The general sent boys to fight. It was unfair to their families. Yes, fix these nasty cuts."

Liu nodded. "Boys criminals. Their only chance to avoid punishment was to fight. General know that you bring justice for him."

"But did they even know how to fight?"

"Not matter. Only matter that you stay alive." Liu helped her to her feet. "I get special dinner from chef. He pray for you while fighting. He like you much."

"Speak to me in Cantonese," Yas said, switching languages. "I need to learn. Besides, I like the chef too."

She winced as Liu sewed her wounds, smeared a cream on her wounds, and wrapped her arm and thigh.

During their next pass over the bridge, they found Orotes waiting for them. The chef sat down next to Yas and dipped his feet into the water. He threw tidbits onto the pond for the swans to gobble them up.

"What are the watchers going to say?" Yas asked.

"You won your fight and now you have privileges. I am your prize." Orotes grinned at the swans craning their necks. "These birds are so much like us. They get a little bit of a good thing and they stretch for more. How much of me will satisfy you?"

"I will not be satisfied until I have all of you." Yas grinned. "I don't think that can happen while we're here, however. From this moment on, I'll be looking for a way to get us back west where we can live freely."

"If you're speaking of Persia, you and I know we didn't really have true freedom. You had to take up your family's fight for the throne. But I would be satisfied to spend any time together with you."

"You say that because you're a man who gets to do what he loves," Yas said. "Men always have it easy. If you're good at something, someone will want you to do it for them. For women like me, we have to work a hundred times as hard—and we still might be overlooked."

Orotes stared at her. "Are you serious? Do you think I'm satisfied to have others tell me what to do all the time? There are so many things men want to do… and when they get to do it, they find that they're still slaves. There is no freedom in helping someone else all the time." He got to his feet and looked toward the emperor's red-tiled palace. "I've got to go. This isn't the way I imagined we would spend our first free conversation. Perhaps we shouldn't spend too much time together."

Yas watched him go, then turned her attention back to the swans.

"The talk is finished already?" Liu inquired upon his return. "What happened?"

"I guess I got too much freedom too fast," Yas told him. "It's not easy trying to be a woman in a man's world. Neither is it easy to be a Persian in a Cantonese world. Neither is it easy to be a leader when you don't have any power."

From the far side of the pond, General Ban Chao emerged from behind the workers' residences and glared at them.

"I hope he hasn't got another test for you already," Liu said. "Your wounds still haven't healed from the last one…."

The arm dragging Ardeshir out of the alley turned out to belong to one of Tertullian's band of thespian assassins.

"Stay silent!" the friendly assailant whispered. "Follow me, quickly."

Before he could react, Ardeshir was being secreted across the warehouse and pulled into a two-wheeled cart on the other side of a street. The man covered him with a tarp, but Ardeshir managed to peek out from under it.

His abductor set himself between the two shafts, lifted the cart, and began to pull it through the streets.

"Dead dogs! Dead pigs! Dead rats!" he called as he moved slowly along.

Ardeshir quivered as a pair of animal carcasses landed atop the tarp blanketing him. A death cart? This was the best these assassins could manage in helping him escape?

It didn't take long for the death cart to turn into another alley and come to a halt.

"Help me bring in the body," his abductor called to someone.

Then another voice: "Stay still."

The cart shifted and both Ardeshir and the tarp were lifted out. A pair of men scooped him into their arms and ferried him out of the daylight and into a veil of darkness. His body swayed as they carried him.

With a thud, they dropped him on the hard ground.

"Well, if it isn't the dead prince," Tertullian remarked. "How many times do I have to rescue you before we even get started on this rescue mission?" He motioned to a colleague at the entrance to the room where they huddled. "If everyone's here, we better get planning how to penetrate that fortress. Everything we've rehearsed so far ends up in our deaths."

Ardeshir gingerly got to his feet and followed the giant out of the room and into yet another warehouse. At the far end of the cavernous space, he came to a circle of stools. In the middle of the circle, three candles had been arranged on the floor.

As he waited, eight men gathered. None of them sat.

Tertullian pulled out a large scroll and spread it on the floor next to the candles. The men huddled over it.

"These are the temple grounds," Tertullian explained. "Here is the courtyard of snakes for the lame and dying." He indicated a space near the entrance pointed away from the harbor. "There are six armed guards at the gate, another six around the courtyard, and six more at the inner court. Dozens of priests and priestesses wander the grounds, willing to die for their goddess." He pointed to a vague marking along the edge of the scroll. "This is the service entrance where they bring the girls, food, and sacrifices. There are only four sentries here, since whoever comes to this place has already passed through the front gate. If we are to access the temple quickly, we need to crawl over this hedge as the shifts change and charge this door."

"Where is the target?" a voice asked.

Tertullian knelt and pointed to a spot on the side of the inner court. "Our contact says that he should be here. The prince will go with me to identify his father. We'll move in and out quickly. Two of you will come with us, bringing a sheet to carry the body. We can't have him slowing us down."

"Are we taking weapons?" Ardeshir asked.

"The usual." Tertullian folded up the scroll. "First team, you'll lead the distraction at shift change. Second team, you'll stand guard to stop reinforcements. Third team, you'll eliminate the four guards and clear the path for us to get the target." He stood and held up his arm. "When the sun kisses the sea, we move into position. Until then, eat, rest, arm yourselves."

In moments, the room emptied apart from Tertullian and Ardeshir.

"What do I need to do?" Ardeshir asked.

Tertullian moved to a nearby crate, yanked off the lid, and pulled out an assortment of clothing. "Put these on and stay out of sight, except to go find something to eat."

After a meal of flatbread, cucumbers, goat cheese, and dates, Ardeshir crept back into the warehouse and went through the clothes. The dark tunic with accompanying trousers and bandana adjusted easily to his form. He found the darkened goatskin footwear light and comfortable.

Twice, warehousemen walked in to retrieve a container, and both times he remained in the shadows—that is, until Tertullian stepped out in front of him.

"Where did you come from?" Ardeshir asked, startled.

"I've been here all along. There was no need to speak or make my presence known. I could have killed you and you would never have been the wiser. Train your senses to be sharp so that you can feel the energy, warmth, and breath of another being. Learn to survive."

"Where are the others?"

"They're in place, waiting for you," Tertullian said. "The sun has kissed the waters. It's time to go."

Six

General Ban Chao disappeared into the hedge maze without stopping or issuing a command. As he marched out of sight, two young girls around the age of ten stepped into the open, clearly following him. When they saw Yas and Liu stepping down from the bridge over the koi pond, they waved shyly.

Yas nodded in their direction. "Who are those girls?"

"The general's daughters," Liu replied. "Look away. They'll only cause you trouble."

The girls approached confidently, so Yas remained in place.

"Why is the foreigner in our garden?" the older one asked Liu. "Why did out father not cut her up for the koi?"

"I can speak for myself," Yas told them in Cantonese. "Your father had me fight six warriors at once and I defeated them. My prize was to walk freely in the emperor's garden. Why has he permitted you in here?"

The girls stood with their eyes wide and mouths open.

"She means no offence," Liu said, prostrating himself on the ground. "She is learning our ways. Let her punishment fall on me."

Yas stepped around the gardener and crossed her arms over her chest. "No! If something is to be decided, it must be focused on me. This man has done no wrong and neither have I."

The oldest girl crossed her arms in imitation of Yas. "How can you, a woman, defeat six warriors? Can you ride a horse or throw a spear or shoot a crossbow?"

"I have done all those things since I was your age," Yas replied. "If you'd like, I can teach you."

The younger girl stepped around her sister. "You can teach us? Even though we are girls? I want to ride a warhorse and throw a spear."

"There are horses in the soldiers' village. This man can take us there." Yas knelt beside Liu and tapped his shoulder. "You can take us there, can't you?"

Liu slowly rose to a crouching position. "It would not be right to take you to the village. The general would cut out my tongue and feed it to the koi."

The oldest one set her hands on her hips and glared at him. "If you don't take us to the horses, we will speak to our father and make sure he cuts the whole of you to feed the koi."

Liu clearly found himself caught in a dilemma. He shifted back and forth on his feet, head down, hands behind his back. His shoulders rotated as he furrowed his brows and considered what he could do.

"There is a farmer nearby, much closer, with a horse," he said. "We cannot have you gone from the garden when someone in your family comes looking for you. What if the general returns and finds you gone?"

The oldest girl smiled. "He's gone to the front now. The emperor sent him to check the farms on the borderlands so he could assign more properties to the next round of returning warriors. We are free for half a moon and will be riding by then. Come! Let's go!"

"Wait!" Yas said. "If I'm taking you away from here and teaching you to ride, you must do everything I tell you without questioning. Riding is dangerous and you could be hurt or killed if you don't do it properly. Am I clear?"

Surprisingly the girls stopped, shoulders back. They looked quickly at each other.

"We will do as you ask," said the older one. "But we will not act against you for as long as we agree."

Yas didn't understand and wasn't sure whether she had translated the phrase properly. But she nodded anyway. The adventure would at least get them out of the garden.

She nodded to Liu. "Lead us on."

Liu led them through a maze of hedges behind the servants' residences. Yas hadn't noticed this part of the garden before and forced herself to trust the man ahead of her.

"Not far," Liu said.

They broke through an opening in a hedge three times the size of Liu and the change was immediate. Farms and rolling hills spread out before them. Wildflowers dotted the borders of the pathway they took.

Liu pointed. "Over the next hill."

At the top of the hill, the quartet looked down on a small herd of grazing mares and colts. One stallion stood among them, head up and staring in their direction.

"We can ride the colts, but the stallion will cause trouble," Yas said. "What are we going to do about that?"

"I'll talk with the farmer," Liu said. "He's my uncle."

It didn't take long for Liu to return with a man who looked a lot like him. The man nodded, called the stallion over, and led it into a paddock. The horse remained calm at first. But when Yas and the girls moved toward his mares and colts, the beast snorted, ran around the paddock, and reared up on its hindlegs.

"He doesn't look happy," Yas said to the girls.

"One day I will ride that great one," the youngest girl said. "I'll lead the emperor's armies like my father."

Yas turned to her. "What is your name?"

"Why do you want to know?" the other one interjected. "I'm the oldest and you should ask me first. You are a disrespectful foreigner who knows nothing of our ways."

Yas stood up straight. "Right now I'm your teacher, and I'm the one who knows how to ride the horse you want. If I end up having to bury your dead body for doing this wrong, I'll want to know who it is I've had to bury!"

The girl stood back, uncertain.

Liu touched Yas's elbow gently and waited for her to turn. "When it comes to naming a child, parents make a careful choice. We don't name children after ancestors, as it would be disrespectful to the dead. We also don't name our children after celebrities or ancient figures, as this could bring bad luck." He bowed briefly to the older girl. "We try to find a Chinese character which harmonizes with our surname. Then, with the other character, we aim to express our hope for the child. A second child will have a name that fits well with the first. The first might be named for the sun while the second is named for the moon or a star."

Yas shook her head. "All I want to know is what they're called. I don't need to know why."

"The name tells you who they belong to and their parents' hopes for them." Liu turned to the oldest girl. "What dream do your parents have for you?"

The girl bowed slightly. "I am Fang, the beautiful fragrance with pure virtue. This is Jing, the peaceful one. We will now ride the big horse."

Yas smiled. "First we'll see if you can gentle something simpler. Go. Stand by that colt and rub your hand along its back. When you've done that, stand in front of it and rub the top of its head between its ears."

"That is the work of servants," Fang objected. "We want to ride."

"Before the horse will let you ride it, you must earn its trust," Yas said. "If you think you can do this by yourself, go ahead."

Jing stepped tentatively toward a colt standing near its mother. She reached her hand out and jumped back as the mare stretched out to nip her hand.

"Bad horse!" Jing shouted.

Yas stepped forward and put a hand on the shaking girl. "Your name says you are the peaceful one, yet your actions won't lead to peace. Watch and I'll show you what to do. You must be patient. You must not think the world is here to serve you."

"We should chop up that horse for the koi," Fang said. "That monster nearly ate my sister."

Yas stepped forward and held out her hand to the mare, holding her pose like a statue. The mare hesitated, then nuzzled the outstretched hand. Yas ran her fingers over the nose and then the horse's head. She gently patted the neck and backed away.

Within moments, the mare stretched out her neck and stepped toward Yas, who patted her again. The colt nestled close to its mother's side.

"Walk up to me slowly," Yas instructed the girls. "You can pat the neck of the horse, but that is all we can do today."

The girls did as instructed and were soon tentatively petting the mare.

"A little firmer," Yas said. "The horse can pick up your fears. She needs to know that you're safe before she trusts you with her foal."

But Liu intervened. "We need to return to the gardens. Their mother has been instructing women in the art of silk-making and will soon be looking for her girls. We can come again tomorrow."

"How long until I can gallop and throw a spear?" Jing asked.

Yas followed Liu away from the horses. "Come, girls. It will take a while before we gallop, but each day we'll learn a little more. We can practice throwing a spear, though, if you want."

They had hardly pushed back through the huge hedge around the garden when Liu's niece rushed up to them.

"The general's wife has sent servants to find her daughters," the girl said. "Hurry! You need a good reason why the girls disappeared."

As they emerged from the maze and approached the pond, a troop of six guardians marched toward them.

Turning to Yas, Liu motioned for silence. "You should go to your room. I'll take care of the story." He sighed. "Girls, what will you tell your mother?"

"I will tell mother that we were petting the farmer's horse," Jing said.

"And who took you to see the farmer's horse?"

Fang nodded and glanced toward Liu. "You alone did."

Yas put out her hand. "I won't force these girls to lie. If the emperor is the lord of truth, as he claims, he will soon learn what is true. It will be worse for us all if we lie. I'll stay with you until this is over."

Fang stepped forward to meet the soldiers but whispered over her shoulder toward Yas: "You have more courage than sense."

Tertullian hunched over on the seat of the donkey cart as Ardeshir limped along beside. Both were dressed like impoverished fishermen with raggedy tunics, old wraps around the top of their heads, and worn sandals. The old path circumventing the Temple of Artemis was easy to follow and the numerous trees and bushes in the orchard allowed them to conceal the cart and donkey.

As the sentries changed shifts, the two intruders breached the main hedge and sheltered behind a large oak on the perimeter of the temple grounds. The daytime priests, priestesses, and sentries faded away as newcomers took their place. There were fewer guardians onsite during the night, although a group of six girls soon emerged with a priestess from the service entrance and climbed into a chariot. The four sentries made lewd remarks on them as they departed.

As the chariot reached the gate, the first thespian assassins sprang their ambush. One assassin sliced the harnesses and spooked the horses to run. Another grabbed the priestess while another knocked the driver unconscious; the final member herded the girls into the bush.

The girls screamed in terror and the four sentries at the service entrance raced to the scene of the trouble. As they ran towards the commotion, Tertullian and Ardeshir crept across the grass and into the abandoned service entrance. They passed a startled cleaner at work and arrived at the room where Ardeshir's father, Nabonidus, was meant to be held.

A single priest stood gazing up at the heavens with a heart in his hands.

Ardeshir gazed in horror at the candlelit scene. "What have you done with him?"

The priest backed away. "Who are you and what are you doing here? The time for favor is past. The sacrifice is done and the entrails have been determined."

"Whose heart do you hold?" Ardeshir asked as Tertullian stepped toward the shadows to examine a dark shape lying there.

"It is the goat of passions." The priest held out the heart. "I'll call the sentries if you don't leave immediately."

"Where is the old man you kept here?" Tertullian demanded.

"He left earlier with the Romans. They were sailing at dusk to Rome. He claimed some right to make his case before the emperor and they took him. I have offered this goat as a substitute."

Loud shouts arose from the yard outside.

Tertullian raised a dagger to the throat of the priest. "We need to leave without being seen. How do we leave this place?"

The priest pulled back a step. "You can follow me, but remove that blade from my neck."

Tertullian grabbed the priest by the collar of his tunic. "The blade stays until you deliver us into freedom. One yell and it will be your last."

"I promise not to scream," the priest said, nodding. "There is a secret entrance for priests which few know about. It will take us to a hidden cave on the beach. We will have to hurry if we aren't to be discovered."

"How many sentries along the way?" Tertullian asked.

The priest hesitated. "There are four. If you were to dress as my assistants, we would not be bothered." He looked up at Tertullian. "Perhaps I don't have anything large enough for you to wear. You can dress as a sentry and your companion can be my assistant."

The man opened a cabinet and withdrew a priest's tunic, which he handed to Ardeshir.

"Wear this. Weapons are in the next room." The priest laid the goat's heart on the altar before him. "The time is past for the sacrifice. Let's do what needs to be done."

Tertullian picked up a spear and shield in the next room but didn't find a tunic large enough for himself.

"Who I am will have to do," the big man murmured. "You lead and I'll be right behind you. Get us to the beach you mentioned, then return to your place without a word."

The trio descended the hidden stairs, followed the secret corridor under the temple, and soon emerged into a cave stocked with golden goblets, jewels, trinkets, robes, and treasures too many to number.

The priest reached into a pile of coins and dropped them into a purse. "Here! It is a gift from Artemis for the life of her servant. Go and do what you must do. The Roman ship has sailed, but if you get to Puteoli before the next full moon you can intercept the traitor and kill him for yourselves. Artemis will have her vengeance by my hand or by the hand of others."

The man opened a series of doors, set aside a curtain, and proceeded to usher them out into the night.

Yas and Liu leaned on the bridge railing, watching as Orotes sauntered in their direction.

"Do you think it will go better this time?" Yas asked.

Liu shrugged. "I guess it depends on what you're willing to do. After what happened with the girls and their mother, though, it almost seems as though you're living a charmed life."

"Fang sure knows how to talk with her mother, doesn't she?" Yas smiled. "She's either confident or arrogant, but certainly not afraid. When those soldiers marched us into the palace courtyard, with the emperor's wife sitting there on that golden throne surrounded by marigolds, I was sure we'd be dinner for the lions. 'No,' Fang says, 'I ordered this foreigner and this commoner to take us to the horses and they did what they were told. We're safe and back in time for our dinner.'"

"Their mother simply nods and waves her hand and it's all over," Liu added. "Of course, we haven't seen the two little maidens since."

"They'll be back. Hopefully before General Ban Chao returns." She stood up as Orotes reached the bridge, switching her language to Persian. "Welcome, chef. Do you and I have anything more to say about our conversation the other day?"

"A conversation? Is that what we had?" Orotes asked. "Living on the edge of death every day sure isn't easy, for either of us. If I make one dish the emperor doesn't enjoy, I'll be fed to the koi. Or the lions. Or the other wild things. I imagine it's the same for you." He leaned against the railing. "The general's oldest daughter told me about your adventure outside the gardens. She said you have more courage than sense. She also mentioned that she saved your life!"

Yas smiled. "She has an interesting perspective. And why were the two of you talking about me?"

Orotes looked her in the eye, then turned away toward the waters of the pond. "It appears she's matchmaking. She asked whether I had any interest in you and wanted to know if I would be willing to poison you. She thought maybe we care too much about each other."

"So that's why the food tastes different lately." Yas stretched out her hand as the swans circled below. "What did you tell her? How tempted were you?"

"To poison you? I told her I'd need a special Greek potion, one which her people hadn't discovered yet." Orotes leaned on the railing and inched closer to her. "I told her that if I only had water hemlock, dried, crushed, and powdered to the size of her smallest finger... well, then I could poison everyone in the garden. I also implied that if I put it in her food, she might fall asleep and never wake up!"

Yas leaned in close. "Are you trying to get us all fed to the lions? You'll have the poor girl terrified."

"That's when she asked about other types of poison. I told her about the Roman emperor's Greek physician using arsenic because of its lack of color, odor, or taste when mixed with food or drink. If she could smuggle you and me out of here... well, maybe I could get her some when I went west."

"And did she agree to let us go?"

"She's young, but not dumb," Orotes said. "She knows we'd probably leave and never come back. It seems her biggest regret would be not getting the chance to learn to ride that horse."

"Sounds like we might have her help if we need it..." She trailed off, lost in thought. "How would someone know if they were being poisoned?"

Orotes straightened and looked around the garden. By now, Liu had moved out of hearing range. "If I mixed a large dose into someone's food, there would be strong abdominal cramping, diarrhea, vomiting, and then death from shock. If I dared, it would be better to mix smaller doses so a person gradually loses their strength, gets confused, and ends up paralyzed. This is the main reason kings and generals keep winetasters to sample their food."

"I thought you said arsenic was tasteless."

"It is," Orotes said. "This is the great secret of chefs. We have power. We determine whether a leader stays or goes!"

"Now you're scaring me," Yas said, backing away. "Am I safe around you? With what I eat?"

Orotes smiled. "You're safe for now. Of course, if you wanted to poison the general, the emperor, or two certain young girls, I may not be able to protect you. You see, I'm both the chef and the winetaster. I'm obligated to tell the emperor if anyone even approaches me in an effort to poison him."

"Let's forget we had this conversation. The more I know you, the less I know you."

"What do I say to our little matchmaker?"

"Tell her you're so committed to me that you'd rather take the poison yourself."

"You know very well that she'll test me on that." Orotes looked toward the palace. "Wouldn't you know it? As we speak of the conspirators, they're already on their way here. I hope you're ready for another horse lesson."

Without looking back, he left the bridge and made his way toward the kitchen entrance.

The girls arrived only a couple of minutes later, strutting like miniature generals.

"Take us to the horses," Fang ordered.

Yas continued to lean on the railing, observing the swans. "Have you ever stopped to consider how majestic these birds are?" she asked.

Jing skipped up beside her and gazed at the gliding white birds. "They're a gift from the gods to the emperor. Fang says she wants to eat them one day."

Yas turned toward Fang. "What would the emperor do if you ate his gift from the gods?"

Fang frowned. "He would feed me to the wild things. They tried to bite my finger when I was younger. But forget those silly birds. Take us to the horses."

"One day you'll learn that it's smart to treat both people and horses with dignity and respect," Yas said. "When you force others to do your bidding, they may begin to resent you and fail to treat you with dignity and respect."

"But you're a foreigner, not even a designated teacher," Fang said. "What do you know about anything?"

"I know how to ride a horse and I know how to teach others to ride. All you need to know is whether you want to learn how to ride or to keep dreaming about it in your garden."

Fang pouted. "I'll tell my father to chop you up and feed you to the koi."

"Okay," Yas said. "Come, Jing. You and I will ride horses while your sister spends time with the fish."

Jing hesitated as Yas and Liu headed for the maze and that giant hedge separating them from the outside world. She glanced at her sister, who hung back on the bridge with her arms crossed.

Finally, Fang turned and followed. The draw of riding was too much to resist.

Seven

The ship lurched into another trough as Ardeshir heaved on an empty stomach.

"You'll feel better after we get to land," Tertullian yelled into the gale of the winter storm. "This is the best ship my fellow shadows could find."

They'd gotten blown off-course near Crete, preventing them from completing this itinerary to Corinth. Now they'd need an extra day circumnavigating the southern tip of Achaea before heading up to Ancona and taking aim for Rome.

Tertullian gripped Ardeshir's shoulder and gave his back a pat. "We need to find your father before he hears that we're looking for him. Fortunately, the priests at the Temple of Artemis think we're trying to assassinate him. They may not be too quick to send word. After all, they'll want him dead before he goes to trial with Caesar."

"Why do they want him dead?" Ardeshir asked. "Nothing about this is making sense."

The giant leaned against the railing as if they were sailing leisurely on a sunny day. "Before your father fought in the arena at Ephesus, he was forced to make a vow of loyalty to Artemis. When he turned his back on her to follow Yeshua, her followers were forced to enact their revenge on him."

Ardeshir nodded and hugged himself. The deck pitched violently and saltwater sloshed over everything in sight. He was drenched, shivering, and exhausted from all the retching.

He stepped toward the stairs which would take him belowdecks just as the ship surged upward into an oncoming wave. Tertullian caught him as he hurtled toward the main mast.

"I'm taking you below," Tertullian said. "You haven't got anything left in your stomach anyhow. Wrap your arm around me until we get to the cabin door."

The two men stumbled as the ship plunged yet again. They fell into a folded sail on the deck.

"Crawl!" Tertullian yelled. "Hurry!"

Ardeshir reached the door and tumbled down the stairs, hurting his back in the process but feeling too afraid to pay any attention to the intensity of the pain.

"Yeshua!" he called. "Help!"

Tertullian grabbed him by the shoulder and pulled him toward his cabin. Inside, the two of them collapsed on the floor.

"Whatever possessed you to go outside in that weather?" Tertullian asked. "We survive the temple, convince the hunters of Artemis that we're on their side and the priest is not, that trying to assassinate your father is the wrong move, and then hire a ship to actually sail despite the storm… and you have to test the fates to see whether they'll drop you into the sea?"

"I didn't want to lose my dinner in here." Ardeshir held his stomach. "I don't think I was made to sail. I hope my father did better than I did."

Tertullian rolled out the sleeping mats, threw a towel and dry tunic toward Ardeshir, who began to change into the new clothes.

"It's amazing that your father is still alive after all this time," the thespian assassin said. "He's got to be strong and determined. Either that, or else he's insane enough to think he can rescue himself."

"My father was a great warrior. You don't get to be the emperor's champion by giving in to trouble. When my mother died, I thought he would fade away. Instead he put his heart into our farm and opened it up to orphans and widows and those who had no place to belong." Ardeshir finished changing and threw his wet tunic into a corner. "The Elamites and Parthians both wanted him to declare himself for the throne on their behalf. He refused and spoke about the true King of Kings who brings peace to all. People didn't understand him, even though he had proven himself. They just turned their attention to others."

"If you're heir to the throne of Persia, why don't you contend for it?" Tertullian asked. "Why don't the Elamites and Parthians come after you to declare yourself?"

"They don't know whether my father is alive or dead, and they think I'm definitely dead. General Ban Chao from the Han Empire chased after me when I married Lu Hou and they destroyed our farm. Now we're in hiding—that is, until we can build our army and rebuild."

Tertullian shook his head. "No one will believe that story. A prince of Persia marries the daughter of the Han emperor but has to run because the same emperor's general wants them dead? The prince has no place to rule, no place to call his own? And his father is in chains, pleading for his life before the Roman emperor while priests for Artemis try to kill him because of his faith in the wrong god?"

"That's about right," Ardeshir said. "I think I'm tired."

"What was that like for you," Yas asked Jing as they skipped along through the maze, heading back towards the emperor's garden. "After riding for ten days, your muscles and balance are improving a lot. Your sister will be jealous when she sees what you can do."

"Fang refuses to talk to me anymore," Jing said. "She creates untruths before our mother and I'm worried I will be punished."

"If you ever need my help, send me a note that says 'I love horses.'"

"How will that get me help?"

"It will be our secret code. If you send that note, I'll meet you where the horses are kept."

Jing hung her head. "The emperor doesn't like us to keep secrets."

"Then we won't tell the emperor." Yas decided to change the subject. "Do you like to ride?"

"Oh yes! More than anything. But it would be much better if my sister could ride with me."

"Why don't you tell her that?" Yas suggested. "She needs an excuse to save face and overcome her resistance."

"I could do that," Jing said. "She's missing out on so much fun. I could teach her how to walk forward and back, how to turn and move more quickly. I can't wait until I learn to trot!"

"What are the most important lessons you need to remember about riding?"

"I need to breathe. I need to sit comfortably and keep relaxed. I need to give clear instructions with my knees and hands. Of course, I need to not surprise the horse. And I need to stay on the horse."

Yas grinned at her pupil. "Well done! Perhaps we can try throwing a spear after the next full moon. You know, a person should only throw spears when they need to. As you grow up, you need to find ways to protect yourself. Like learning this maze. You never know when understanding the places around you can help to save you."

As the two emerged from the maze, they stopped. In front of them stood Fang and her father, General Ban Chao. Fang's arms were crossed and she wore a wicked grin on her face. Ban Chou stood with his hands on his hips, wielding an impressive length of bamboo.

The general pointed to his side. "Jing, here, now!"

Jing ran and stood behind him, head bowed.

Ban Chou walked toward Yas with his bamboo stick held high. As he swung, she turned and the bamboo struck with a sharp sting. Again and again the bamboo fell across her back, arms, and legs until Yas fell onto her knees and covered her head.

Liu found her there some time later, long after the beating, accompanied by his niece.

"Come," he said gently. "Come to my home. We'll care for you there."

That's when two young gardeners arrived with a sheet. They carefully rolled her onto it and lifted. The pain was so intense that Yas hardly noticed the jostling until she found herself at rest in a dark, cool room.

She looked up and recognized the visage of Liu's wife. The woman slowly removed Yas's robe and rubbed her welts with a healing balm. Tears rolled down her face and fell on Yas's cheeks.

"This is not the way your brother taught us," the woman murmured.

A trio of thespian assassins, dressed in black, shuffled down the Roman street outside a small military outpost. Two of them carried a stretcher while the third, an extremely tall man, emitted a wail of mourning. Four legionnaires marched in front of them.

As the procession reached the gate to the outpost, the legionnaires engaged in a ritual of exchange with the sentries on duty. Once the exchange was complete, the four new legionnaires opened the gate and allowed the mourners inside.

Once they were within the walls, the mourners set down the stretcher and Ardeshir rolled out onto the cobblestone plaza.

Tertullian, the tallest mourner, motioned for the pair of stretcher-bearers to stash the stretcher behind a building. Those dressed in black shed their robes to reveal the armor of legionnaires. They formed a unit and marched toward the barracks.

Without hesitation, they walked through the doors and entered the assembly hall where they were met by a centurion.

Tertullian raised his hand toward the centurion.

"I'm Brutus Legunus, from Caesar's legion, here to collect the prisoner," Tertullian said. "According to the rumors, special assassins are planning to murder him before the trial. We'll relocate him closer to the tribunal hall. What are your instructions on how we should collect and transport the man?"

The centurion frowned. "I have received no such order. Are you new here?"

Tertullian held out a scroll. "I'm on special assignment. This is an urgent matter. Here are the orders from the Senate, containing the emperor's seal. You should have heard from a messenger by now! Hopefully the assassins didn't dispatch him in order to delay the transfer."

The centurion opened the seal and examined the scroll's contents. "All seems to be in order. I'll bring you the prisoner, although he will need a stretcher or a carriage. He is weak from his travels."

"I will order a carriage."

As the centurion departed, Tertullian lifted his thumb toward one of the other men in his cohort. The man left through the gate. The rest of the group stood like statues awaiting orders.

The centurion finally returned with another sentry.

"The physician says that your man is too weak to travel or to get off his bed," said the Roman. "This man with me is the one who accompanied your charge all the way from Ephesus. There is quite some concern about releasing him to anyone since he's been marked for assassination."

Ardeshir stepped forward. "Perhaps if I speak to him, things will be different. He knows me and understands that he can trust me. Would you allow me to at least see him?"

The centurion looked briefly at his colleague and then nodded. "Leave your weapons behind. I'll escort you to his room. It seems his body and sight are both weak. He may not recognize you as you wish."

The path led through darkened basalt stone hallways lit by occasional flickering torches. The passageway was so convoluted that Ardeshir wasn't sure any of them would have found their way to the right cell.

When the centurion stopped, he unlocked a door and swung it open.

An old man, thin and curled up under a blanket, lay instead, moaning from a mat pushed into the corner.

"No, I can't go," the prisoner said. "They're trying to kill me. I appealed to Caesar…"

Ardeshir knelt down and placed a hand on his father's bearded face. "Shalom to the emperor's champion," he spoke in Persian. "I am your son, here to take you home."

Nabonidus clutched onto his son's hands and began to sob, convulsing.

"What did you say to him?" the Roman asked. "Why is he crying?"

"I spoke to him in his own tongue and told him we were here to take him someplace safe," Ardeshir said in Latin. "I think he'll find the strength to go with us now. Would you see if the carriage has arrived?"

The centurion left and Tertullian showed up alongside two others, who carried a stretcher.

"Come Abba," Ardeshir said. "These friends have travelled a long way to protect you. Once we get you out of here, you'll be safe and won't have to state your case before Caesar."

Nabonidus struggled up onto one elbow. "But I must have my day in court," he whispered in a raspy voice. "I must tell Caesar about the good news of Yeshua. My life means nothing if the emperor won't release us from this iron fist of his."

The old man collapsed back onto his mat in a fit of coughing.

"There are others, stronger than you, who will find a way to present the good news you desire," Ardeshir said. "Your people in Persia need you to come home."

"I'm not afraid of Caesar, his cross, or his lions," Nabonidus said. "I've come this far and I must finish my journey. Caesar must know."

"Abba, there are people who have taken an oath to kill you before you speak to Caesar. If we found a way to fool his guards, then you must know that others will do the same. They may poison you, strangle you, or find another way… but they will not allow you to have your day in court." Ardeshir rested a hand on his father's forehead. "Your life in the arena has been your lasting witness. The church you started in Ephesus is your witness. Now is the time to rest and be with your family."

"But the journey is too great… let me die here, fighting for what is true…"

"Abba, I have a wife and a son." Ardeshir helped his father up into a sitting position. "They need to see you. I've come all this way to find you! Come with me. We'll go slow for you."

Nabonidus breathed heavily. "How is the farm and all the orphans? How is my sister, Laleh?"

"The situation is very unsettled in Persia, as they were in your time. Come, find your place again. Bring peace back to our people."

"I'm too weak," Nabonidus said, trying to lie down again. "Go with my blessing and take your rightful place."

"No, Abba. I've come so far for you. Come with me."

The centurion marched into the room at that moment, sword drawn. "Who are you men?" he demanded. "A messenger from Caesar's palace has come, informing me that a group of thespian assassins has been dispatched from Ephesus to kill the prisoner. Where did you come from and where did you get your orders? My messenger says that no orders have been issued to move the prisoner."

Tertullian stepped forward from where he had been leaning against the wall. "It is as I told you when we arrived. This man has been marked for assassination. If we aren't who we say we are, how do you suppose we acquired a scroll with Caesar's own seal? Likely, this new messenger is an imposter. Let me confront him."

Ardeshir followed the centurion and Tertullian out to the plaza. He needed to find a way to get his father out of here before someone else found him.

In the plaza, the messenger in question stood watching the disguised thespian assassins.

"Centurion," Tertullian said, nudging the man's elbow. "How would we move this man if others were trying to ambush us?"

The centurion turned toward him, wearing a frown. As he did, Tertullian wrapped an arm around the messenger's head, jerked, and let the man fall to the ground.

In moments, the big man was standing back amongst his own men as if nothing had happened.

"What have you done?" Ardeshir said.

The centurion pivoted and ran to the fallen man. He then looked suspiciously toward Tertullian. "His neck is broken!"

"He seemed to fall," one of the assassins said. "It seems you can't trust anyone around here. Anyway, we have a task to perform."

The centurion appeared distraught. "Whether he lives or dies is no matter. But if the prisoner leaves on my watch, it will be my neck Caesar chooses to sever!"

Tertullian stepped forward, towering over the soldier. "Perhaps you may simply report that you prisoner died of natural causes. Say that you released him for cremation. We'll give you some ashes to confirm the story."

The others closed in around the centurion.

"Take your prisoner and bring me the ashes as soon as you can," the centurion eventually decided. "I will also need thirty pieces of silver… to cover any hidden costs."

Tertullian nodded as one of the assassins stepped forward with a leather pouch and counted out thirty pieces of silver. The centurion accepted the payment and walked out through the gate of the outpost.

As Ardeshir watched, two of the men proceeded to retrieve Nabonidus on a stretcher. Two others carried the deceased messenger around the building to the cremation slab. Meanwhile, Tertullian and Ardeshir settled Nabonidus into the carriage, covered him with a blanket, and joined him.

Moments later, the carriage was on its way.

They were less than a stone's throw away from the gate when the centurion rushed out again. "Stop!"

Tertullian handed his dagger to Ardeshir. "Slice his throat quickly and we'll ride hard before we're caught."

Ardeshir stepped down from the carriage, the dagger concealed.

"What is it you need?" he asked the approaching centurion.

"You need to take the papers for the cremation of the body," the soldier said. "And you forgot the fee for delivery."

"Thank you." Ardeshir accepted the small leather scroll and the money pouch. He did his best to conceal his relief that he wouldn't need to use the dagger. "The empire is stronger because of men like you."

Eight

Mercifully, weeks passed without further visits by General Ban Chao. Yas's welts healed slowly as Liu's wife applied the cream and damp cloths to her wounds.

"The Way is the way."

The woman chanted this over and over until the words worked themselves into Yas's nightmares. In these torrid visions, the general yelled this as he hit her. Her brother yelled the words as he taunted her from the lion's den where he had last been seen. Fang yelled at them as she stood on the back of a horse, taunting her.

There was no question that the phrase had to do with her brother's fascination with Yeshua, but what did it mean?

The babblings of Liu's wife revealed several things. The Han were fascinated with talk of the way of truth, especially the notion of the emperor being the way of truth. But Ardeshir had confused them by speaking of Yeshua. East and west met at Yeshua's cross, but neither side was willing to set aside the alternatives they had learned to lean on through the centuries.

After the second full moon, Jing appeared at the doorway of Liu's home. She walked in without hesitation and looked down on Yas.

"My father says you should be walking by now. I haven't had a horse lesson in almost two moons." Jing knelt beside the mat. "My father says you can take me as long as you also take Fang. There can be no favorites if it brings shame on the oldest child. You must learn our ways if you are to live here."

Yas covered her eyes with her arm. "I cannot walk anyplace where your father will see me. I cannot bear to be near your sister. I need to go back to my home… where I know the way of things…"

Jing laid a hand on Yas's wrist and gently tugged. "Let me see your beautiful eyes. The eyes show the soul."

Yas closed her eyes as her arm moved away.

"Liu has told me about how your brother, the one who spoke of the Way before he was eaten by the lions," Jing pressed. "What is this way?"

"I don't believe my brother was eaten by lions. I think he escaped, which is why your father came to my land to kill everyone I loved. He's the dragon who consumes everything in his way."

Jing pulled away. "No! My father is not a dragon. He is a kind and gentle man to those who deserve it. And he is a stern and righteous warrior for those who defile the ways of the emperor." She stood and backed toward the door. "You speak untruths in a foreign tongue. Fang was right. It's only a matter of time until you seek to turn us against our leaders… to turn us toward darkness."

Yas propped herself up on an elbow and eyed the defiant child. "I'm the one who can teach you to ride. I'm the one who suffered because of the untruths your sister told your father. I am the one who can't walk because your father beat me for no reason."

"No!" Jing covered her ears. "You suffer because you have wronged the emperor in your ways, in your speech, in your thoughts, and in your choices. To blame others is to defy what is."

"Go play with your Koi," Yas said. "You are choosing not to hear, and not to learn, what is true. Run to your sister and to your father. Let them teach you what you want to know."

The girl turned and ran.

Once they were alone again, Liu's wife knelt down beside Yas.

"She is a child," the woman assured her. "We use a feather on a child and a stick for a man. The Way teaches us to treat others in the right way."

Afterward Yas set her back against the wall and wept. No matter what she wanted, there seemed no way to get it. She was trapped and alone in this land.

"I'm not sure my father is going to make it." Ardeshir hopped out of the carriage and approached Tertullian, who was getting down from his mount. "It's a long journey and he's so weak."

"At least he won't die by the hand of someone who wants to mock and destroy his reputation," Tertullian remarked. "I'll purchase some bread and fruit from the vendors here. Speak to your father. Encourage him."

As the giant man walked away towards a line of nearby stalls, Ardeshir turned back to the carriage and removed the blanket from overtop his father.

"How are you doing so far?" he asked.

Nabonidus smiled weakly. "Your face is the last one I expected to see in Rome. How are you doing and why have you come?"

"I married the Han emperor's daughter and I have a son," Ardeshir told him. "The farm was destroyed, but we're rebuilding it. Yas has been taken back to the Han Empire too… but once I get you back home, I'll go after her. I will need your word in order to raise an army."

"I'm not sure I can make it back. Take me to Ephesus where members of the Way can care for me. How is my sister?"

"Queen Laleh is dying. The country needs another Maimonides to secure the throne. We're a divided people, with others taking advantage of us."

Tertullian strode back up with a bag of purchases. He leaned over Nabonidus while handing to Ardeshir a handful of flatbread, dates, and figs.

"We can take you both back to Caesarea, but the rest of the journey would be up to you," the giant said. "We'll travel overnight to Ancona. There will be a ship there ready to sail at dawn."

"Leave me at Ephesus," Nabonidus whispered. "I'm too weak to go further."

"We're not stopping at Ephesus," Tertullian said. "We'll get you to Caesarea, though. Then you can decide where to go. At least the weather is supposed to be much better in the next few days."

Nabonidus moaned. "What is the point of my life? I can't defend my faith before Caesar and I can't help the church in Ephesus. My body has betrayed me and I don't even have the strength to walk. I'll die a stranger in a strange land."

"Abba, you will live to see your grandson," Ardeshir assured him. "Yeshua has rescued you for a greater purpose than you know. In the meantime, I've brought you something to eat. So regain your strength, get some rest, and thank the Almighty for what he has done through these men who have risked their lives for you."

A fresh blanket of snow smothered the emperor's garden as Yas limped toward the bridge over the koi pond.

"Are you sure you're ready to go back to your room on your own?" Liu asked. "The general can come by and find you anytime if no one's around. Remember that he threatened to have you thrown over the wall to be consumed by the wild things. The emperor is still too sick to sit on the grand council and cast his deciding vote."

"I'm more worried about those two girls," Yas said. "I promised to teach them to ride, and no arrogant old man should take that away from them. And if Fang keeps up her attitude, she'll likely join me when I'm thrown over that wall!"

She kicked snow off the edge of the bridge onto the thin sheet of ice covering the pond.

"I need to go back home, but I don't want to escape without Orotes," she mused. "Do you think you could help us get away?"

"The general would go after you if you tried to leave," Liu said. "Then my family and I would be killed. No. We must wait for the emperor to make his decision. But why do you think your home is the only place you can be happy?"

Yas leaned back against the railing. "Home is where I can be myself. I don't have to prove how good I can speak another language or how well I can perform a task. The people there know me and accept me."

Liu's niece emerged from a path near the residences. "Hurry!" she called. "Smoke is rising from your home. Did you leave your fire on?"

Yas limped behind Liu as he raced ahead of her.

"Send help!" Yas urged the girl. "We need water, snow… anything. Hurry!"

By the time they arrived at the scene, flames were already licking the cedar shingles on the roof. Smoke billowed out the windows and a dozen workers were busy scooping up snow to throw it on the flames. She watched as Liu rallied a group of servants to form a human chain to carry water from the pond. Four men had already shown up with their own buckets.

Yas stepped into line and helped pass on the buckets, but after an hour it was clear that the home was beyond help.

General Ban Chao arrived as Yas and Liu were sorting through the smoldering ruins.

"What is the meaning of this?" he shouted, raising his bamboo rod. "You ungrateful dog. Is this how you treat our mercy? Destroying what we have shared with you?"

Everyone prostrated themselves on the ground—everyone, that is, except Yas.

"Your servants can tell you that I was nowhere near this place when the fire started," Yas said defiantly. "I haven't even had the chance to come here since you beat me for no reason. Ask your sentries who might have been around. Surely, you have observers watching all of us."

The general barked an order and a young man rose to bow before him.

"The woman was not here when the fire started," the young man confirmed.

"Who have you seen around here?" the general asked.

"Only your oldest daughter."

Ban Chao raised his bamboo rod and struck the young man once on the side. "How dare you accuse a child of such an evil. You and your family will feed the wild things today. This destruction must be avenged."

Yas stepped forward. "General! Your youngest daughter says you are a gentle and merciful man, and this young man has done nothing but help us put out the fire. If this kingdom centers itself on what is true, you need to release him from this unrighteous sentence."

The general raised his bamboo stick and took a step toward Yas. As he did, Jing stepped out from amidst the hedges. He stopped when he saw her.

He lowered his stick. "You can find your own place to rest. This isn't your home. The sooner you leave, the better we'll all be. Your foreign ideas have warped the minds of my people. Even my own daughters have been infected."

Yas nodded. "Are you saying I don't have to wait for the emperor's permission to go home?"

Ban Chao shifted uncomfortably. "As soon as the emperor gives his assent, it would be good for you to be gone. If I see you with my daughters again, I'll send you to the wild things."

"I will take the chef with me when I go," Yas hastily added. "We'll be gone as soon as the snows melt."

The general stepped toward her again and whispered harshly, "The chef stays."

The shipping yards at Ancona swarmed with sailors and builders. The ribs of a quinquereme under construction towered above the drydock. Next to it, a newly launched naval vessel measured forty-five strides in length and five strides wide. Around three hundred rowers were prepared to board with a hundred soldiers armed and waiting behind them. The ship's sailors and crew were already aboard, yelling instructions to a train of slaves hauling sacks of grain, vegetables, and salted meat up the gangway to a gap for the hold. The men dropped their burdens only to join the never-ending circle to carry another load.

The second-floor warehouse window was the perfect place for Ardeshir and Tertullian to observe the shipyard without being seen.

Tertullian pointed toward the ship's captain, who stood near the hold. "They'll load the weight of a thousand men into the hold. If any enemy ships get in our way, they'll ram them. Carthage used to rule the seas, but in the last wars the Romans sent a hundred thousand rowers and more than forty thousand soldiers in three hundred ships. The pirates are slowly being pushed out of the Great Sea."

Ardeshir glanced toward the form curled up under a blanket. "The Romans didn't do it quick enough to save my father from those pirates."

"At least they got to him before he could be sold at a slave market. And we got to him before the priests of Artemis or the courts of the emperor. You should thank whatever god you worship that you weren't alone in your quest."

"I do thank you, as well as the other shadows," Ardeshir said.

The slaves completed their loading of cargo and the rowers marched aboard to take their places, their strong shoulders and backs evidence of the consistent strain the work exacted on their bodies.

Ardeshir glanced back toward Tertullian and noted the big man's own substantial upper body strength.

"You will get your payment in full," Ardeshir assured him. "I've been thinking that I won't be happy until I get everyone home again. But all I can think about is whether my father will survive the journey."

"I can see you have little faith in this god of yours," Tertullian said. "Perhaps you should try another god. There are plenty to choose from. Your friend Arsama assured me that this Yeshua was a great god and our mission would be successful because of it. Perhaps our fortune has come from another source."

"No! Yeshua *is* a great God. It's just that I'm not a great believer. I've seen too much of this world, but I know that Yeshua is still the Way."

"Perhaps you should offer more costly sacrifices to him. That way he'd pay better attention to you."

"There is no more need for sacrifices," Ardeshir said. "He ended all that when he sacrificed himself."

Tertullian chuckled. "A dead god? No wonder you don't need sacrifices. What good is a dead god when you're in trouble?"

"He was dead, but he's not dead now. He came back to life after three days. He hears our prayers and helps us because he loves us."

"If you learn of any real god who can defeat death, follow him," Tertullian said. "If this god of yours is real, why are you afraid?"

The warrior shook his head in wonder and walked away.

Ardeshir watched him go. The man had a point. Why worry so much if Yeshua was so powerful? Why work so hard? Why wrestle so much to earn the approval of his father and others?

He stepped aside as a fisherman pulled a cartload of fish across the wharf to the ship. It was time to get his father settled for the long trip home.

Three of the emperor's gardeners swept the snow from off the pathway ahead. Liu and Yas walked behind them, deep in conversation.

"What hope is there for me to leave if the chef has to stay and the emperor refuses to get up from his bed?" Yas wondered. "When will I find justice?"

Liu clenched his hands behind his back and nodded thoughtfully. "The one who knows all truth will decide when the time is right. We can only wait."

"What if he dies before he makes a decision? What will happen to me then?"

The sweepers cleared the bridge and waited for the pair to cross before taking up their duties again.

"The successor who alone knows all truth will decide," Liu said.

"And how long will it take to find a successor?"

"When the swans nest and bring forth their young. At that time, the grand council will choose the next emperor of the Han dynasty."

"I've been here three times and have never seen the swans nest," Yas objected. "It could be years."

"And yet the sun will rise and set. The moon will cross the night sky. The stars will shine. The snow will come and go."

Yas sighed. "All that may be true, but I will be here without a man to marry. I'll be without children. I'm getting too old to fight… too old to give birth."

"That is your truth then. You must know your truth so it can guide you. Perhaps your man will be someone from here. Perhaps you don't have to go somewhere else to have a child."

Yas crossed her arms and stepped into the great stretch of untouched snow lying over the great lawn that sloped down to the covered lake.

"I was made to walk where others are afraid to walk," she said. "I fought alongside my father and brother and led the great cataphracts in battle. Orotes is the only Persian here, though, and the general is keeping us apart."

"Why is Orotes your only choice"

Yas spun around to face him. "Who else could there be?"

The look in his eyes told her all she needed to know. Her mouth hung open before she turned away, warmth running up her cheeks and into her ears.

"When the emperor dies, all his servants will be set free," Liu said. "I will go wherever I wish and marry whomever I desire."

Yas slowed her pace and gritted her teeth. What could she say? No, she couldn't stay. Her whole world was wrapped up in the land south of Susa. How could she even think of remaining here in a world where a man such as the general could be so determined to destroy her?

"Liu, you're better than a brother to me," she began. "Once I go west and find my brother again, perhaps he will give his blessing for a man to marry me. And perhaps he'll rescue our father…"

Liu stopped walking. "What are you saying?"

The sweepers stopped to stretch and Yas waited for them.

"I'm saying that I have dreams and desires," she answered at last. "But there are parts of my life which demand the input of my family. I cannot give an answer to a question that is not mine to answer."

He smiled. "Of course. You're right. If the people of this land must await the nesting of the swans to know their new emperor, then it is right that I await the right timing for the one who is for me. This is a true truth. It will guide you as others notice your beauty and grace."

Yas glanced sideways with a smirk. "My beauty? You think I'm beautiful?"

"You are as beautiful and gracious as the swans on the lake," Liu said. "Your beauty is lovelier than the spring flowers. Your grace is like the flow of a gentle stream. Your movement is the flow of dancers under the harvest moon."

She nudged him in the side with her elbow. "If you're trying to convince me to favor you before others, then let me assure you that there may be no others. You've already learned that we Persians love poetry, song, and dance. Continue speaking to my heart like this and I won't be able to resist. That is, if my brother gives his blessing."

"That's all I need to know."

Nine

As the ship rounded Crete and headed for Caesarea, the seas offered a rolling swell to guide it on its way. The sails billowed under a cloudless sky and the gulls floated calmly overhead. A pod of playful striped dolphins rose on their tails to glide by, chittering at the naval vessel. Bottlenose dolphins bobbed in and out of the ship's wake, feeding on fish spooked by the vessel's shadow.

Ardeshir watched all this from the deck, leaning into the railing as a large whale spouted off just below.

"Your father still isn't happy we're passing by Ephesus," Tertullian said, coming up behind him. "I can't believe the old man wants to go back there. Don't the Ephesians want to kill him? If he placed one foot on that shore, I doubt they'd give him a second chance to get away."

"His deep faith in Yeshua drives him to think he can change the world," Ardeshir said. "I'll talk to him again. If he's got enough emotion to get upset about Ephesus, perhaps that means he has enough strength to get home. But I can't imagine how he'll hold up for the next three months on the road."

"Perhaps you should wait with him in Caesarea. He'll need to regain his strength. Just send a message to your wife to let her know you're coming. Wouldn't want her to worry. In the meantime, the shadows and I will be moving on to an assignment in Damascus, so we can't guard you once we reach the shore. I'll collect our fee as soon as we catch sight of the harbor."

Ardeshir pushed away from the rail and stretched. "I've left the coin with a friend in Caesarea. You'll have to come with me to collect it. Remember what we agreed? That I'd pay you once the task was complete."

Tertullian towered over him and lowered a hand on each of Ardeshir's shoulders. The weight of those hands was significant.

"You've seen us work," Tertullian said. "We don't play games when we take an assignment. If you think you're going to get away without payment, think again. I'll throw you overboard right now."

"Relax!" Ardeshir said. "You can guard my father at the harbor while I retrieve the money. Or you can come along. Believe me, you've been worth every shekel. The fighting techniques you've taught me might even impress my sister!"

That didn't seem to fully satisfy the giant.

"If you're trying to insult me, I'll throw both you *and* your father overboard," Tertullian muttered. "The men are expecting a quick payment and you're not making this easier on either of us."

Still, he released his hold on Ardeshir and leaned back against the rail.

"Tell me where the money is being held and I'll try to convince the men to be patient. We're already late for Damascus and need to move fast."

Ardeshir took a step back and eyed a gull dipping down to fly level with the deck. "Arsama and Mariam guard my coin. Send someone with me on horseback and we'll be back before you've packed for your next assignment. I can meet you at the warehouse where you store your supplies."

Another member of Tertullian's band stepped up beside him.

"The old man is having trouble with his breath," the shadow reported. "He's gasping like a fish out of water. What do you want us to do?"

"We're still two days from land," Tertullian said. "Carry him up to the deck and let the wind blow into his face. He may need some sunshine, not to mention all this briny air."

Ardeshir rushed down the stairs ahead of the thespian assassin and knelt beside his gasping father in their cramped cabin.

"I can't... I can't... I can't do this," Nabonidus said.

"Abba, you can!" Ardeshir urged. "We're almost to Caesarea. We'll take time for you to regain your strength before we travel farther. I need you to be strong so you can meet my son."

Nabonidus rested his head against Ardeshir's chest. "I have... beaten... every enemy... along the way... but this one... this one... is too much."

Ardeshir made way for the much bigger and stronger Tertullian.

"Abba, this man will carry you up to the deck so you can get some fresh air," Ardeshir said. "It will help you to see the blue sky and to breathe in the fresh sea air."

Nabonidus struggled to adjust himself as the big man lifted him. "Ardeshir. Say goodbye... to your sister... Nothing but Yeshua... can help me... now..."

The emperor breathed his last as the full moon rose above the red-tiled palace. Yas heard the first wail, a keening noise from the maiden assigned to meet his final needs. The sound was then picked up by other members of the house staff.

As the cries drifted across the emperor's garden Yas sat up to absorb and understand the meaning of this disturbance of the sacred space.

Urgent knocking prompted her to slip on her house robe and slippers. The knocking continued until she acknowledged the guest wanting her attention. It was Liu.

"The emperor has taken his final journey," he said. "We'll need to hide you until his successor is chosen. My niece recently heard a chambermaid tell a vendor that General Ban Chao planned to help you 'disappear' as soon as the emperor left us."

"Where will we go?" Yas asked. "What do I take?"

"Take everything you can carry in one bag. I only have a small bundle, but tie it to your back to keep your hands free. We'll hide among the unseen and unwanted until we're meant to be found again."

"I have no idea what that means, but I trust you to keep me safe."

As she packed her clothing, personal items, and trinkets, Liu's niece arrived at the door, breathing hard.

"The general has sent two of the guardians to arrest the chef," the girl announced. "He'll be sending two more to get you. Hurry!"

Yas stopped her packing. "We need to help Orotes. They'll blame him for the emperor's death and execute him. Find me a weapon."

Liu stepped forward and grabbed her wrist.

"No!" He reached down and grabbed her bag. "We need to hide. Then you can plan for whatever needs to be done. If you're dead, you'll never be able to help him. Besides, he hasn't shown any interest in you. Let him go."

Yas shook off Liu's hand and snatched her bag from him. "In my family, we care for everyone who matters to us." She took a step toward the door. "But you're right. I need to get to safety first."

Her sleepiness faded in the cool night air and she pressed against the hedges and bushes in an effort to closely follow Liu. Meanwhile, the wailing throughout the gardens rose like a tsunami of grief. Torches flickered as people gathered. In the distance, a gong clanged from the palace, crushing the night back into silence.

Yas turned at the shouts of guardians pursuing them.

"Quick, through the hedge to the horse pasture," Liu instructed. "We'll ride from there."

They pushed down the hill toward the barn, where Liu's uncle had already taken the horses out of their stalls.

"I thought you might be coming," the man said. "The road is clear and no soldiers have come this way. Ride over the hills and through the forest until the sun rises. Then hide. The horses will last until then."

Without a word further, Liu clambered aboard his mount and Yas followed, clinging to her bag as the horses shot across the pasture.

Ardeshir breathed a sigh of relief as he watched Tertullian and his crew ride out of Caesarea at a gallop. The coins had been enough and his father had survived to reach Arsama and Mariam's home.

Upon returning, he sat next to his father as Mariam spooned broth into his mouth. The food was reviving his strength, but the biggest boost to his energy seemed to come from the little one, Hananiah.

"Hananiah… wasn't that the name of one of Daniel's crew in Babylon?" Ardeshir asked, searching his recollection of the scriptures.

Arsama nodded. "He was one of the courageous few who stood in the fire with Yeshua. Nebuchadnezzar called him Shadrach. I hope my own son will be able to stand strong when others around him bow to pressure."

"Israel will need men like him," Ardeshir said. "So will Persia. My son, Artabanas, will grow up with the combined fury of the Han Empire and the Persian Empire in one heart and somehow find his peace with both."

He fell silent, watching his father play with young Hananiah. The sight made Ardeshir miss his son even more.

"We'll be with you only until my father is strong enough to travel," Ardeshir said.

Arsama set a hand on his shoulder. "Stay as long as you like. My home is yours. Who knows what opportunities we may have to honor Yeshua?"

"I've heard about a centurion here who follows the Way." Ardeshir turned to look him in the eye. "I think he's named Cornelius. Have you heard of the gathering in his place?"

"Yes! The group has grown rapidly and is looking for other places to meet. Mariam and I thought about joining them, but then Hananiah came along. We're not certain of all the rituals involved in hosting a group like that... which is why we've stayed quiet."

"My father helped start a gathering of the Way in Ephesus," Ardeshir said. "He could help get us started. Perhaps this Cornelius can help us build up our numbers. That way you'll have others to keep you encouraged after my father and I leave."

The sound of footsteps made him look up. Mariam had left his father's side and stepped close.

"I couldn't help overhearing, and it sounds like a great idea, but your father is calling for you," she said. "If you can spare a few minutes away from your dreaming, this would be a good time to listen to him."

Ardeshir crept over to Nabonidus, who lay on a mat in the corner of the room, his back propped up by some cushions. The old man feebly lifted his arm, but then let it drop at his side.

"Son... I can't go on."

Ardeshir knelt at his side and reached for his hand. "But just a moment ago you were with the child..."

Nabonidus frowned in confusion. "You are a good son... but I need to go to Yeshua."

"You've accomplished so much, Abba." Ardeshir held his father's hand against his cheek. "I need you for one more task. Arsama and Mariam want to start a gathering of the Way." He laid his father's hand back across his chest. "You started that gathering in Ephesus with the apostle John and the mother of Yeshua. Can you help us here... stay long enough to ensure we do it right?"

The faraway look in his father's eyes captured a glint of hope. "Perhaps I can stay... for a few more days... to guide you... in this great risk. The Way is caught... in the middle of the battle... between the religious leaders... of this nation... and the political leaders of Rome. It will not be easy... and may cost more... more than newcomers might realize. Nevertheless, I will help."

Ardeshir stood up, smiling. "Together we'll do more than we can dream. Abba, a short time from now, if you get stronger, I'll take you home. And then I will find Yas."

Nabonidus sighed deeply. "I must get stronger. You must see your son. We leave Yas... to the Almighty."

The unseen and unwanted proved to be an entire village of lame, lepers, and a tribe living among the caves and ravines of a mountain range two days from the emperor's garden.

At the outskirts of this community a one-armed man with half a nose stopped Yas and Liu with an upraised hand. His Cantonese sounded distorted, but it was clear to Yas that he wanted to know why they had come.

Liu dismounted and led the conversation. "The emperor has died and General Ban Chao is taking out his revenge on those he dislikes before a successor is chosen. We're among those who will be fed to the wild things if we're caught."

The sentry pointed toward a grass-thatched hut nestled among a copse of trees.

"Go!" he said.

A woman who lounged on a bench outside the hut had no legs below her knees. Without waiting for them to ask, she said, "A wild thing ate my feet."

She whistled low and a young man hobbled out of the hut using two canes.

"You want a place to live?" this man asked. "All the caves are taken, but you can build your own place near the blue forest on the other side of the hill. Someone will show you the way. Since you are among the whole, though, you will have to leave once the emperor's successor has been chosen."

"But we are among the unwanted," Liu said.

The young man hobbled closer. "Two feet, two hands, two eyes, everything in place. You will never remain unseen in this place. You don't fit and can't stay."

Yas stepped forward. "We are happy for your hospitality. Who will show us the way?"

"He will come. Wait!"

Halfway through the afternoon, Yas had curled up under a tree to nap when Liu nudged her arm.

"Wake up," he hissed. "We're in trouble."

Yas rubbed her eyes as the blurry form of Colonel Wei gained focus.

"Well, if it isn't the Persian rebel," Wei said. "What brings you to this hidden refuge?"

"You're a hard man to find," she answered.

The colonel raised his eyebrows and smirked. "This land does have some surprises, doesn't it?" He dismounted from his horse and dismissed the young man with a wave of his hand. "You were wise to come here. Ban Chao will be looking to take his revenge while he can."

"He destroyed my home and all that I loved," Yas said. "What are you doing among the unseen and unwanted?"

"Few people realize that I was among the unwanted," Wei said. "My mother took me while I was young to another, more favored tribe. Her sister had married a man of that tribe and they raised me as their own. I joined the military. Only at my mother's death did I learn my true identity."

"So why are you here and not with the military?" Yas asked.

"I come here to oversee and provide for this community. They're my hidden family. Many who hide among us are escaping their fate with the wild things. General Ban Chao is suspicious that a place like this exists, but so far we don't think he knows where it is." He turned to Liu. "I hope you weren't followed."

"We didn't see anyone," Liu assured him.

"If you need help building your home, there are some who will help. You met Wai Ling upon arrival. Check with him whenever you come or go."

Two young girls in colorful costumes quick-stepped up to them, set their hands on their knees, and bobbed their heads. Their smiles were like sunshine in a gloomy place. And as Yas watched, they began to wave their hands in the air.

Wei angled his head toward Yas and Liu. "They cannot speak with their mouths, so they speak with their hands. We aren't always sure what they're saying, but I think this time they're directing you to the tall grass behind their home. I'll ask them to weave roof flats together so you won't have to worry about that. You may have a home by tomorrow."

"What do we do tonight?" Yas asked.

The colonel shrugged. "The same thing you did last night."

Ardeshir grunted from the burden of hefting the chair from the back of the donkey cart. The cart's driver, a corpulent Ethiopian man, had parked the loaded vehicle in front of the door to the home of Arsama and Mariam.

"What did you do?" Ardeshir asked. "Did you fill this chair with solid gold?"

"Let that be our secret," the towering black man whispered. "After I was converted, I determined to move here and learn all I could about the Messiah. There was no easy way to bring my wealth without drawing attention to myself. Living under the protection of Cornelius has been a gift from the Almighty. But if I am to help you start a new gathering, I'll need to utilize some of the resources entrusted to me."

"What brought you to faith in Yeshua?" Ardeshir probed. "Why would you even think of leaving your homeland?"

"I might ask you the same question." The Ethiopian deposited his bulk into the chair. "Several decades ago, I came to the temple to pay homage to Adonai. My people have a long history going back to King Solomon and the queen of Sheba. I happened to be the treasurer of Queen Candace at that time."

"Don't tell me you stole the queen's treasure to finance the work of Yeshua!"

The big man chuckled. "There was no need. She compensated me well. I spent a small fortune on a scroll written by a prophet called Isaiah and read it aloud as I returned home. A Hebrew named Philip joined me and asked whether I knew what I was reading."

"And what did you tell him?"

"That I didn't understand. So he stepped up into my chariot and told me about Yeshua, the fulfillment of the prophet's words. We continued our journey together until we arrived at an oasis. There, I was immersed as a sign of my acceptance into the new people of Adonai."

Ardeshir nodded in understanding.

"I shared the good news I knew with many of my own people and we began a gathering of our own," the Ethiopian continued. "Each week we looked at the scroll and tried to understand what was written. The people expected me to teach them, but it became clear that my knowledge was limited." He shifted in the chair and readjusted the colorful cap on his head. "My people used to say, 'Ahmose, you are a big man with a big heart, but you have little knowledge. How can we become students when we have no teacher?'"

"So you came here to learn!"

Ahmose lowered his head in acknowledgement. "Yes. I stay here for half the year and return home for the other half. Others have arrived to teach my people, so I no longer feel the pressure to know everything. Cornelius has suggested that I spend time establishing this new community with your father."

"My father isn't well," Ardeshir said.

"We will trust Yeshua for this new family of followers." Ahmose looked up at the sound of approaching footsteps. "Ah. Here are the others."

Two men and two women were strolling down the cobblestone street in animated discussion. They returned Ahmose's wave and stopped several strides away from the front door of the home, bowing as they did.

"Shalom to the brothers of our Lord," trumpeted one of the men, sporting a bushy beard. "We have come to join our Ethiopian brother in establishing a new community of faith in this neighborhood. What would you have us do?"

Ardeshir stepped forward. "I am Ardeshir, son of Nabonidus, the emperor's champion and the founder of our community. We welcome you to the home of Arsama and Mariam, where we will gather to break bread and worship. Come in and wash your feet."

"I am Joab," the bearded man said. "I was a teacher under Cornelius, a companion of the apostle Shimon, and a distant relative of a man named Lazarus… whom Yeshua raised from the dead."

"That is quite the pedigree," Ardeshir said. "And who might your companions be?"

Joab opened his palm toward a bronzed young man, clean-shaven and sporting a multicolored robe. "This is Yoseph, a rider for the emperor's postal service. He came to faith after reading a letter sent by the apostle Paul from the prison in this town. He is new to the community but eager to learn."

"Shalom, my brother," Ardeshir said in welcome.

"Shalom," Yoseph replied.

Joab indicated the women. "These two sisters are from Thyatira. They are daughters of a woman named Lydia who helped the apostle Paul found his church in Philippi. They understand the importance of hospitality and compassion and we are grateful for their willingness to join us. But come, we are here to meet the man of faith who fought in the arena for Adonai and who helped found the assembly in Ephesus."

The group turned just as Mariam scurried out of the house and into the street.

"Hurry," Mariam summoned. "The old man is struggling for breath. He may not have long."

Ahmose stretched out his arms and Joab and Yoseph stepped forward to pull him to his feet.

"This is the moment for Yeshua to prove himself," the Ethiopian said. "Take me to the one who has learned to defy death."

Ten

Yas and Liu sat back-to-back, shivering under a blanket donated by Colonel Wei. The maple tree they rested their shoulders against had sheltered them from a light rain, but the moisture seemed to seep into their very bones.

Liu worked to distract his companion. "Among our people, the trees speak truth to our innermost being. We have trees for greetings and trees for farewells."

"Are you trying to take my mind off of how cold I am?" Yas asked. "Do you have a tree for that? If we burned a few trees, I think that would help more."

"Before you burn a tree, consider what it symbolizes," Liu said without judgment. "The blossoms of the pine tree, the bamboo, and the plum are considered the three friends of winter. Our poets and scribes admired the ability of these plants to survive and thrive in harsh conditions. You can see that some pines look to have open arms. They are trees for greeting."

Yas rubbed her shoulders up and down under the blanket. "I assume you're saying it would not be appropriate to burn down a tree that wants to welcome me. Okay, I won't burn a pine tree. What other tree shouldn't I burn?"

Liu tugged the blanket tighter around his head. "The word for the willow tree sounds like our word for *stay*, which is why many poets connect it to the grief of farewells. We give willow twigs as parting gifts. We hand them off on bridges to our soldiers and relatives who prepare to travel away. If we were permitted to cry, the willow would soak in our tears."

Yas nodded. "So I can't burn the willows because it would leave nothing to give to those who are departing us. I can hardly imagine your people feeling such deep sorrow. Why didn't you give me a willow branch last time I left?"

"You left suddenly. I still have a wilted branch beside my bed from the last time. My mother continues to ask me why I don't throw it away."

"And what do you tell her?"

"I tell her that it's saved for a special friend and I hope to never have to give it away."

Yas shifted and leaned a little closer to Liu. "I promise I won't burn your willows."

When the rain slowed to a mist, the two shed the damp blanket and rose to their feet, rubbing their hands for warmth.

Liu pointed toward a forested area nearby. "That is a mulberry tree and a catalpa. They represent a person's hometown because of how practical they are. They are necessary because they provide wood for our furniture and tools." He folded the blanket and laid it at the base of the maple tree they had sheltered under. "We use the bark and leaves for medicine—and to repel bugs."

Yas stepped lightly through the damp grass and mud toward the shrubbery at the edge of the forest. "What else shouldn't I destroy? I can see that you will find reasons why I shouldn't touch anything in your world."

"Since you ask, let me tell you about the red bean tree and the parasol tree. The red bean tree captures the essence of love and desire. Its seeds are shaped like the tears of a woman whose husband has died as he guarded the homeland. We send them as tokens of love to our distant lovers, or we make them into bracelets or jewelry."

"So you're saying that these are love seeds of some kind."

"Yes. Love seeds. That is a good way to describe them. The trees can live for over a thousand years, so this is an enduring love."

"If someone were to send me these red bean seeds, it would be a message I shouldn't ignore?"

Liu probed her eyes with a look of longing. "Yes. Do you wish that someone would send you these seeds?"

"Maybe someday." She looked away. "What about the parasol tree?"

Liu's sigh was impossible to miss. "The parasol often goes with the red bean seeds because it stands for devotion. We have a legend that the phoenix rests only on these trees. Somehow they have a magical quality. Devoted couples recognize the importance of this tree. We make each other special carvings to express our enduring commitment."

Yas stepped toward a nearby settlement of five huts. "I hope we can build our huts today, because it's becoming clear that your people would rather die of exposure than harm their environment. I won't burn down your pines, willows, mulberries, catalpas, or red bean trees. What other trees could you possibly leave for me?"

"Permit me to tell you about two last trees." Liu jogged to catch up. "The scholar tree is connected to those who learn and those who lead. The brightest minds among us gather to make decisions that affect the rest of us. We plant these trees in royal courtyards to mark the spots where such people meet to make a difference."

Yas stopped in her tracks. "That seems unfair. Your leaders set up a system to determine what the brightest minds must know. Then they only allow certain others to learn that knowledge so they can rise to the position of decision-makers. How can women learn and make decisions? I think this is the tree I will burn."

"Please guard your tongue," Liu pleaded. "If you must attack the pillars of our culture, please don't attack those who have the power to destroy you. I couldn't bear to see you harmed or destroyed."

A group of four women welcomed them as they approached. They bowed at the base of a maple tree.

"What are they doing?" Yas asked.

"They are Miao people," Liu told her. "They have worshipped the maple tree since the beginning of time. They tell a story that the original butterfly mother came from the core of a divine maple. She laid twelve eggs from which the gods, humans, and all animals hatched. This tree is planted around their homes to secure protection and benefits. You should definitely not burn this tree."

A horse-drawn cart suddenly appeared on the road. It was led by Wai Ling, the community's gatekeeper, with his one arm and half a nose.

Wai Ling smiled and nodded in their direction.

Yas observed that the cart was loaded with lumber and covered with a heap of grass-woven mats to serve as thatch roofing.

"It looks like someone has figured out which trees are okay to sacrifice," Yas mused. "Let's get our huts built and get some kind of fire going before we both perish."

By nightfall, Nabonidus was continuing to fight for breath while the assembly of eight believers knelt around him, beseeching Yeshua for mercy on this fallen champion. Soon after all semblance of light had slipped from the sky, reinforcements arrived; six more prayer warriors joined the ranks, mounting torches in alcoves along the wall. Meanwhile, Ardeshir kept massaging his father's shoulders and whispering words of life into the old man's ears.

Mariam rallied the group, slipping in and out with mugs of water and strips of venison. Some of the group preferred to fast. The entire time, Ahmose towered over the prostrate figures, punctuating the intercession with his own thundering pleas for restoration and healing.

As the night wore on, the Ethiopian withdrew a vial of oil from a hidden pouch. He raised it up.

"While the Lord himself is our healer, he has instructed his people to call on the elders for prayer," Ahmose prayed. "He says that the prayers of faith will make the sick person well. So we believe and so we will do."

He gently poured a generous portion of oil onto the head of Nabonidus and looked upward.

"Adonai, King of the universe. Yeshua, Lord of all things. Spirit of the living Christ. Hear us, we pray. As you raised Lazarus, so raise Nabonidus. As you healed the deaf, the dumb, the blind, and the lame, so restore this servant of yours. He has faced death in your name, so give him life through your name. He has given up everything for you, so restore all he needs in this moment. Give him breath. Give him hope. Give him strength for the journey ahead. For your glory and for the good of your servant, we pray. In Yeshua's mighty name."

An echo of amens arose from the circle of kneelers. Then all was silent.

As the moments passed, Ardeshir grew restless. His father seemed quieter, less panicked for breath, but otherwise there was no evidence of healing. One by one, the intercessors got to their feet and moved to the edge of the room. Some even stepped outside.

When Ahmose stepped away, Ardeshir spoke. "Where are you going? You can't give up now."

Ahmose placed a large hand on Ardeshir's shoulder and gently squeezed. "No one is giving up. The prayers have been given and the answer has been given. We wait now for the result."

Mariam arrived with water and lifted the mug. "It is time for life," she said.

Nabonidus breathed deeply for the first time in hours and set his lips to the task. He sipped slowly and finally waved Mariam away. He squeezed Ardeshir's arm and made an effort to shift his body.

Yosef and Joab knelt by his side, one supporting him by the arm while the other moved his feet. The stricken gladiator finally swung into a seated position and nodded.

"It looks like I will be with you a little longer," he said.

A rumble of heartfelt celebration rolled through the believers and several surged forward to hug Nabonidus and hug each other.

"We praise Yeshua, the healer," Ahmose said.

As the group chattered in excitement, a new voice entered the room. The out of breath young man hunched over in the candlelight before speaking.

"You need to leave, now!" the newcomer declared. "The Roman watch commander has ordered his soldiers to break up whatever is happening here. Take the alleys toward the market. They will be here soon."

Joab and Yosef hoisted Nabonidus into Ahmose's chair and strolled into the street.

Ardeshir followed, looking over his shoulder. Shadows slipped into the darkness as silence reigned again.

When the group sheltered in an alcove a few hundred feet away, a dog barked, then another. The thump of heavy feet reverberated off the basalt walls of the alley.

They all heard the heavy knock on a door, accompanied by a loud command.

"Arise and produce your guest in the name of the emperor!"

A few moments later, the watch commander repeated his knock and the command.

Someone must have answered, as a muffled conversation ensued. The sound of a baby crying arose and then stilled. Gruff voices conversed. Ardeshir, Yosef, and Joab pressed up tight against the walls of their refuge. Nabonidus lay still.

"Find out who issued this complaint and have him beaten," the watch commander shouted, his irritation plain. "We aren't here to chase every whine and whimper. Back to your posts!"

The heavy thud of military sandals faded into the night as even the dogs stilled again under the starry heavens.

"Looks like Yeshua came through right on time," Nabonidus said. "Help me to my feet. I can feel the energy in my legs again. Let me walk from here."

Ardeshir took a step back toward the home. "I need to thank Arsama and Mariam for their hospitality."

"No!" Joab said, grabbing Ardeshir's elbow. "There will be a spy planted out of sight. You'll be seen. The soldiers are setting a trap for us, so we need to move quickly away. Arsama and Mariam will understand. The believers here know how to function without us."

"Then what good am I to the starting of this church?" Nabonidus asked. "There was no purpose to my return."

Yosef clamped his hand on the gladiator's shoulder. "Do you not see Yeshua's plan? Your illness drew these believers together in a prayer of deep faith and trust in God's healing power. They have been heard and will be united now to see what else Adonai can do in this place. You have accomplished your mission. Now it's time for you to move on to your next one."

"And what might that be?" Nabonidus mumbled.

Ardeshir stood in front of his father. "Abba, it's time to go home!"

Yas raised a rock and crushed the nut before her. The shell shattered and flew upward in a small arc.

"Who could have imagined that the tree acceptable for sacrifice here is a common Persian walnut," she remarked. "This is the best wood of all and we use it for most of our building back home. From one tree we get lumber for shelter and food for our bellies. It's the best tree of all."

"And we burn it for warmth," Liu added, holding his hands over a flickering pyramid of flames. "I cannot confirm whether it came here from your country, but it grows easily enough in our land."

Yas poked through the crushed shell and picked up small bits from within. "These nuts are some of the earliest foods recorded in our writings," she said. "Some of our ancestors likely traded walnuts for silk. There are walnut trees as far west or as far east as you might travel."

Liu crushed his own walnut and munched on the edible meat inside. "We too have writing which shows this is an ancient tree in our own forests. One of our ancient officials brought such a nut and cultivated it for our emperor. One of our main tasks is to grow this foreign plant to sustain us in our towns and villages."

"I'm glad my people were able to help," Yas said smugly. "Perhaps it's time to return the favor by finding a way to release me."

"Only the new emperor will decide when to release you. It's best that we are thankful to the one who gave us this time together."

Yas smiled. "You don't give up, do you? Well, neither do I. It's time for me to start planning how to rescue Orotes. If you want to help me, that's fine."

"I need to finish our shelters, gather more food, and speak with Colonel Wei," Liu said. "When your plans are complete, let me know. I'll do what I can as long as you're safe."

Surprisingly, Nabonidus had made it through an entire week since the trip over the sea. The barren landscape they rumbled across now was harsh as they aimed south towards the end of the newly laid Roman road.

"Why are we going so far this way?" Nabonidus grumbled. "We haven't seen an oasis for days, the sun is scorching, and the Romans are too sensible to drift this far into the land of the Bedu."

"Abba, you know what I told you," Ardeshir replied. "This camel caravan had the only sheltered seating which could carry you the distance. With two hundred camels back-to-back, we aren't going to be stopped and inspected by any Roman patrol who dares to travel here."

Nabonidus shifted on his perch atop his proverbial ship of the desert. "I still think the Via Maris, along the Great Sea, would have been cooler and more comfortable."

"Perhaps if you were going to Egypt, we might have chosen that route. But the Roman patrols would have been alerted to watch for you there, and you know it. We didn't have it so bad when we travelled through the Galilee and Jezreel Valley. Megiddo was a nice stop."

"Yes, if you count having to disguise myself as a crippled Bedu. This King's Highway is longer than I remember. At least the dates at Megiddo were sweet and the water refreshing."

"Praise Adonai that you only had to pretend to be crippled," Ardeshir said. "You needed to wash in that mikveh. I for one am glad I didn't have to carry you into the bath. By the time we see your grandson, you'll be refreshed and whole and strong again."

"That Arab said we'll have two days before we reach Wadi Musa. It looks like Roman roadbuilding has come to an end. From here on in it will be dust and grit."

Ardeshir turned in his saddle. "Since when did you ever complain so much? I remember you as a determined fighter who could face anything without a single negative word. You aren't the abba I recall. Remember to drink your water before you shrivel up even more than you are."

Nabonidus's jaw sank against his chest. He remained silent as the sun crested in the heavens and then slid toward the distant sea.

Ardeshir settled into a rhythm. The arid landscape went on forever and only twice did they come across other caravans of camels sauntering through the sands. The tang of frankincense, myrrh, cardamom, and other spices hung in the air as the first caravan passed. The second held the aroma of cinnamon, cassia, pepper, nutmeg, and cloves.

Visions of his earlier travels across Hindustan filled his mind, the good and the bad. What was happening with Yas? How was she faring at the hands of the brutal warriors of the Han? Would she be left at the mercy of the grand council? What would become of his own empire now that his father was little more than skin and bones? He hardly recognized the imposing champion who had once commanded the attention of friend and foe alike. Yes, his father had rallied after their prayers, but would his strength be enough to carry him across this desert?

His daydreams were interrupted by a chorus of shouts from the front of the caravan. A dust cloud loomed ahead, but Ardeshir could see this was no desert sandstorm. He heard a dull thud and suddenly recognized the sound.

Just then, an army of warriors appeared at the base of the dust cloud. They were riding hard in the direction of the caravan.

"What's going on?" Nabonidus asked.

"I think they're trying to beat us to the watering hole ahead," Ardeshir said. "These camels have come as far as they can without replenishing their water. I hope we aren't going to have trouble with the Nabataeans. The last thing we need now is to go into battle."

Eleven

Four sleepless nights passed as Yas pored over the crude drawings she had sketched out on the peeled bark of a pine tree. Liu had objected to wounding the tree for such a pointless purpose, but after sharing this he could focus on the task of improving their shelters and securing food.

They debated whether it was wise to involve the colonel in the plan. The Han official had shared with them that Orotes had been called before the grand council to face the trial of five. One thing was clear: the chef wasn't a warrior and would never survive such a challenge.

Memories of her brother's ordeal flooded her thoughts. It had been fascinating to hear him share of his triumph against all odds. As for the twelve council members in their bright red garb marching across the koi pond bridge… well, it was a familiar sight for her now. So was the march of the unfortunate participant, surrounded by the golden-robed guardians.

Only once had she stood before the ornate cedar table boasting the carved images of dragons, snakes, monkeys, oxen, pigs, and other members of the animal kingdom. Bright lamps had lined the walls of the judgment hall. When the council members had removed their red garb and stood in their white robes, the only thing that had stood in the way of life and death was the choice of a black stone or a white stone. She was glad she hadn't been tasked with having to come up with four noble truths like her brother had. His leading truth, that the Way was the way, hadn't impressed the collective wisdom of the ancients.

A shadow fell across the drawings in front of her. Liu's shadow.

"A swan's egg for your moment of truth," he said.

Seeing the sincerity in his eyes, she stretched out from her kneeling position and shelved her bubbling lava of rage. What could this poor gardener do to overturn an empire of tradition? What point was there in returning his desire when her end was inevitable? Once she moved against the council to free Orotes, her fate would be sealed. To give Liu any hope would be cruel.

"What a ridiculous thing to say," she retorted. "What does that even mean?"

The pain shot through his expression like lightning. He stepped back and hunched his shoulders. "I meant no harm. I only wondered what you were thinking… to see if I could help."

She looked away. "This is something I have to do myself. With your niece and other family members, you can't afford to end up as food for the wild things."

Liu slouched away and walked toward a forest path.

The evening shadows had already fallen before he returned. Yas sat alone in her refuge, feeling alone and abandoned.

"Serves me right," she muttered over the flickering candle.

She pulled the blanket tighter around her shoulders and shuddered. She would have to act soon if Orotes stood any chance of survival.

The Nabataean commander and the caravan leader understood the way of the desert and quickly worked out an arrangement so both parties could access the precious water of the oasis. The warriors and their mounts lined up along the southern edge of the pond while the caravan and its camels lined up along the northern edge. While both groups had to manage their own ranks, these negotiations saved a costly skirmish from breaking out.

Ardeshir meandered toward the center of the oasis where the Nabataean commander and the Bedu leader stood side by side shouting instructions to their assistants.

"May the Almighty bless your land, your rulers, your people, and your dreams," he said in Arabic to the Nabataean.

"And may he double your blessings through this journey," the commander responded.

Ardeshir inclined his head. "What is the news of your family and your home?"

"My two sons have taken their vow to the goddess Allat and my daughter has been dedicated to the virgin goddess Chaabou and her son Dushara. We are waiting for the rains to bless our sanctuary. What is the news of your family?"

"My son awaits his anointing as the prince of Persia and my father is returning home to be honored. We are followers of the Way and Yeshua, the anointed one."

The commander straightened, turned, and bowed at the waist. "My prince. It isn't every day I meet someone of your stature out on these trails so far from home. How may I serve you?"

Ardeshir glanced back toward his father, who had descended from his camel and now stumbled toward the water. "That old man is my father. He is weary from the journey and unsure whether he'll survive the rest of the way. We only seek shelter in one of your caves until his strength increases."

The commander bowed again. "My names are Thabet Hatem Uday Turfa Nebaioth Ishmael Avraham. The history of my people is revealed in who I am and the names I carry. My people have eaten the dust of this land for as long as anyone can remember."

Ardeshir nodded. "My names are Ardeshir Nabonidus Mamonides. You well know that Mamonides is a royal line. And my wife is the daughter of the Han emperor."

Thabet pivoted and motioned for Ardeshir to walk with him. "You can wield huge power over the eastern trade routes with such a lineage. You know that we covet your horses and the silk of the Orient. Perhaps while in my home we can consider how to combine our efforts to share our resources."

Ardeshir kept pace with the Bedouin but held his silence.

The commander finally broke the impasse. "Your wife is a woman of great influence. Among us Nabataeans, we hold men and women of equal ability to rule and operate their own business. King Aretas IV is gone and his mausoleum has been sketched out of the stone, but his wife Chuldu continues on the throne with their son. She has championed the arts, culture, law, and the economy of trade."

"I know your people control all the trade routes for the distance of two moons' journey," Ardeshir said. "From Arabia to Gaza, you alone are lords of the sands. You alone know how to collect the water from flash floods, to store it and provide the hospitality trader and warrior alike might need."

"It is so," Thabet said.

"You control many of the sixty rest stops and cities protecting and providing for caravans. Your people have grown wealthy helping others deliver their merchandise. Your fortress in the desert is a wonder of men and nature working together."

"It is so."

"Your city of Mamshit is famous for its Arabian horses and my kingdom is famous for what the Han emperor has called our heavenly horses. We can never supply the emperor with enough horses for his warriors. Perhaps we can work together to share our stock when the need arises."

Thabet grunted. "You'll need to speak to the governor with such specifics. Why don't you plan to join me until our business can be concluded to everyone's satisfaction?"

"My true need is an escort across the desert, so I may link up with the silk road again. I know you have hidden cisterns and an unmarked passage for your camel drivers. My only request is to be included on one of these unofficial journeys after my rest with you is done."

The stroll ended abruptly.

Thabet held up his hands. "Only the gods can help you with that."

Without a further word, he marched away.

A few minutes later, two fully armed Nabataeans marched up to Ardeshir.

"We will escort you and your father from here," the first man said.

She hadn't intended to betray Liu, but that's what it felt like as Yas crept away in the middle of the night. The one-armed Wai Ling had become her confidant, and it was he who met her as a guide outside the village. He had placed the donkey cart far enough away from the sleeping village so as not to wake anyone. The light of the full moon would be more than enough to help them along the journey.

"Take me to the horse farm and I can find my own way from there," Yas said.

"What will you be doing?" Wai Ling asked.

"Trying to rescue someone I care about. If all goes well, I should be on my way home within a few days. Thank Liu for me when you return to the village."

"I will come with you."

"No!"

"You can't do this alone," Wai Ling asserted.

"I will find help inside," Yas said. "There are others who know the ways and protocols of life inside the emperor's garden. If you're discovered, they will guess where to find Liu. Then all of you will be at risk. Bringing me here has taken enough courage. Return home and take care of your people."

"Your acceptance of me has given me life. You will not be forgotten."

The two parted near the horse farm.

Yas skirted the property, using the fence to draw her in the right direction. It didn't take long to travel towards the emperor's gardens and locate the breach in the hedge. Once slipping into the maze, she maneuvered her way until she caught sight of the first rays of sunlight cresting the hills behind the palace.

As she considered what to do next, she watched Fang and Jing step onto the koi pond bridge and throw something down for the swans. They jabbered excitedly.

Seeing no one else around, Yas stood on a rock and allowed herself to be seen over the top of the hedges. Jing was the first to notice her and tugged at her sister's sleeve. Yas waved and then lowered herself out of sight.

Within minutes, Fang's voice drifted over the maze. "You are a traitor to the emperor and will be chopped up for the koi."

Yas moved deeper into the maze, keeping out of sight.

Again, the voice drifted over the hedges. "The new emperor will give you a black stone and feed you to the wild things." The pause was brief. "You have no truth in you and know only how to disrespect the people who matter here. You are a simpleton and an arrogant fool."

Fang's voice revealed that the girls were on the move through the maze. Yas proceeded to exit and skirt the outside of the tall hedges.

"Fang, don't go so far," Jing called. "Do you know the way? I'm scared."

"Stay where you are while I find this traitor. I'll turn her over to the beaters so they can chop her up for the koi. She must be crying in fear like a small child."

Jing pleaded, "Don't leave me."

Fang ignored her sister until the younger girl's cries grew louder.

"Jing, you are the general's daughter, not his baby. Be strong as a tiger and fierce as a dragon."

But Jing was neither strong as a tiger nor fierce as a dragon and Yas continued to listen to her whimpers through the bushes.

Yas found a gap in the hedge and slipped through, finding her way to a row near the young girl.

"Do you want me to take you out of here?" Yas whispered. "Do you want me to show you the way home?"

Jing's whimpering stopped. "What about my sister?"

"She can find her own way home," Yas said.

"Yes, I want to go home."

"If I help you, you need to help me."

"What do I have to do?"

"Follow me now and meet me back here tomorrow morning. I will need a basket, a blanket, and a dagger."

"What do you need a dagger for?"

"To stay free. Can you get me one?"

"I don't know. I can try."

"Then follow me."

As the two allies crept out of the maze and took the path toward the emperor's palace, Fang's voice could be heard in the distance: "Jing, where are you? I need you to show me how to get out of here. Jing, come here this instant!"

Jing glanced back, smiled, and reached for Yas's hand.

The Nabataean commander reined in his horse as Ardeshir took in the grandeur of the scene before him. A bleak mountain range marched toward the horizon, forming a basin around a monstrous outcropping of rock.

"The Arabah valley," Thabet said. "Through these hills around us, my people have built an endless fortification of caves and hidden trails should anyone attack. We have learned to harvest the flash floods that come through these parts and trap the water in cisterns for the dry times. We'll ride through the Siq and into the heart of the rose city that the Romans call Petra."

The closer Ardeshir rode, the taller and closer the Siq walls seemed to grow.

"Can we make it through the gap on our horses?" Ardeshir asked.

"That's the exact question we want our enemies to ask," Thabet said. "The top of the rocks is more than ten times your height on horseback and no more than two riders can fit through this shaft at a time. If my men don't want you to get through here, they have at least a thousand paces to convince you to turn back."

Carvings of stone gods lined the passage at intervals. And when they broke into a clearing, the sight was stunning. A pillared wonder carved out of sandstone stood twenty times the height of a man and thirty paces wide. The masterpiece could have come straight from the heart of Alexandria or Corinth, or even Athens.

"The tomb of King Aretas." Thabet gave the structure a cursory nod. "Don't worry. We have tombs for all our kings and noble citizens. Up ahead you'll see an entire village carved into the rock. We'll walk from here. When you see the maidens with water, take advantage of their offerings."

He pointed at carvings near the base of the monument.

"Those are carvings of Castor and Pollux, intended to protect travelers on their journey." He pointed upward. "I don't know if you can see the top, but we have carved an Egyptian and a Greek goddess for good fortune. One is Isis and the other is Tyche."

Two young men took control of the horses and the lone camel on which Nabonidus rode. The camel lurched to its knees, groaning, and allowed its rider to disembark.

At Thabet's nod toward Nabonidus, two warriors crossed their arms and carried the former gladiator away. Ardeshir followed and soon came upon a garden, a pool, as well as musicians and vendors of all sorts.

"Every pleasure can be yours in this place," Thabet said with a smirk.

The path opened wider to reveal a rock-carved amphitheater capable of seating over eight thousand. Hundreds of tombs and residential caves surrounded the site.

Thabet turned to Nabonidus. "This is where you would have fought our champions if you had dared. We have always longed to see an emperor's champion stand in front of our people. None of our warriors lasted long enough to fight in the arenas."

Ardeshir also took note of the many places of worship and sacrifice. Dancers and religious leaders practiced their craft in every nook and cranny. Ardeshir recognized the whirling dervishes from his homeland.

Thabet pointed at a particularly imposing structure. "Our largest space is twenty-five times the height of a man and almost sixty paces wide. It too is carved deep into the rockface."

He glanced back at Nabonidus, who was trying to sit in a dignified fashion upon the hands of two warriors.

"But come, you can stare later," Thabet beckoned. "We must get you out of this heat and into my cave. You'll be amazed at the luxury we can create inside the rock."

As the small group moved toward a large cave entrance, Thabet continued to point out newly constructed edifices with clear significance.

"That massive temple is dedicated to our recent King Obodas. He is now a god. The other temple complex was carved by King Aretas IV and finished two moons ago. At the end of this colonnaded street is our sacred quarter. The Temple of Winged Lions is one of the two main buildings there."

The warriors stopped at a small plateau twenty steps up the main street. Ardeshir saw that his father was breathing heavily, as though he had been forced to walk up to that plateau himself.

Ardeshir looked out across the wide city square and pointed. "Soldiers and priests are coming this way fast. Looks like news of our arrival has spread."

It was well into the morning before Jing skittered across the koi bridge and broke into a run toward the hedge maze. She carried a small sack, which Yas presumed carried treasure. Yas crouched low enough to hide, yet high enough to keep her watch on the general's youngest daughter.

Fang soon appeared at the end of the garden, at the palace door. Yas watched as the older girl looked for her sister. Jing had played this game before, Yas knew, sheltering in place behind a flower bush or fountain.

When Jing was close enough to Yas's hiding place, she abandoned the sack and ran off again toward the far side of the pond. Fang spotted her in the motion of ducking behind a fountain.

"Black jaguar!" Fang yelled. "I found you and now it's my turn to be the jaguar. Your turn to be the general looking for his cat."

The game demonstrated so clearly that these girls had little concept of how their father's behavior struck terror into the hearts of the servants.

As Fang raced towards her sister, Yas retrieved the sack left by Jing. Upon looking inside, she smiled. Its contents did not disappoint. There was a large ball of rice, some carrots, an orange, a chunk of meat, and a small ceremonial dagger hardly bigger than her hand.

Yas ate quickly, not reserving anything for later. This was an all-or-nothing mission.

The garden was busy most of the day with workers coming and going as they went about their daily tasks. Two chambermaids passed as Yas crouched near the entrance to the maze. They noticed her and nodded but continued their activity without a word. She was a familiar sight and most just assumed that if she wasn't meant to be in the garden, she wouldn't be there.

By midafternoon, Yas's stomach grumbled, but she remained in place. Leg cramps and back strain tested her patience. Sweat trickled along her spine.

Toward evening, a contingent of golden-robed guardians emerged from the judgment hall. Every muscle in Yas's body tightened like springs, for the group carried a six-foot board. And on it lay what appeared to be a body covered in blue silk. Was it Orotes? Had the five trials already begun? Was she too late to save him? Or herself?

Twelve

The amphitheater continued to fill as Ardeshir stood beside Thabet in the heart of Petra. The city's welcoming committee hadn't waited long to make its request known. After all, disturbing rumors had spread about this prince of Persia; he needed to explain his presence.

A bevy of priests carried pots of burning frankincense and myrrh around the perimeter of the venue, chanting as they moved. Men and women dropped small coins into a basket hanging off the priests' shoulders.

"They will want to hear what you have to say," Thabet informed him. "For a few years, we had a Jew called Paul who used to debate with the other religious leaders here. He was also a follower of the Way and this Yeshua of whom you have spoken. Most of the time, the soldiers keep the riots to a manageable pandemonium."

"My father knows much more than I do," Ardeshir said. "But he is weak and not always clear in his thinking. I hope I can communicate well."

Thabet chuckled. "You are the prince of Persia. Start by speaking of your exploits in the Orient. My people are always interested in news from abroad. If they don't believe your message, at least they'll think you are an interesting storyteller."

Thabet started to back away, but then he stopped to add something.

"Remember, we call this place Rekeme, after the first king who ruled here. It's important to address the residents of Rekeme to show respect. Then you can draw attention to all the markings and goddesses you have noticed."

"I think I'll focus on the similarity between the virgin Chaabou and her son Dushara," Ardeshir said. "According to your wife, this is a new teaching for your people and it aligns in small ways with our understanding of Yeshua."

"Our people are quick to listen to the teachings of all and find a way to incorporate new truths into old beliefs. We have gods and goddesses for everything. We accept everyone."

A stout priest with a smoking pot of frankincense shuffled forward just then and positioned himself between Ardeshir and Thabet.

In fluent Persian, he addressed Ardeshir. "If you are a true prince of Persia, we expect an acknowledgement of Zarathustra, the twenty-one holy books, the importance of the law, and the supremacy of truth." He tripped and bumped hard into Ardeshir. Regaining his balance, he bowed slightly. "My pardon, are you okay?"

"Thank you for your concern," Ardeshir responded. "I'm here to speak of my own experiences and understandings. Perhaps we can discuss these matters after my testimony. I would like to find the shortest way back to Susa from here—that is, if you know of any travelers heading that way."

"Perhaps I can help you," the priest said. "But first let me listen to what you have to say."

Thabet was generous with his introduction, acknowledging the heritage and experiences of both Ardeshir and Nabonidus.

The crowd thumped their feet in welcome as Ardeshir stepped forward.

"Noble citizens of Rekeme," he began, "citizens of the world who long for truth, thank you for coming to hear this humble prince of Persia, this son of a gladiator who was the emperor's champion, this husband of the princess of Han, this poor wanderer who also longs for truth."

As he spoke, he included testimony of his journey toward truth, his quest for love, and his escape from the emperor, not to mention his efforts to rescue his father. Amidst all this, he sprinkled confident assertions about Yeshua. Apart from a few shouts for him to speak louder. His words were well received, as evidenced by the frequent foot-thumping.

That all changed when a rider galloped into the plaza and dismounted with his sword drawn.

"This man is a fraud!" the rider yelled. "He's a thief who has stolen the sacrifice from the Temple of Artemis. He's in league with Roman assassins. He has come to uncover the secret routes of the Bedu and steal the treasures of the devotees of our moon goddess Allat."

Ardeshir was too stunned to speak. For a moment, there was only silence as this warrior marched purposefully toward the platform. Murmurs in the audience soon turned to shouts of anger.

Thabet motioned for a few of his men to step up and intervene with the swordsman. Ardeshir tried to get the attention of the crowd, but by then the turmoil and pandemonium had already turned into a tsunami of rage, dividing the crowd into those who were for him and those who were against.

Thabet grabbed Ardeshir by the arm and two other men scooped up Nabonidus. As the residents of Petra surged forward to take hold of the two Persians, the small group of protectors hurried them away into the Siq.

"That is one show these people won't forget," Thabet shouted as they reached the horses. "I hope your father can find enough strength for what comes next."

Gripping the dagger so hard unleashed pain in every joint in her right hand. Yas eased the weapon to the ground and stretched her fingers out for relief. Her stomach rumbled loudly and she instinctively put her hand over her mouth, taking note of the covered body still lying in the middle of the garden.

As the sun reached the hilltops in the distance, four young men in black approached the body. They shuffled in close and removed the covering. She had no way of being able to tell who it was from her hiding place, but she feared it was Orotes. Had he failed in his trial of five? Was she keeping vigil for no reason?

A fifth figure in black arrived carrying a uniform. The four firstcomers worked to dress the corpse in slow and deliberate movements, as if to show respect to the one who had passed. It was dark by the time their task was completed.

Yas stepped up behind a tree to survey the rest of the garden. There was no one else in sight, and soon even the men in black departed, taking the body with them.

This was undoubtedly the longest night of her life, and it continued far beyond her endurance, yet she persevered and waited behind the trunk of the tree, waiting for whatever would come next.

At dawn, the gardeners and chambermaids scurried about the garden, taking on their usual roles. The same two chambermaids nodded at Yas as they passed, showing no emotion at her strange location.

And then Jing appeared. The girl carried another small sack and left it in the same location as the day before. Two rice balls and a few vegetables lay inside, and beneath them? A pair of metal stars, the kind used by martial artists. The girl seemed committed to doing everything she could to help.

Her belly satisfied, Yas moved back into the maze. She knew every twist and turn by now and felt confident that she could avoid any pursuers.

When the sun was directly overhead, Liu's niece arrived at the entrance to the maze and scanned the hedges. Twice she moved towards the koi pond and twice she returned. Glancing over her shoulder, she seemed to make a decision.

"The one who loves you has returned," she called. "The one who met the trial has failed. A new emperor will be proclaimed as the new moon rises."

This was a cryptic message. What did it mean? Who was the one who loved her? Was it Orotes, or was it Liu? Or both? Who had failed the trial? Orotes? Liu? Someone else? What was the significance of a new emperor being proclaimed at the rise of the new moon?

Perhaps the best place to start would be finding out who had died and been dressed.

Scurrying behind bush and hedge, Yas made her way to Liu's home to see whether his mother was there. She was. The old woman pulled her into the darkened interior and sat her down with a hot cup of tea and a rice ball.

"Where you be?" the woman asked in halting Persian. "Where Liu?"

Yas answered in Cantonese. "We had to ride away. Liu will return."

Freed to speak her native tongue, Liu's mother spoke quickly. "There are many rumors. Someone said Colonel Wei has died. He fought alongside the chef and failed to win the trial of five."

The old woman ducked her head out the door of the shack for a moment and then ducked back inside.

"No news of the chef," she added. "No one has seen him. Perhaps he is eaten by lions."

The clench in her gut paralyzed her tongue for a moment.

Why would Wei have died? What would now happen to all the suffering people in the village he had tried to help? Where was Orotes now if the trial of five was already done?

Both camels loped farther and farther behind the galloping quartet of horses as they departed the Siq. Dark clouds hovered overhead and heaven-sent drops fell first by the dozens, then hundreds, then thousands. A torrential downpour soon unleashed a flash flood on the settlement.

The timing was too perfect to be anything but divine intervention.

"Praise Adonai," Ardeshir shouted as he pulled his mount to a stop.

Thabet lifted his hands toward the sky, smiling. "We can stop and soak in this moment. By now, most of the people will be proclaiming you as the latest god in their collection. The rain is a sign of divine blessing."

"I hope they credit Yeshua," Ardeshir said. "He's the one I was trying to tell them about. The virgin-born son they speak of has appeared in the flesh as Yeshua the God-man, the same one the apostle Paul has spoken of before me. He should be honored for who he is, not confused with a nonexistent god."

Ardeshir waited for the camels to catch up. When they got closer, he saw that his father was hanging on for dear life; he was also smiling like he hadn't in days.

"Now that is something those people won't forget," Nabonidus shouted. "They'll be too busy now capturing their water to bother us. Where do we go from here?"

Thabet pointed to a lone camel lingering far behind them. Atop it sat the stout priest who had been swinging the pot of frankincense and urging loyalty to Zarathustra.

"He will be your guide for the next part of the journey," Thabet said. "He'll show you the secret trail of the Bedu, which you will be sworn to deny if ever you are asked. His name is Adar, a name which means 'fire.' Do not cross him or his men will ensure that you perish at the Temple of Fire."

Adar slowed his camel when he eventually caught up, scanning the heavens. He coughed and lifted a gourd to his lips. The smell of frankincense was still strong around him.

"Your timing is to be noted," the priest said in Persian. "Dushara would be pleased that you're drawing more attention to his prominence, regardless of the name you use for him. We have carved many statues in the rock of all the gods and goddesses we have heard about—and now we have reason to build a temple that will stand the test of time. The Midianites, the Edomites, and now the Nabataeans will be recognized as residents of this rock forever."

Ardeshir urged his mount forward a few steps. "I came only to proclaim Yeshua and find a quicker path to my home in Susa."

"Tonight a train of fifty camels will pass through this place," Adar told him. "They will stop briefly for supplies and then follow me along the secret Bedu trail. We have buried cisterns hidden across this desert. Know that you will pay dearly for this adventure."

"I'm prepared to pay whatever is needed," Ardeshir said. "I'll give you a sampling of my own hidden treasure, to ensure that you don't abandon us in the middle of the trek."

"Did you realize that tradition tells us this is the place where the Hebrew Musa struck the rock and split it to produce water for his people coming from Egypt?" Adar asked. "To this day, we call it Wadi Musa. His brother Aaron is buried on the hill above us, and he too is honored with yearly sacrifices. Anyone who produces water is honored as godlike by some and as an enemy by others. You have little choice now but to leave this place, before the guardians lose control of the mob."

"But first we have to wait for the caravan of camels to arrive tonight."

Thabet motioned to his two men. "My men will take you to a refuge in the hills, where you can wait until evening. There is a cave where you can be refreshed and find something good to eat. It is my brother's home, so I thank you in advance for your generosity."

Ardeshir raised his arm. "Your brother will not be disappointed." A deep dread wormed its way into his soul as he reached inside his robe. He slid off his horse. "Wait! I've misplaced something."

He tore apart the saddlebags and shook out his robe. Turning in circles, he frowned and held out his hands.

"Did I give you the money pouch?" he asked as he stepped up to his father, still seated on his camel.

Nabonidus shook his head and glanced over to Thabet and Adar. "Did you leave it at Thabet's home?"

"No," Ardeshir said. "I had it with me when I went up to speak at the amphitheater." He patted his chest. Then his eyes turned to slits as he looked at Adar. "You! I had my money pouch until you bumped into me at the amphitheater. Turn it over now."

Adar didn't even hesitate. He smiled, held up the money pouch, and chuckled. "Most merchants are too smart to allow such a heist. There's enough in here to get you halfway across the sands, but if you give a generous share to Thabet and his brother you will owe me much more than you can spare."

Ardeshir stepped toward Adar, but two soldiers intervened with drawn swords.

Thabet dismounted and faced Ardeshir. "It seems you haven't come prepared for your journey. Such poverty isn't fitting for a prince. Perhaps you are not who you claim to be."

Nabonidus urged his camel forward until he was next to Ardeshir. "This is not the time or the place to start a fight with the emperor's champion," he said deeply. "Mount up and let us settle this in a way that will leave us with dignity and respect."

Nabonidus produced his own bag of jewels and coin.

"Where did you get all that?" Ardeshir asked.

"A wise man is always prepared for his journey," his father said. "Never let your hosts regret their relationship or time with you. Be generous early and late."

There was a new arrival in the garden soon after sunset.

Yas had already stretched out on a mat provided by Liu's mother. In the darkness, she hadn't even been aware of the presence until he was suddenly crouching next to her, reaching for a blanket. When he pulled on her robe, she instinctively pulled away.

In a moment, she found herself pinned.

Fearing capture by the emperor's guardians, she thrust up a knee and twisted. Her attacker grunted, then loosed his hold on her wrist just long enough for her to pull her arm free and elbow him in the jaw.

His grunt encouraged her to drive her fist into his ribs.

Liu's mother called through the chaos. "What is happening in here? Yas… Liu? What are you doing?"

The attacker pushed away and stood to his feet. Yas kicked out, striking his legs… but he was already out of reach.

"Yas!" Liu's mother said. "Yas! It's okay. Liu is home. It's okay."

A moment later, the woman lit a candle and Yas saw well enough to realize the attacker was none other than Liu himself, clad in his underclothes.

"What are you doing in my bed?" he demanded. "Why did you leave me in the village?"

Yas sat up in bed, pulling the blanket closer around her shoulders. "I came to rescue Orotes, but it seems as though it was Wei who died. Why were you attacking me?"

Liu bent over with his hands on his knees. "The pain in my body says *you* were the attacker," he said. "I was just trying to quietly find my bed so I didn't disturb anyone. It's never been my experience to have a beautiful woman lying in wait for me!"

"That's not what happened," Yas said. "I thought you were one of the emperor's guardians coming to take me to the wild things. I told Wai Ling to give my farewells to you. Why did you come?"

Liu reached for his robe and wrapped it around himself. "If you don't know the answer to that by now, then I have no words left. From now on I'll support you in any way you need, but I won't pursue you. I'll sleep on the upper floor and hope we didn't just wake the whole village with our tumble together."

"We both need sleep," she pointed out. "When the sun rises, we can sort out what happens next. If you can find out from your contacts what took place at Orotes's trial of five, that would be very helpful.

Liu's mother merely snuffed out the candle and shuffled away in the dark.

Yas reached under the bedroll and pulled out the fighting stars she had stashed there from Jing. She cradled them in her fist and snuggled back under the blankets.

That's when the sound of crashing thunder shook the home. Liu's mother screamed and Yas rolled to the far side of Liu's bedroom.

Dark invaders pushed their way inside—and although the newcomers attempted to be stealthy, the stench of unwashed bodies filled the room. With her keen senses, Yas determined that there were at least three of them. But she dared not move. The slightest movement would alert them to where she was.

Thirteen

The caravan of more than fifty camels plodded under the starlit skies on a shifting road of sand which none but the Bedu could follow. Ardeshir watched and Nabonidus dozed as the rhythmic chanting of the Arabian traders took effect.

"Adar!" Ardeshir called. "How did your people take control of these routes? There have got to be thousands of Arabs moving in these caravans."

Adar slowed his mount to draw abreast. "Generations ago, our grandfathers became the middlemen for salt, gold, horses, slaves, copper... for anything and everything. We met people at the limits of where they were willing to go and brought them what they wanted in exchange for what they could trade. Our people took as much time as necessary to travel since we had no cities to tie us down."

"But you've become philosophers and artists and builders as well," Ardeshir said. "Your wealth is envied by many."

"We've learned to sit around the fires while people talk, and we know how to listen. People share with us ideas, and we carry those ideas along with the goods we trade. The world grows closer because of it." Adar lifted his leather pouch of water and quenched his thirst. "We were also smart enough to take control of Damascus. Once we held the heartland of the trade routes, we controlled the silk road to the east, the frankincense road and the king's highway to the South, and then the sea routes to Hindustan and beyond."

Ardeshir glanced back at the caravan. "I heard somewhere that your people used to use horses and donkeys. Why did you change?"

"We've been using camels long before others," Adar said. "This beast can travel farther in a day, carry more, and live longer than a horse or donkey. We use camels because we're wise businessmen who know how to invest in what lasts."

"And how did you become a leader of such a large caravan?"

Adar moved his camel closer to Ardeshir. "The secrets are passed from father to son. I'm a khabir, a position that's earned through the wise use of power and responsibility. A man maps the stars in his mind as clearly as he marks the streets in a city, or the villages in a country." He set a more aggressive pace. "A khabir must know the rules of the desert, of health and hygiene, remedies for snake bites or scorpion stings, cures for sicknesses or the fixing of broken bones. He must have good relationships with the chiefs and shamans of every tribe and village. He sometimes marries a woman from each tribe so he always has a home to call his own."

"So how many women do you have?" Ardeshir asked. "How many homes?"

"Five," Adar said. "But I don't count the women who comfort me without obligation."

"I have one. I miss her a lot."

"All the more reason why you shouldn't be selfish in sharing your comfort and care." Adar stopped his camel and held out his hand. "Do you smell the change in the sand? Do you notice the vegetation, the shifting direction of the wind, the mountains on the horizon, the shadows of the dunes in the moonlight, the spray of the sand from the peaks of the dunes, the eroded gullies, the distribution of rocks and small stones? Do you notice the mirages, the camel dung which always points toward the next water source…?" He chuckled. "Once you learn these things, you will never be lost in the desert."

Four days passed with only one other caravan passing them. At the end of each day, the Bedu guardians gathered with Adar and settled on where to camp. Each time, the group produced sufficient water for the camel train and its passengers. Ardeshir never solved the mystery of where the water came from and he never asked. The Bedu secrets were theirs alone.

A week into the journey, the caravan halted on the outskirts of a huge tented city called Teyma at the northern end of the Nafud desert. Thousands of camels stood or knelt around small gatherings of tents.

Adar stopped as Ardeshir slid off his kneeling camel.

"We camp here for three days, then turn north to Dumah at the south of the Syrian desert," the khabir said. "After that, the next great civilization will be Susa. Whatever supplies you need should be purchased here. We will take you to the watering hole when it's our turn. Be patient."

The day before their group was taken to the watering hole, the camels grew irritable—and so did their drivers. As Ardeshir urged his beast forward, he noted another camel train moving toward the same location. He noted these men's Oriental makeup.

And as he sheltered from view, one face stood out: the one belonging to General Ban Chao. What was he doing out in the middle of the Arabian desert?

The faint moonlight slid in through the broken door, silhouetting first one then another intruder. The bulky leader dropped to his knees and aggressively hacked at the bedroll where Yas had been just moments before.

"She's not here," he mumbled in Cantonese. "Check the other room."

The second man slipped out of the room. The first stood to his feet and kicked at the darkened corners.

From her hiding place, Yas remained perfectly still, her back pressed up against the wall.

When the attacker stepped within reach of her and kicked, she grabbed his ankle, lifted his leg as high as she could manage, and took out his other knee. The man tumbled with a grunt.

"Here!" he yelled as he fell. "She's here."

A shadowy figure darted into the room and kicked at the man on the floor, no doubt mistaking him for their target.

"Hey! It's me," the first man snarled. "She's hiding against the wall."

As the two struggled to their feet, Yas crawled out of the room towards the back door. The bright moonlight made it easy to swing up onto the roof and out of the fracas.

Where was Liu? This wasn't a good time to be running from a fight.

Liu's mother limped out from behind a tree at the edge of the garden pond. Yas jumped off the roof and ran to her aid. Just then, she heard a dozen steps from the house as a figure emerged.

"Stop!"

Yas pivoted, fingered her fighting stars, and let one of them fly in the direction of her pursuer. The resulting yell proved she had hit her target.

"Run," Yas urged the limping woman. "Run!"

As Liu's mother vanished into the hedge maze, a figure emerged from the home. Yas launched a second star. It thudded into the doorpost of the house.

Fortunately, the two men tripped over each other, going down in a tangle of elbows, knees, and feet.

Yas backed away as a third man, dressed all in black, appeared from the shadows and quickly dispatched the pair of attackers.

"Whoever you are, it is best if you leave quietly," she breathed into the stillness.

The man removed his head covering. "It's me, Yas. It's me."

"Liu?" Yas sank to her knees in relief. "I thought they'd got to you. What did you do to those men?"

"I took care of them. They were expecting a woman, not a master of martial arts."

"I think your mother is hurt," Yas said. "I saw her running toward the maze."

"She'll be okay," Liu said. "We need to remove these bodies before the others wake up. I'll need your help if you can spare the time."

Yas bent over the two prone men. "I'm not sure they're going to wake up," she said. "They're not breathing."

"Grab their feet," Liu said. "We'll leave them in the maze for now… and find my mother while we're at it. Maybe I'll toss these poor excuses for men over the wall into the home of the wild things. Then we'll see how brave they are."

"Ah, the gentle gardener," Yas noted. "I see you've changed a little since the days when my brother first met you."

"I wonder who sent them. With the general gone, it's possible someone else is making decisions before the new emperor can be crowned. It's likely a member of the grand council manipulating things to his own advantage."

Liu halted as Yas lowered her burden to the ground.

"Usually the emperor has a son who takes up the position when it becomes vacant. But our previous emperor dismissed his daughter as an heir. Now the council must decide who leads us… who understands the most noble truths."

"Thank you for coming back to rescue me," Yas said. "I'm not sure I could have beaten these men."

Liu lifted the first dead man by the shoulders and waited as Yas lifted the feet. "You could easily have taken four of these unskilled oafs. Remember that day in the arena."

"Still, I'm thankful you stayed with me."

Liu nodded. "You know I'd never leave."

As soon as Adar gave Ardeshir the signal to water his camel, he inched close to the khabit.

"Why is General Ban Chao this far west?" Ardeshir asked.

"Apparently he's hunting pirates," Adar said. "From what I've heard, he claims a Nabataean ship has been stopping his merchants and taking their best cargo. He says he's tracked the silk, jade, and porcelain along this route."

"But I thought this was a secret route, one only the Bedu know. If no one knows the way, how could a Han general find us all the way out here?"

Adar sighed. "Life is the same everywhere. Wealth is persuasive. And if it's not wealth, power and pain can loosen people's lips."

Ardeshir held out the rope restraining his camel. "That man has been hunting me for a long time. I cannot let him find me. Can you get someone else to water my camel? I'll be waiting in my tent until it's time to leave."

Adar took the rope and shrugged. "I heard him speaking of a Persian woman who's been giving him trouble back home. He also says that his emperor had died and they're looking for a successor. I don't suppose you know anything of that Persian woman?"

"I'm sure she's my sister," Ardeshir said, smiling. "But this is the first I've heard that she's alive. I need to share the news with my father. He'll gain strength at the thought of seeing her again."

Ardeshir returned to his tent, where he found Nabonidus resting by a small fire.

"I have good news," Ardeshir began. "I've heard that Yas is still alive and causing trouble in the Han kingdom."

Nabonidus perked up. "How did you hear this?"

"It turns out that the other camel caravan includes a familiar Han general." Ardeshir sat next to his father. "The bad news is that he's the same man who destroyed our farm and tried to kill my wife. I'll have to stay in hiding until he leaves."

"Perhaps I can pay this man a visit," Nabonidus said, stretching and standing. "He may need to meet someone like me. Someone who can instill fear."

"This man fears nothing and no one. It might be best for us to stay quiet and get home as quickly as we can."

"If we don't face him now, we'll only have to face him later." Nabonidus turned and began walking away.

"You may be stronger then," Ardeshir called.

"Son, you know that I never walk away from trouble. You took me away from Rome, from Ephesus, and from Caesarea. I cannot let this go on."

Ardeshir rustled through the bags until he found enough dried fruit and bread to sustain himself. He then shed his outerwear and lay down in his tent, sweating. What would his father do against the general? What *could* his father do? He was weak, long absent from the arena, and unable to even brandish a sword for any length of time.

Still, he was the emperor's champion.

The news might have been expected, but it shook Yas to the core nonetheless. Hearing from Fang didn't make it better.

"The grand council chose my uncle as the next emperor. His first act was to purge the ranks of those disloyal to our family. Since Wei made the mistake of speaking up for Orotes the chef at his trial, both had to go."

Yas fell to her knees, looking up at the glowering face of the general's oldest daughter. "How did they die?"

"The council made them drink poison and then threw them over the wall into the pit of wild things."

"Do you know what will become of me?" Yas asked.

Fang crossed her arms. "Am I the emperor to know such things? I only came because my sister told me that she'd seen you. My father will soon return. Then they will chop you up for the koi. Jing has spoken up in your favor, but I'm the older one and my word will be honored more."

"And what will you say?"

"That you annoy me."

"Why?"

"You dishonor our protocols and culture by putting my sister before me. You favor those who are weak and have no honor. You speak of truths which are neither noble nor familiar."

"And for these things, I am destined to die?"

Fang dropped her arms to her side. "This is my dilemma. I still want to ride those horses, and you won't be able to teach me if you are fed to the koi."

"How is it that you have the power to turn the heart of your uncle or father?"

"This is why you annoy me," Fang said. "You know nothing. I was born during the full moon at the chrysanthemum festival and the emperor's wife anointed me the eternal flower. Last week was the flowering of my womanhood and I shall be the new emperor's wife. What I think and say will finally matter."

Yas's heart quickened as she realized that this young woman had the power of life and death over her.

"No one as young as I should have such power," Fang said, kneeling. "I want to play and ride horses and feed the swans. I may not even be able to see my sister again. Next week the tutors will come to prepare me, and at the fall festival I will be wed."

"My heart is too sad to care anymore."

"What right have you to be sad in my presence? I need you to teach me to ride a horse. I'm supposed to be the source of joy and hope for my nation."

Yas shrugged. "And yet you are my source of sadness, bringing me news of the colonel and the chef. One was my helper and the other was the man I intended to marry. What joy or hope could there be left for me?"

Fang stood up again and placed her hand on Yas's shoulder. "I can be your hope and joy. I will find you a new helper and a new man to love."

Yas lay on the grass and rested her head on her arms. "No flower stands tall under the foot of the elephant."

"What is the meaning of such words?" Fang asked.

"The powerless have no power under the weight of the powerful."

"Are you speaking of me? Are you saying that I have no power?"

"Not everything is about you," Yas said. "I congratulate you on your womanhood, on your position as the emperor's wife, and as the one who will decide my fate. If you ever see my brother again, let him know that I tried to bring honor to our family and our nation."

Fang crossed her arms in annoyance. "Do you dare to give up in front of me?"

"Is there a choice?"

"You must claim me as your advocate."

Yas looked up from the ground at the girl standing over her. "What do you mean?"

"When your brother stood before the grand council, he chose Liu to represent him. When Orotes stood before the council, he chose the colonel. You must choose me."

"But you're a child!"

"Not anymore! Are you not listening?" Fang backed away. "I am now a woman and soon to be a wife. My word will be more powerful than most. Choose me and then do exactly as I tell you when your trial comes."

Yas looked towards the koi bridge and saw a group of six guardians in golden robes moving in their direction.

"Are you betraying me?" Yas asked.

"For the sake of my sister, I'm saving you."

The shuffling outside alerted Ardeshir with just enough time for him to duck under the shelter of a cape in the corner of the tent. He didn't know who was about to enter.

The flap swung open for a moment and then he heard his father break into a belly laugh.

"Is this the depth to which the Maimonides clan has fallen?" his father said. "To hide from our enemies? Son, come out here and show your courage."

Ardeshir dropped the cape and stood to face his father. "What happened with General Ban Chao?"

"We fought to the death." Nabonidus chuckled. "What do you expect?"

"You won?"

"No! That khabir of yours told the Han general that he saw a Persian matching your description just a few days ago in Petra. So Ban Chao ordered a few of his best riders to race after you. He left with them. It seems that he's sentenced his own soldiers to death, since there's no chance of them getting there in time."

"He'll strike back at me with a vengeance when he finds out I was here all along."

"By the time he finds us, we'll be ready."

The ensuing trek to Dumah and beyond lasted another moon cycle. By that time, another two hundred camels had joined them from Ethiopia. The caravan pressed on toward Susa.

"It'll be only a few more days until we emerge from the desert," Adar promised.

Sand clung to every stitch of Ardeshir's clothing and every pore. His parched throat and cracked lips combined with weariness to drive him to the edge of despair.

Surprisingly, his father rode with quiet anticipation and perseverance. The old man understood suffering.

When one of the traders slipped off his camel and broke his neck, the accident struck hard, reminding Ardeshir of the risks of failing to focus while travelling. Two slaves dug a shallow grave in the sand and dumped the body. No one else even slowed to acknowledge the tragedy. Death was the plight of every man who failed to respect the challenges of the desert.

More than a few mirages had spiked his hopes during the journey. So when a shimmering haze appeared ahead, Ardeshir just closed his eyes and let his camel walk on. Lu Hou's face faded in and out of his mind, and he couldn't even remember his son's face. How long had it been? Would Yas still need rescuing by the time this was over?

The chatter up ahead pulled him back into the present.

His father pressed his mount closer. "An oasis up ahead," Nabonidus said. "This is the last stop before home. We made it."

The entire train surged with a burst of energy as they took their final steps. Smoke arose to blur the horizon and hills appeared, tinged with blue and green. White clouds hovered in the air. Bells tinkled. Dogs barked. Sheep mewed.

They had entered another world.

Fourteen

Despite Fang's promise of salvation, Yas found her time in the dungeon to be a horrifying experience. Groans accompanied the cries of those whose minds proved incapable of overcoming the damp, dark trauma of this place. Even worse were the screams of those who were questioned by the torturer's hand as he probed for loyalties and names.

Twice a rat scurried over her feet as she hunched against a slimy wall. She kicked at it.

"I killed and ate a rat like you once already," she threatened. "I'm going to last longer than you, so don't test me."

Somewhere around the third day, she heard the sound of scuffling feet. She looked up and saw Fang holding a flickering torch just outside the cell door.

"It seems you won't be as easy to represent as I hoped," Fang said. "I must wait until I'm wed before my word carries any power in the empire. For now you will be a guest in my home. My sister will be your companion until I arrange your marriage."

"My marriage?"

"Yes! I have chosen the one whose life will be tied to yours. If you're sentenced to death, he will join you. If you're given life, he too will live."

"Who would ever choose to die with me?" she asked. "When will I leave this place?"

"You will come now." Fang nodded to the guardian. "Open the gate and let her out."

Light had never looked so good. Flowers had never smelled so intoxicating. Birds had never sounded so much like an orchestra. The very ground vibrated with life and energy. If her limbs hadn't been so shaky from the cramping and hunger, Yas could have danced across the koi pond.

A young woman stood at the door to a large residence behind the palace, near the wall which contained the wild things.

"That is Yun," Fang explained, gesturing to the woman. "She will be your maid until the sentence is passed. She will dress you, feed you, bathe you, and tutor you. Whatever you need."

"I think I can take care of myself," Yas said.

"If that is so, I'll put you back into your cell. Yun needs to be of service to earn her way for her family. You're the only one I can give her to. Choose now."

Yas nodded. "I'll be happy to have Yun teach me the things I need to know."

"Bathe quickly," Fang instructed. "I will go and alert your future husband that the time has come for a wedding."

The stars seemed to penetrate the night sky with more intensity than usual as the last of the sand faded from view. At dawn, the sight of the first river unleashed a melee of enthusiasm as men rushed for the water, stripping off their robes as they went. Camels and cargo alike were abandoned to slaves for caretaking. The cooler air coming off the Zagros mountains chilled the air and water alike.

Ardeshir emerged from the rushing current and whooped with joy. Spotting his father still on the bank, he splashed water in the old man's direction.

"Come, father," he called. "Forget your dignity. Wash your past away. We're almost home."

Nabonidus sat on the bank with his feet in the river and rubbed his face and hair. "I've been dirtier than this in the arena. A little grit isn't going to slow me down."

"Wash up for your grandson."

Ardeshir dunked under again. His skin felt vibrant and renewed. The scent of jasmine hung in the air like a cloud. Images of Lu Hou nursing their son with a flower in her hair grabbed his mind so strongly that he was sure it was more than a mirage.

"If you don't get dressed and get these camels across the river," Nabonidus said, "your wife and son will never get to meet you. I'll put on a fresh tunic so your family will still welcome me."

As the caravan reorganized itself, camels waded through the chest-deep water single-file until all of them had crossed.

Adar approached Ardeshir and Nabonidus. "We have kept our promise to take you through the Bedu trail and we have done so safely. It's time to pay your balance. You can go on your own from here."

Nabonidus handed the khabir a small leather pouch and Adar emptied the contents into his hand. A gold ring, silver coins, three rubies, and two other gemstones lay in his palm.

Nodding with satisfaction, Adar turned back to his caravan without a further word of farewell.

It was sundown by the time they reached Susa. Nabonidus was stumbling from dehydration and exhaustion.

"Wait here, father," Ardeshir said. "I'll run to the guesthouse and bring a cart to take you the rest of the way."

"I should have given him another gold coin and kept the camel," Nabonidus murmured. "I forgot how far this walk could be."

"You left as a man full of strength and health. Now you're an old man, hardly more than a skeleton. I'll bring you food and water."

The long journey had taken its own toll on Ardeshir and his run quickly slowed to a walk. His parched throat grew scratchy, but the shops had closed and most people had shuttered and barred their doors against thieves and vagrants.

In desperation, he knocked on a door where a lamp still flickered within.

"Go away!" a harsh voice responded.

"My father and I have crossed the desert and we need water," Ardeshir begged.

"You should have got your fill at the river. Go away!"

He turned away and stumbled toward the center of the city where the guest-house had been set up. Would Lu Hou, Farzana, and other members of the Way still be there? Had the authorities shut them down? Had they run afoul of priests from the Temple of Fire? Had the Magi or the Elamites stirred up trouble and made them run?

A hand shook his shoulder and roused him to his senses again. He found himself facedown on the ground.

"Get up, vagrant," a stranger spoke in a gentle voice. "We can't have our streets littered with bodies."

Ardeshir rolled over. "I've crossed the desert and need water. My father is outside the city. He's old and can't walk any further."

"I have a cart," the stranger said. "It's used to pick up the dead, but for a small fee I can bring it. First we need to fill you with water and food. Your face looks like it has spent far too long in the sun."

The moon hung directly overhead by the time they had mobilized the cart and rumbled out of the city towards the road where Nabonidus lay. The old man remained huddled right where Ardeshir had left him, shuddering in the cool air and sounding delirious.

"Good sirs," Nabonidus rasped. "Spare me a sip of water or a blanket. I have nothing to offer except my blessing."

Ardeshir stumbled to his father and hugged him. "Father, I have food and water and a cart to take us the rest of the way."

The old man snatched the water gourd from his son and guzzled it. A short time later, he took the bread and nibbled it.

"I thought you had died out there," Nabonidus said.

"Come! Get in the cart," said the driver. "We'll get you to a place of rest before the night is over."

"In your wanderings, have you by any chance seen any sketches of a fish?" Ardeshir asked the stranger as they returned to the city. "We've been away for some time and need to reorient ourselves."

"Why would you need to find such sketches?"

"It's a sign to help me find people I know," Ardeshir said.

"I've seen a fish near the market, but there are only one group of people who use them."

"Do you mean the followers of the Way?"

"You know of them?"

Ardeshir nodded. "I'll pay you double if you take me to any of those signs."

"There is no need," the man said. "I too am a follower and can take you to the shelter you desire. It seems that Yeshua has brought us together for a reason."

The tension in Yas's shoulders eased when she saw Liu step into the wedding chamber. She drew a deeper breath and looked for his smile. He attempted to huddle in with the other fifty or so guests mingling along the edge of the space.

It was a relief that Fang had allowed Liu to come to her wedding. The man had proved to be a strong friend to her brother and a good ally for her. Perhaps he had been chosen as a witness or advocate for what might still lie ahead.

Liu stood patiently by the door with a guardian, not acknowledging her attempt at eye contact.

Beside her, Jing giggled. "Not knowing the groom must be fun. Today is your big surprise."

A small band of musicians flowed into the room lined with chrysanthemums. Flutes, bamboo panpipes, bells, mouth organs, zithers, and drums created a joyful melody which she would have enjoyed had not the occasion been so personal and life-changing.

Fang had insisted that this marriage was one of two conditions which would save Yas' life. She had no emotional capacity left to resist. Not with Orotes gone.

The large doors at the back of the arched chamber opened and Fang, accompanied by a retinue of red-robed council members and a train of golden-robed guardians, paraded into the hall. As she stood, she saw from the corner of her eye an ivory-studded golden throne placed behind her. She sat in it, feeling erect and stiff.

Two of the guardians stepped in front of her with a blue robe embroidered with yellow dragons, cranes, and horses. They approached Yas, stood beside her, and grasped her elbows.

At Fang's nod, a red robe appeared in the hands of another pair of guardians. This robe was wrapped around Yas.

Fang then rose and nodded again, this time toward the entrance.

Yas hung her head. She closed her eyes and tried to breathe. Whoever had been chosen would now share her fate. If the man was a criminal, he was already doomed to die. If he were a soldier, he might be away for long periods of time and die in battle. If he were a farmer, he may be fodder for the wild things.

If he were a scholar, there may be hope.

Shuffling at the entrance betrayed the approach of the man who would be her husband. She hoped he would be gentle.

"Keep your eyes down," Yun had instructed. "The favor or disfavor of your husband can help decide the favor or disfavor of the emperor when the time of his decision comes."

One of the grand council members stepped up, helped her stand, and turned her so that she was aligned back-to-back with her future husband. She could feel that he was slightly taller.

A silk draping was placed over their shoulders and a small golden cord tied her left hand and the man's right hand together. Music played as their head coverings were put in place. The end of her life was growing closer.

A guardian approached with a silver tray on which was perched a single crystal glass filled with red wine. Fang lifted the glass and handed it to Yas's prospective husband, and then to Yas herself.

"Sip for life together," Fang said.

Yas raised the glass with her unbound hand and took a sip. Fang then took the glass and held it out to a tall man in a large coned hat.

"The shaman will now determine the match," Fang told her.

The shaman held the glass up to the light and rotated it slowly. Within minutes, he placed it back on the tray and turned toward the group of witnesses.

"It is a match," he declared.

The group clapped three times and then stomped their feet once.

Yas waited in trepidation as a blindfold was wrapped around her—and the eyes of the groom as well, she could only assume.

She felt herself being moved into a new position, perhaps so she and her husband-to-be stood side by side.

"I declare you children of the lotus, workers of the empire and builders of family," the grand council member chanted. "Do your duty and live in peace."

Someone grasped Yas by the elbow and led her out of the hall, down a path, and into a room. All the while, her new husband held her by the wrist.

Once she heard the door close behind them, leaving the two alone, she didn't know what to do. In fact, neither of them moved for a while.

She closed her eyes and held her breath.

The man gently grasped her blindfold and tugged it away. He unfastened the cord on her wrist. Then he wrapped her in a strong and lasting hug. He smelled of roses.

"At last we are together," he said.

Yas jerked in surprise, then opened her eyes. Standing face to face with her was Liu.

Stepping back into his home city brought a flood of memories from the last time Ardeshir had been with his wife and son.

"Adrina died of fever a few months ago," the cart driver told Ardeshir and Nabonidus as they parked outside the house. "There's a new hostess, but I don't know her name yet."

Once they'd unloaded, the man left with three silver coins in his palm. He nodded to the father and son with gratitude before returning to his work of collecting the dead from the city streets.

"Should we wait until morning to disturb them?" Nabonidus whispered.

Ardeshir shook his head. "I can't wait a moment longer."

They didn't even get a chance to approach the door when a shadow slid through to greet them.

"Welcome, if you are brothers," spoke a young woman. "It is late and the house is asleep. Would you be willing to lay on these mats until the daylight comes?"

Ardeshir took a step towards the familiar woman. "Farzana? Is that you?"

"And who is it that asks?" she said.

"It's your prince, Ardeshir."

"Oh, Prince Shir!" Farzana threw herself into his arms. "And who is with you?"

"It is my father, Nabonidus, the emperor's champion."

"I will bring your wife," Farzana said. "She recently delivered another son and hasn't had much sleep. She hoped you would be back before the babe was born. I don't think you even knew she was with child when you left to go west!"

"This is a blessing from Yeshua." Ardeshir turned to his father. "Father, we have another prince for you to bless and welcome into your kingdom."

He opened the door and helped his father to a stool inside.

Moments later, Lu Hou shuffled into the room carrying a clay lamp. The flickering wick revealed enough of her face for Ardeshir to see that his wife was weary and disturbed.

"Farzana, why are we receiving strangers in the middle of the night?" she asked.

She lifted the lamp higher and focused on Ardeshir's face. Her expression changed abruptly and she charged forward, dropping the lamp in order to wrap her arms around her husband. The clay shattered and a brief spurt of fire splashed onto the floor.

Farzana retrieved another lamp and lit it to clean up the mess.

"All this noise will have the little ones up and screeching. You two will need a room to yourselves for a while." She turned to Nabonidus. "Come with me and I'll show you where to rest. You look exhausted. We can catch up with everyone in the morning."

Lu Hou grabbed her husband and pulled him deeper into the house. "Walk with me. We have so much to share."

"I'm tired of walking," Ardeshir said. "Can't we sit somewhere?"

"The garden has a bench. Come and share your love with me."

But Ardeshir stopped, unwilling to walk one step further. "Tell me about our new son."

"I named him Farshid, if you approve. You'll see him in the morning and I can tell you how much trouble he gave me on his arrival. And how is your father? What took you so long? Your face looks like it's been tormented by the sun."

She eased him down onto a pile of cushions near the wall.

"Stay here in the family room," she said. "Your feet must be dirty from the journey. Let me get a basin."

"I missed you every day," Ardeshir said through cracked lips. "Yeshua was gracious, but there were many days when I thought we'd never find my father... and many others when I thought we'd both die. But the Almighty blessed us with great friends who shared their provision and protection. We came down to the last of our resources to get home."

Lu Hou ran her hands through his scraggly beard. "We've all prayed daily for your safe return. It's hard not to hear news or to know what's happening. I can't bear to be away from you that long ever again."

She slipped out and soon returned with a basin.

Ardeshir hesitated before speaking next. "I'll soon need to go east to save my sister."

"No! I can't have you leave us. Your boys need you." She filled the washbasin with water and set it at his feet, kneeling to wash them. "Why did you come if you're only going to leave again?"

"Shhhhh," he said, gently running his fingers through her hair. He sat on a stool and set his feet in the cool water. "I'm here now. We can talk about all this another time. Right now, this moment, is just for us."

"If you have to go, take us with you," she pleaded, looking up at him. "I cannot look after these two little ones on my own."

She handed him a towel and stood to her feet.

He took it and rested it on his lap. "A trip that long would be too hard on the boys."

"Let's talk about this tomorrow after you've seen your sons. Right now, you need to wash, to eat and to sleep."

Nabonidus stepped into the family room with Farzana right behind him. "Son, this young woman just shared some disturbing news about your sister.

General Ban Chao came through here a month ago looking for you. His intentions for you don't sound good…"

Yas's tears continued to flow even as Liu tried to wipe them away and calm his new wife. Her body went into convulsions of relief, then laughter. When she caught her breath, she drank in the vision of this friend who was risking his life for her.

"Tell me truthfully," she said. "Are we truly married or is this a drama created by Fang to take my mind off my trouble?"

"We are truly husband and wife," Liu said. "I've never been married before, but is this the usual way that a wife responds to being alone with her husband?"

"Did you manipulate her into setting up our marriage?"

Liu stepped back, frowning. "I don't understand. I thought you would be happy that the man who gives his life for you is also someone who honestly loves you."

"I'm as happy as I can be." Yas removed her head covering and set it aside on a basket. "The man I thought I would rescue and marry has been killed. The girl who threatens my life now tries to save me by marrying me off to someone I can't even see. A friend of my brother says he has deep feelings for me. This is all so sudden and unexpected."

"How can I help you learn to be loved by me?"

The look in his eyes was so sincere. He seemed almost pained in confusion.

He sank to his knees and bowed. "Although Fang chose to bring us together without my help, I don't regret my role. I've been called on to face life or death with you. If I have only days, or ten weeks, to share my life with you, it is enough."

She knelt next to him and ran her fingers through his hair. "No woman could have a greater friend than you. I'll learn to love you as you teach me. Our time may be short, but I offer you my devotion, friendship, and hope for what is ahead. I don't die easily."

Liu squeezed her hand, then raised his head and focused on her face. Then he smiled. And laughed.

"What man could hope for more?" he said. "To live with a warrior who believes she will not die easily? Come! I think we need to walk in the garden and learn to love each other from the start… before we die."

"I remember the love my father and mother shared with each other," Yas said, "but I have been a warrior since I was young. My instincts are not to caress you and whisper sweet words into your ears. You'll have to be patient with me."

Liu took her hand and brought it to his lips. "Perhaps you could teach me to fight well enough so we can live. And I can teach you how to love well enough so you really live."

The smile erupted from deep inside her. "You do have a way with words. I think we will be more than friends very soon."

Fifteen

The next few weeks passed quickly and Ardeshir enjoyed every moment he spent with his young sons. The chill of winter eased, the first blossoms of spring decorated the trees, and an uneasy truce developed between him and Lu Hou, neither making any mention of heading east to rescue Yas. It didn't take long for them to fall into a natural rhythm of passion and intimacy. Soon it felt as though they had hardly been apart.

Nabonidus had relished spending time with the little ones, but it soon became apparent to all that his health was failing. It was getting harder for him to rise from his mat and nibble at his food. The aches and pains of the past showed up in his moaning from trying to get around.

"I don't think my father has much longer to live," Ardeshir confided to Lu Hou as they strolled in the garden with the little ones. He hoisted Artabanas onto his shoulders while Lu Hou held the newborn. "Hearing that his sister died stole the life from his heart. There will be increasing pressure on me to take on my royal duties, but I don't want it."

"You know they'll come looking for you in the same way that the bees come to these flowers," Lu Hou said. "You can't hide out here forever."

"I can manage taking care of a small family. Taking care of a nation requires a lot more."

"With my father's death and a new emperor on the throne, everything has changed for us. I have nothing left back home, yet I have nothing here except for you and these two boys. Why don't we find out what's happened to your sister before making a decision?"

Ardeshir looked up and saw Sanjay and Farzana huddled in the far corner of the garden talking with their son. The couple waved them over.

"We have good news for you," Farzana called. "We're now expecting our second child. We will have a playmate for your little one."

Ardeshir hurried over and sat on the bench beside Sanjay. He held out his son Artabanas toward the son of his friend.

"Davit is growing fast," Ardeshir said. "These two little warriors of ours will soon be wanting to have their own sword fights. We should fashion wooden ones for them to play with."

Sanjay pulled his own son, Davit, onto his lap. "Farzana and I have decided that our son will be a man of peace. We've seen enough violence in the world."

"But how will he protect you if you don't teach him how to fight?" Ardeshir asked.

"We've come to believe that violence chases after violent men," Farzana spoke up. "We know you don't want it to chase you, but it does anyway."

"Are you saying you don't want your children to play with my children?" Lu Hou asked. "We've known each other since our boys were born. They don't have to be violent with each other."

Sanjay stood with Davit, rocking him in his arms. "We will always be grateful, and we will always be friends. We only want to be people of peace. We've studied more of the teachings of Yeshua with his followers and we think that shalom will change people faster than force."

"You know that the Magi will press Ardeshir to take on his role as King of Kings." Lu Hou let out a sigh. "And the Elamites are already claiming him as their native son. There will be a struggle for power and control. Hard decisions will have to be made to protect our sons. Of course we would like to have you with us on that journey."

Farzana stood, gently rubbing her abdomen. "We will visit when we can. We now have the responsibility of looking after this refuge for followers of the Way. Life will continue to be difficult in this country for us and we want to provide shelter and help."

Ardeshir stood up and placed Artabanas on his shoulder.

"We would like nothing more than to stay here and to promote shalom," said Ardeshir. "Sometimes life doesn't always let you embrace the choices you want. At times you have to step into the role set out for you. But we'll be relieved to know there's an oasis of refuge for those who flee their persecutors. We'll support you in any way we can."

"Will you be going east soon?" Farzana asked. "To rescue your sister, I mean?"

Ardeshir took a moment before answering. "We're waiting for news from a messenger."

Just then, a young woman raced into the garden, waving her hands.

"Hurry!" she called. "Something is happening with the old man. Come quick!"

Waiting before the grand council as husband and wife didn't make it easier. Yas and Liu wore black robes and knelt in the sand of the arena, shoulder to shoulder. The same men who had presided over their marriage three months earlier would now decide whether they lived or died—and so far they gave off no hint of compassion or empathy.

The couple watched the elders parade up behind the judgment table. The box with black stones and white stones sat at its center.

This time, there would be no outside advocate. Liu understood the process and had prepared as best he could for the ordeal ahead. He'd instructed Yas to remain silent and trust his work on her behalf. Their marriage ensured that he was highly motivated, since they would share the same fate now.

If she lived, he lived.

If she died, he died.

Fang sat on her throne, watching the proceedings from the side. Her wedding to the new emperor had been set eighteen months in the future, in line with a prediction made by the shaman. The new emperor would take his position after seven fool moons had graced the heavens. These dates would align with the appropriate astrological signs.

If the grand council deadlocked again at six black to six white stones, the final judgment on their fate would be decided by the emperor after his coronation.

Yas and Liu had discussed their strategy over and over. How would they present their case? Tying her exploits to her brother's seemed like a flawed approach due to his condemnation to the lion's den. Reminding the council of her heroic efforts on behalf of the former emperor had potential, but it was clear from other recent rulings that the elders were looking for a more current angle more advantageous to the new regime.

"Your willingness to train the new emperor's future wife to ride a horse may be something to highlight," Liu had suggested a few weeks earlier while in their cell.

Yas had shaken her head. "That girl can't wait to see me chopped up for the koi. She hates me."

"Then why did she intervene and arrange our marriage? She's just a young girl trying to live with the burden of becoming the empress."

"Why don't we ask her how to move forward? If not her, maybe Jing. We need some clear advice on how to present ourselves. Do you think Fang could talk to the future emperor on our behalf?"

"That would be highly improper and outside protocol."

"If he were already emperor, we wouldn't stand a chance," she had said. "But right now Fang is still just Ban Chao's daughter."

To her surprise, Jing had been a willing messenger—and Fang had then agreed to provide some advice. The advice had come within a week: "Share four noble truths that draw attention to the greatness of the Han Empire."

This advice had seemed both simple and overwhelming at the same time. Yas recalled that her brother Ardeshir had failed to impress this very same council, and he had been the princess's teacher at the time.

She and Liu had lost much sleep debating which four truths could bring glory to the empire and the new emperor. They had discussed it right up until the moment they had been covered in bulky black robes to be brought before the council.

Now they bent their foreheads to the ground and opened their palms.

The lead member of the grand council banged on the table. "Your judgment has been put off long enough. It is time to hear your final plea. Speak."

Yas clenched her teeth as her husband spoke on her behalf.

"Our only defence is to present four noble truths for the glory of the empire," Liu announced.

"An interesting defence," the leader said. "Remember that your life is forfeit if you fail. Stand and speak clearly. It may be your last opportunity."

Yas exhaled so sharply that she swayed. Lui bowed until his forehead touched the jade floor.

The high councilor smiled. "It is your fortune to live until the new emperor's decision. Your truths may serve us well until then."

The cart rattled along the rutted road toward the farm as Ardeshir and Sanjay drove, putting Susa far behind them. Nabonidus had requested to see the farm one last time before his passing, regardless of its condition, and Ardeshir had pledged to do everything he could to honor his request. Lu Hou had asked to stay home, as the little one had kept her up all night, and Farzana had chosen to stay as well; her morning sickness had become debilitating.

Sanjay had insisted on joining them. He hadn't been to the farm in months, since the winter, and wanted to deal with the weeds he knew would be overrunning the property. There was also the matter of chasing away any vagrants who had moved in.

"I know that you want to be a man of peace," Ardeshir said to Sanjay, "but we need to arm ourselves. What if we have to defend the farm when we get there? My father and I can fight."

"Your father can hardly stand," Sanjay said. "How can he fight?"

"He has the pride of being the emperor's champion," Ardeshir said. "He may have a weakened heart, but he's driven. Don't underestimate him."

The trio had been on the road since dawn and by midafternoon their destination still wasn't in sight. Caravans, traders, pilgrims, and locals filled the roadways; they seemed almost in a festive mood. The rich scent of spices drifted in the air as a long train of camels plodded by. Ardeshir felt truly alive amidst all this beauty.

"Father, what are your best memories from all your years of life?" Ardeshir asked. "I'm sure they don't have anything to do with your days as a slave, and probably not even your days in the arena. What gave your life meaning and significance?"

Nabonidus coughed. "Such deep questions for a trip like this?"

"What do you remember best?"

"Meeting your mother," his father said with a smile. "Seeing you for the first time. Starting the assembly in Ephesus. Establishing the farm."

"What about finding out that you were the prince of Persia?" Sanjay asked.

Nabonidus shook his head. "Not one of my best memories. The price of power is high. It tests men to their limits. I already knew I was a child of the true King of Kings, so settling for being a prince mattered little to me."

"But what was your toughest battle?" Sanjay persisted.

"Not the one you might think," Nabonidus said. "I had to fight the temptation of unfaithfulness to my God and wife. The internal urges are sometimes stronger than we realize. We live in an arena where temptations, lies, emotions, misbeliefs, assumptions, and old wounds team up to ambush and attack us when we're not alert or prepared. You're young still, but there will come a day when you'll remember my warning to guard your heart and mind while you can."

"When that day comes, you can stand up and remind me yourself," Sanjay said. "You'll live to see my sons marrying your granddaughters."

"Look!" Ardeshir broke in. "The farm is up ahead. Looks like there has been a lot of heavy traffic through this area."

Nabonidus held up his hand. "Let me see those tracks."

The old man lowered himself slowly from the cart and knelt, feeling the indents in the mud.

"These aren't local horses," he noted. "There were twenty or thirty in the group and they were carrying heavy weight. Could be military. They weren't plodding along like a caravan."

Sanjay looked nervous. "Maybe we should go back."

"We're almost there," Ardeshir said. "We'll take a quick look and then move on."

They halted at a single post rising out of the dirt, marking the former location of a gate. A field of mud and weeds spread out before them.

"Doesn't look like much anymore," Nabonidus remarked. "Who can believe that this was once the foundation of a potential kingdom?"

The sound of dull thuds marked the approach of riders. The trio took up a defensive posture at the gate post, waiting as ten riders approached with lances, swords, and shields. To Ardeshir, they had the demeanor and armored garb of cataphracts.

The leader gave a head bob to Nabonidus. "We heard you had returned, oh prince. We've also heard that an enemy has marked you for death. Your time is short. You need to hide."

"We'll soon head back to Susa," Nabonidus told him. "Thank you for letting us know."

"There will be no return to Susa," the cataphract leader said. "The enemy is almost here. We wish we had more to fight on your side, but there are only a few of us left to defend your honor."

"Is it the Magi?" Ardeshir asked. "Who is this enemy who dares to attack us?"

"They are from the Han Empire. They have been here before and show no mercy."

"We will fight then!" Nabonidus said.

Ardeshir unwrapped the weaponry in the cart and distributed it to those in need.

"It's General Ban Chao," he said to Sanjay and Nabonidus. "He's tracked us down. Sanjay, take my father and see whether there are still tunnels in which to shelter. We cannot put him at risk."

"No!" Nabonidus said, looking horrified at the suggestion. "I have never run and I won't run now. Hand me a crossbow, a lance, and a sword."

Ardeshir looked up to watch the lead cataphract charging around the perimeter of the farm.

"We'll shelter behind the ruins of that old building," the leader said upon his return, pointing at a heap of timbers. "Those of us on horses will take on the enemy's first charge. The three of you without horses can try to take down as many as you can with crossbows."

The sun was already setting when a scout charged into the farm.

"Horsemen approaching fast," he yelled. "Prepare your arms!"

Within moments, a thundering chorus of hoofbeats on the roadway announced the arrival of General Ban Chao and his host of Han assassins.

A shiver snaked its way down Ardeshir's spine. The destroyer of life had arrived with a vengeance.

With methodical intent, the enemy spread around the perimeter of the farm, sealing off the Persians' escape. Ardeshir kept his eye glued to the general, who took up a position in front of the front post.

No one spoke a word.

The sun set and still none of the enemy had attempted to enter the property. The chill of the night was setting in and all was still, apart from the occasional snort of a horse. The silence grew as thick as the darkness.

It soon became clear to Ardeshir that the final attack would come at daybreak.

"How are you doing?" he whispered to his father. "They must know we aren't going to be able to defend ourselves very long. Maybe they're hoping the cold will paralyze us first."

"Let's rearrange this lumber to form a circle around us," Nabonidus suggested. "If we keep active, our blood will circulate better. But tell me—who is this Han general and why is he so determined to destroy us?"

"His father wanted him to marry the emperor's daughter," Ardeshir explained. "But she wanted me instead. He used to patrol the emperor's garden with a leopard and feed on anyone who couldn't escape. I killed that leopard and the general promised vengeance. The time has finally come."

"I'm afraid to die," Sanjay said as he shuffled closer. "I know we believe in the Way, but I want to raise my son and love my wife. This is exactly what we didn't want for our lives."

"If you want to raise your son and love your wife, you had better aim carefully and often with that crossbow," Nabonidus said. "What you and the enemy want are two different things. This fight will be over before you know it."

The sun had hardly cast a ray over the first hill when the Han assassins began to move, closing ranks in a tighter and tighter circle around the farm. They banged their swords against their shields in a deafening attempt at intimidation.

The cataphracts stood until the attackers got to within a stone's throw. Then, without any clear signal, they galloped their horses in a circle. It took one shout and the ten riders bunched together, lowered their lances, and charged at one point of the circle. The Han turned their horses to move out of the way, but five fell before escaping.

The cataphracts regrouped and charged again. Three more Han riders fell, along with one of the cataphracts.

Ban Chao called his assassins together and charged the cataphracts head-on. In response, the cataphracts pulled away and charged toward the ruins where Ardeshir and Nabonidus were hiding. Four more Han assassins fell to crossbows, at which point the general divided his troops, twenty warriors focusing on the cataphracts and another dozen focusing on the archers hiding in the ruins.

Despite how many arrows Ardeshir, Sanjay, and Nabonidus dispatched, there were just too many Han. Six of the assassins got into close range, thrusting their flailing swords as Nabonidus stood to confront them.

Ardeshir tried to draw the attackers away, and three of them did step up to meet his challenge. Sanjay continued firing his crossbow, felling another two assassins in the process.

Ban Chao isolated Nabonidus as the two stepped away from the ruins at the center of the farm.

"And now we end this ridicule," the general roared. "I will return to destroy your daughter, rest assured, but first I will destroy you."

The general lunged forward, swinging a warhammer. Nabonidus parried each blow with his smaller sword; with his other arm, he probed the enemy with a lance. Ban Chao's thick armor seemed impenetrable.

At one point, Nabonidus seemed to stumble. Ban Chao raised his sword to deliver the final blow, which is when Nabonidus threw a handful of moist sand into his face. The Han killer reached up toward his eyes and the prince thrust a lance into the blinded man's thigh.

Stumbling, Ban Chao roared in rage, pulled a dagger-axe from the loop on his saddlebag, and charged. Nabonidus then hit him in the side of the head with the lance, but he endured a slash across his arm.

Both men had delivered a killer blow at the same time. While they fell, mortally wounded, the battle continued to rage around them.

By now Ardeshir had taken out one man and faced the final two. Sanjay took out one of his opponents, causing the remaining assassin to back away and charge for his horse in order to flee.

In the aftermath, Ardeshir reflected that the cataphracts had done well—and yet none of them had survived.

He and Sanjay watched as a few Han stragglers trotted away from the battlefield. Either they would find reinforcements or else abandon the onslaught, Ardeshir couldn't say.

As he turned back to assess their casualties, he saw his father, lying still in the embrace of General Ban Chao's corpse.

"Your father's gone," Sanjay said. "He saved you."

Ardeshir knelt over his father's body and wept until Sanjay nudged his shoulder.

"We need to take his body and get back home," Ardeshir said at last. "There's no one left to help us now."

Sixteen

Two weeks after the grand council, spring was in full array. Birdsong filled the air, butterflies flitted among the flowers, the koi skittered under the surface of the pond, and long-dormant insects made themselves known again.

With the council once again deadlocked over Yas's fate, the duty had fallen to the new emperor to decide. But his coronation was still more than six months away. In the meantime, Yas and Lui were freed to roam the gardens and surrounding fields.

They spent less time on walks and more time inside—that is, when they weren't taking the girls out to ride the horses.

Whispers began to circulate about the unexpectedly long absence of General Ban Chao. His return had been anticipated a month ago and the lack of his elite forces around the garden was noticeable. Fang and Jing speculated on their father's great victories, which were taking longer than normal. They expected him to bring the notorious Persian outlaws to justice and return with even greater wealth than ever as a result of new trade deals. In their eyes, he could do no wrong.

"I think my father is bringing home an elephant from Egypt," Jing commented one afternoon as Fang and Yas trotted beside her along a trail on their ponies. "I think he'll bring a camel train of gold for the emperor and a baby lion for me to play with."

"Elephants don't come from Egypt," Fang pointed out to her sister. "If he brings one, it will probably be for me to ride at my wedding. The camel train of gold will be to line the doorways of my new palace. You can keep the baby lion until he grows up and has to join the wild things."

"Why do you think the whole world revolves around you?" Jing asked.

Fang jutted out her chin and smiled. "Because it does."

A week later, Jing broke out in tears as they rode on another trail, this one running near the wall that contained the wild things.

"I had a bad dream about father," Jing said.

"What happened?" Yas asked.

"He was chasing a snake, but it turned and bit him." Jing broke into tears. "He killed the snake, but the poison was killing him. He called for me. I couldn't reach him. Do you think something terrible has happened?"

"Don't be a child," Fang said. "Father would never miss my wedding. Besides, the emperor couldn't run the empire without his general. Criminals would take over this whole place if it weren't for him."

Yas halted the horses. "Fang, you must be patient with your younger sister. In my country, we take dreams very seriously. What if something has happened to your father and this dream is one way to prepare you?"

Fang scowled. "I thought you had learned to respect those who hold your life in their hands. But now you act like someone who's destined to be nothing more than koi food. I'm working hard to change the culture of this kingdom and I won't have foreigners warping the minds of our children."

"Thank you for reminding me of my place," Yas said. "I've always wondered. What made you choose Liu to be my husband? I never would have imagined such a match."

Fang grinned. "I saw the way he looked at you and thought he would be happy to die by your side. I didn't think the marriage would have to last so long."

"The emperor will be very fortunate to have a wife like you," Yas said. "You can matchmake, change the culture, determine how people think, and sort out the noble truths that are acceptable from those that are not. Perhaps your husband will be happy to let you do all the ruling so he can relax."

"Perhaps I shall ask him to let you live," Yas said.

Two months after Ban Chao's expected return, a pair of riders trotted into the outskirts of the emperor's garden. Yas and Liu had wandered to the vegetable shops to purchase their weekly groceries when they saw the new arrivals.

The men looked ragged and weary, not at all up to the dress code demanded of the empire's most elite protectors. They were, after all, part of the general's platoon.

Two golden-robed guardians stood at the entrance to the palace.

"What is the news?" one of them called to the riders. "When can we expect the general?"

The riders dismounted and looked around, not seeming to notice Yas and Liu standing behind the hedge.

"General Ban Chao is dead," the first rider said. "We crossed the desert chasing the Persian prince but found him instead near Susa. A great battle ensued, but he was too strong for us. The general did kill the enemy snake, but the hordes overwhelmed us. We are the only two who survived."

The golden-robed guardian drew out his sword. "You alone have survived when the general sacrificed his own life?"

"Yes!"

"Then kneel."

The two men knelt. A moment later, the guardians beheaded the two assassins. They then stripped their bodies without hesitation, threw a blanket over them, and sent for a cart. When the cart arrived, they dismissed the driver, loaded the covered bodies, and drove away.

"Now we need to make the mother and girls disappear," one of the guardians said.

Yas and Liu froze, open-mouthed at what they had witnessed.

"He's dead and no one will know," Yas said. "We have to warn the girls before the guardians go after them."

Trying not to arouse suspicion, they walked with purpose toward the general's home, even though they didn't know how they'd get past the guardians at the door. They paused at the koi pond, taking a few moments to study the walking patterns of the men strolling before the sprawling home.

Liu put his hand gently atop Yas's hand. "When the riders said that the General had first killed the Persian snake, do you suppose he meant your brother?"

"My goodness!" Yas cried out, crumpling to her knees. "I didn't even think of that."

"Well, I don't know for sure who it refers to, but it's terrible news," Liu said. "You've lost your mother, your father, and now very likely your brother. Maybe his family too."

Yas grasped Liu by both wrists. "You are the only family I have now, and our fate rests in the hands of a girl who will soon learn that my brother's army killed her father. But her own fate lies in our hands now, since we alone know that the guardians plan to kill her. Yes, we have to do something."

As they stood watching for an opportunity, the two golden-robed guardians walked down the path toward the general's house. They walked with great haste and a sense of purpose.

"Perhaps we're already too late," Liu said.

Upon the news that a trio of elegantly dressed noblemen had arrived in Susa, Ardeshir's mind began to race. The visitors didn't seem to arouse the suspicion of the locals, at least not at first. Their accents and mannerisms marked them as having come from the north, but the city was very international in makeup.

Nonetheless, they asked a lot of questions about the farm where all the recent fighting had occurred. Why were they so curious about that?

Ardeshir followed the nobleman to the marketplace. As they spoke with a potter, he sheltered himself in the weaver's stall next door. He pressed his fingers to his lips and shook his head to silence the weaver's curious glances. He also wrapped his face covering tighter.

"We are here to honor the former prince," one of the three noblemen was saying. "Although he never took his position, we are obligated to demonstrate proper respect to the Maimonides clan. If you know where we can make contact with the family, let us know. We will be at the main inn."

Shadowing the three as they meandered to their lodgings wasn't difficult. Along the way, one of them stopped to barter for a jeweled pendant. Another peeled off to barter for fruit. The third just continued on his way.

Ardeshir waited for the one interested in the pendant. As the man finished his purchase and stepped away, Ardeshir stepped up behind him and clamped a hand on his shoulder.

"Keep walking," Ardeshir spoke in a low voice. "It's clear you know something of our business."

It didn't take long to reach the inn, where Ardeshir ushered him into a back room.

"Who are you and what do you need to tell us?" the nobleman asked.

Ardeshir breathed deeply, rotated his shoulders, and closed his eyes. "What makes you think I know anything?"

"You seem to have hidden from us," the man said. "You attempted to follow us discretely. You also seem ready for a fight."

"What is your business with the fight at the farm?" Ardeshir demanded.

"Rumor came to us that the prince of Persia died near here in a fight with a group of Han assassins. Before that, we heard that he had been taken by the Romans. We seek truth. We also seek to honor him with a proper burial. We need to find his successor."

Ardeshir lowered his head. "The man who died… was my father."

The man knelt with a hand over their heart. "We have been sent by the court of the Magi. Show us this prince who has passed away and we shall do our duty. The Circle of Ancients calls you to come and declare yourself, to take your proper place in the nation."

"What of the battle with the Elamites?" Ardeshir asked. "I don't wish to step into a civil war that will destroy my people."

"Allow us to first bury the prince. We can negotiate the terms of your position once we have done what is necessary. We have buried your father's sister and we shall place him beside her with full honors for his status."

Ardeshir leaned against a wall. "There are many who come as pretenders with their own agendas. Once you have proven who you are, I shall tell you where we have placed him to rest."

The door to the back room opened and Ardeshir looked up. The other two noblemen quietly entered.

"Our apologies, but we overheard," said one of the newcomers. He knelt and held out a small pouch. "This is the ring guarded by your father's sister—the lion ring of our ruler. It belongs to the one who will be proclaimed King of Kings. It is yours… if you can prove who you are."

"My father took a merchant ship west and was captured by pirates," Ardeshir explained. "That ship was taken by Romans and he was left at Ephesus, where the priest wanted to sacrifice him. He appealed to the emperor and was taken to Rome to stand trial. I helped rescue him and bring him home. Then the Han ambushed us at the farm."

The first man, who appeared to be the group's leader, stepped toward him. "That story is hard to believe. And what of your own story?"

"I was sent east to the Han emperor, where I survived a trial of five and married the royal daughter. The Han general destroyed our farm in retaliation, chased us across the Arabian desert to Petra, then hunted us down. My father killed him, and he killed my father."

"Another story that seems too amazing to believe," the leader mused. "But it's worthy of a prince. Come, let us finish what we have come for—"

The third man abruptly changed the topic of conversation. "Why don't you bring your wife, the Han princess. Bring your son as well, so we can honor him."

Ardeshir fell silent. He had made no mention of any son.

The slight hesitation in his posture was enough to alert the three noblemen to his suspicion. Ardeshir saw it in the quick eye check that the leader made with the questioner.

Still, he tried to play ignorant.

"That reminds me," Ardeshir said. "My men are waiting for me not far from here. Why don't I meet them and direct them to where we should go? Where do you want me to go?"

The leader stepped in front of the exit as casually as he could. "There's no need for you to rush off. Why don't you tell us where your men are? Where your father and family are? We can take care of everything without troubling you further."

A knock at the door stiffened them all.

"Honorable sirs," a man outside said, "the innkeeper requests a meeting to know why there are twenty armed warriors outside looking for you."

To Ardeshir, the voice sounded strangely like Sanjay.

The leader turned toward the door. "Tell him we're busy and will join him in a moment."

Determined to use the distraction to his advantage, Ardeshir elbowed the leader's face into the door. At the very same moment, Sanjay pushed the door open.

Before the nobleman even dropped to the floor, Ardeshir spun and kicked the second man in the jaw while punching the third.

By the time Sanjay had squirmed his way inside, all three of the newcomers lay on the ground.

"Looks like I came in time," Sanjay said. "Who are these men?"

Ardeshir snatched up the lion ring now lying on the floor. "They claim to be messengers from the Magi, coming to declare me the King of Kings. But they seemed to know a little too much about my family."

He tore strips of cloth from a bedsheet and tied the men together just as they began struggling for consciousness.

"You don't think they could be legitimate, do you?" Sanjay asked.

"I guess they could have known about my family from my aunt," Ardeshir conceded. "If it turns out that they're legitimate, at least we didn't kill them."

As Yas and Liu stood near the hedge maze, hiding in the underbrush and watching the golden-robed guardians approach General Ban Chao's home, the door suddenly opened and Yun walked into view. She held a bundle of laundry.

For a moment, Yun made eye contact with Yas, who motioned for her to come quickly.

The young maid walked towards their hiding place, careful not to give away their position.

"Listen carefully," Yas told her. "The general has been killed and we need to tell the girls. You see those two guardians? They're going to kill the entire family. We need you to warn the girls that they're late for their riding lessons and should come immediately. Tell them to bring their mother!"

"Will these guardians harm me?" Yun asked.

"Not if you hurry," Liu said. "They'll try to convince the family to leave the house so the deed can be done elsewhere. There are too many servants here to act as witnesses."

Yun walked back toward the home, nodding to the two guardians as they reached the front door, then went around the side and slipped into a side entrance.

It seemed like forever before she emerged again with Fang. After a brief discussion, Fang marched in the direction of the hedge maze.

When she found Yas and Liu, she stopped and spoke firmly. "Why are you still spreading deception? We didn't schedule a ride today. We're busy with our lessons. Besides, we've just gotten word that our father has called us to meet him at our country house."

"We're hiding because your family is in great danger," Yas whispered.

"What do you mean? How is our family in danger? We have guardians all around us."

Liu lowered his head. "Noble princess, hear us so you may live and reign in glory."

"Speak!" Fang said.

"The news we bring is hard but true," Liu said. "Two riders from your father's elite brigade have returned with bad news. Those two guardians who brought news about your father? They're lying to you. They want to draw you out so they can end your lives."

Fang seemed unconvinced. "What is this news?"

"Your father has been killed in battle," Yas said gently. "After the guardians killed the messengers, we heard them say that they would kill you also."

Fang stomped her foot. "You lie! Nothing has happened to my father."

"We're only telling you what we heard and saw," Liu said. "Your father may be fine, but we did hear these two guardians speak about ending your lives. We hoped to warn you before it's too late. Check for blood on their robes."

Fang looked back towards the house. Did she believe them?

"I will test these guardians," she said at last. "I'll tell them that the three of us have to attend our riding lesson first. If they let us go without trouble, I will be back to deal with you for your lies. If they find reasons to stop, I will reward you when we have put them away."

The young woman straightened her shoulders, set her jaw, and strode down a path toward the barracks of her family's guardians.

It didn't take long before Jing stepped out of the house accompanied by one of the treacherous guardians. She jabbered away with abandon as they walked towards the entrance to the hedge maze.

Yaz's stomach churned with fear as the pair moved toward the maze. The guardian kept checking over his shoulder.

They disappeared into the maze.

"I don't like this," Yas said. "They're isolating the girls in case anything goes wrong. The mother is in there alone with that last guardian."

"What do we do?" Liu asked.

"Stay here and wait for Fang. I'll follow Jing to make sure nothing happens to her."

It didn't take long for Yas to catch up to Jing and the guardian. The girl was practically shouting to make her voice heard throughout the maze.

"Wait here!" Jing called, presumably to the guardian. "I know the way through. Fang must have gone ahead to start our lesson. Go back and tell my father that we'll meet him soon."

Yas peeked around a hedge and saw them stopped in the middle of the path ahead.

"No," the guardian objected. "Your father is worried about your safety and wants to see you immediately."

"My sister would never go without me." Jing placed her hands on her hips. "Just wait here and I'll be back after my lesson."

Jing began to walk away, but the guardian followed.

"You will come with me now!" the man demanded.

Jing spun on her heels, ducked low, and raced away into the maze as fast as her legs would carry her. The guardian gave chase, but after a moment he slowed down and fully stopped amidst the towering hedges.

Jing had lost him.

Seventeen

Groans echoed in the night as the trussed-up trio of noblemen regained consciousness. A single clay lamp flickered, casting shadows on their faces as the first fingers of dawn slipped through the window.

Ardeshir and Sanjay sat on stools against the door and waited.

"Looks like you've all survived," Ardeshir said at last when he had the men's attention. "Perhaps we should start off with some truthtelling. Who are you and where do you come from?"

The leader glared. "We are who we say we are. I'm Rapana, the protector of truth. The ringkeeper is Humayak, the smart one. The other is Husravah, the one with a good reputation."

"I showed you the ring as proof," Humayak said. "I didn't expect to lose a tooth to bring you this good news!"

"We've been ambushed, chased, beaten, and threatened for such a long time," said Ardeshir. "You can understand why we'd be suspicious of unexpected visitors."

"Especially when they have knowledge we didn't share with them," Sanjay added.

Rapana waggled his shoulders. "Your aunt told us all about you and your family before she died. She told us that as soon as her funeral was over we needed to find her brother to crown him prince of Persia. That's when we heard about the ambush on your farm and came to see if the news was true."

"I'm glad you survived," Ardeshir said. "It wouldn't look good for me to start killing off my advisors before I even take the crown."

"Will you release us?" Husravah asked. "If you don't want the responsibility of the throne, all you had to do was tell us."

Ardeshir nodded to Sanjay, who proceeded to release the men one by one.

"Perhaps we can offer you something to eat," Ardeshir said. "That way we can start this conversation over again."

"For now, let's focus on giving your father the proper burial rites." Rapana gestured towards Sanjay. "Your servant can get us the food we need."

"He's not my servant," Ardeshir said. "He's my brother."

"Whatever you call him is no matter to us," Rapana said. "As long as you're the rightful heir."

Sanjay stepped towards the door. "He is the rightful heir, and I will bring your food. I'll try hard not to poison it."

Yas made her way back to the entrance of the maze, choosing a spot where she could keep one eye trained on General Ban Chao's house and the other on the maze.

The door to the barracks opened and Fang stepped out, followed by four guardians. They confidently returned to the house.

She sighed and looked back into the maze, where she caught a glimpse of the lost guardian, retreating towards Yas's hiding place. He appeared irritated and frantic.

"Young woman," the guardian called, swiveling and calling into the maze. "Your father will not be happy if you keep him waiting like this. There's no time for horses today. Come out now!"

A moment later, Yas heard the slight rustling of bushes and looked to her left. There was Jing, right behind her, giggling.

"How long do you think he'll look for me?" she whispered.

"Hopefully long enough so your sister can deal with that other guardian." Yas placed a hand on the girl's shoulder. "These are bad men. They killed two of your father's soldiers after those same men brought news that your father is dead—"

Jing gasped. "It's not true, is it?"

"We don't know. All we know is that your family is in danger."

"Where's Fang?"

"She's gone into the house with reinforcements."

They remained crouched, side by side, peering through a break in the hedge. Finally, the door of the house opened and three guardians emerged—two of them loyal to Fang. The man in the middle was enraged and struggling.

Fang followed them out, leading her mother into the garden. Another pair of loyal guardians trailed behind them.

Fang pointed toward the maze. "Another of them went in there," she ordered. "Go after him!"

As the loyal guardians hurried off, the captured one tried to shout a warning for his friend.

"Run!"

Yas looked back into the maze and immediately located the guardian who'd been trying to deceive Jing. He did run, as instructed, but it appeared he could only move in pointless circles, unable to find his way.

As the pursuit began in earnest, Fang marched up to Yas.

"You were right," she said. "The one inside was threatening my mother, trying to convince us to go to my father's cabin immediately. But it turned out he didn't even know where the cabin was. And of course I saw the blood on his robe, as you said."

All of them took a moment to watch the chaos unfolding in the maze.

"You are courageous and wise," Yas remarked. "You've saved your family."

"I only hope I've saved my father as well," Fang said. "If he is dead, my hopes of becoming the emperor's wife may never be realized." She cast her gaze down at the ground. "I don't think I'm in the mood for a riding lesson right now."

"It's okay. We can save it for another day."

At that moment, there was a flurry of movement at the entrance of the maze as the frantic golden-robed guardian raced out. Desperate to escape, he dove straight into the koi pond and began to swim across. His heavy robe weighed him down, though, and soon more loyal guardians arrived to surround the shoreline. There was no escape.

After a short time of paddling to stay afloat, the drowning man slipped below the surface.

Fang turned away. "Koi food."

Nabonidus's funeral procession turned out to be one worthy of celebration. His body was dressed in royal robes and paraded for two days through the towns and villages between Susa and Babylon. Crowds lined the street to pay homage to the emperor's champion, throwing flowers and chanting the age-old songs.

The Zoroastrian priests and magistrates from the Temple of Fire started a small riot when the Magi agreed to let Ardeshir bury his father in the way of Yeshua. The Zoroastrian traditions, taken from their Vendidat scripture, determined that naked corpses be laid out in the open air and eaten by vultures and dogs. Ardeshir hadn't wanted to see that happen to his father.

As a compromise, the funeral procession had traveled to a patch of barren ground where vultures circled in anticipation. A slain lamb was left in place of Nabonidus's body.

Ardeshir stood next to Lu Hou, watching the spectacle.

After this, the plan was for the procession to continue towards a small nearby cave that Ardeshir had purchased in recent days. The tomb would remain sealed for one year, after which time the bones would be taken to the place of the kings to be stored in an ossuary.

"I don't suppose you're expecting a resurrection," Lu Hou said as the vultures finished their feat.

Ardeshir shook his head solemnly. "Only one man has raised himself from the dead and that is enough."

As they turned to leave, two members of the Magi stepped up behind Ardeshir and draped a royal robe over his shoulders.

"We give you this gift for your consideration," one of them said. "Members of the royal council of ancients must still confirm your pedigree and standing, but much work has already been done to determine the legitimacy of your family line."

Next, Ardeshir oversaw the wrapping of his father's body in a specially woven mat. He then watched as a crew of assistants laid it on a cart for the ride to the cave.

As he prepared to step into place at the head of the procession, a messenger rode up on a warhorse.

"Elamites are approaching quickly," the messenger said.

"Are they here for war or peace?" Ardeshir asked.

"They're dressed for war but are riding slowly and in formation."

Ardeshir glanced out towards the horizon. "Allow me to ride out to meet them."

Rapana stepped forward and offered his own mount. "Take my horse. It's already dressed for statesmanship. Do you want a delegation of Magi to ride with you?"

"I'll go alone," Ardeshir insisted.

"You better move fast," the messenger said. "The Elamites have already reached the edge of town."

The other guardian was soon captured and forced to give a confession in exchange for a chance at survival in the enclosure with the wild things. He confirmed the truth of Yas's story, that General Ban Cho's messengers had arrived with news of his death at the hands of the Persian prince.

Fang and Jing stood outside their home with their mother. Fang was furious when the news was confirmed.

"Your father killed my father!" she screamed.

Yas hung her head. "And your father killed my father."

Liu, standing silently beside her, squeezed her hand.

Fang stomped away, only to come back a few minutes later with a new accusation. "Your father must have been a criminal."

"My father was the emperor's champion, the prince of Persia, a follower of the Way, and a loving man."

"How can two fathers kill each other when their daughters are trying so hard to help each other stay alive?" Fang demanded. She then turned toward her younger sister. "How can you sit beside this enemy of our people? Her father killed a hero of our nation. Her brother stole the emperor's daughter and took her away. Our father died trying to make things right."

"How will you make things right?" Jing asked.

"There's only one way to make things right: a life for a life." Fang clasped her hands behind her back and paced in circles around Yas and Lui.

"That's already been done," Yas said. "Your father took the life of my father and my father took the life of your father."

Fang raised her chin in defiance. "You should have to face the wild things, like the guardian."

"My life is now in the new emperor's hands," Yas reminded her. "Thanks to you."

"You should take the honorable way out and jump into the koi pond," Fang said.

Jing looked at her sister pleadingly. "Then who will teach us to ride?"

"We can find another teacher, a better one."

"But she saved our lives by stopping the bad guardians," Jing added.

Fang stopped her pacing. "Yes, she did do that. But who will bridge the gap so I can marry the emperor? Without my father, I will be nothing."

"The arrangements for your wedding have already been made," Liu said. "The shaman has confirmed the match. The previous emperor's wife has anointed you as the eternal flower at the chrysanthemum festival. The grand council has approved the match and set the date. They will face shame if they change their plans now and say that the stars, the emperor's wife, and the shaman were all wrong."

Fang lowered her head again. "Yes… yes. You are a wise and discerning teacher. I should choose you as my advisor."

"That will be hard," Liu murmured. "Especially if my wife receives a black stone from your husband on judgment day. If she dies, I die."

"You have tied up my life in knots," Fang said, shaking her head in frustration. "I have to mourn my father's death while celebrating my own upcoming marriage. I should condemn the family of my father's murderer, but in doing so I would condemn the very advisor I need by my side. Apparently I can no longer trust my own guardians, but I also cannot live without them." She turned to her sister. "Why isn't this so hard for you? This woman's father killed our father."

Jing leaned her head against Yas's shoulder. "She's my friend and she teaches me how to ride. I don't have to marry the emperor. Besides, Father's bamboo cane scared me."

"You're such a child," Fang spat. "I can't stay any longer. I have new guardians to choose."

But before leaving, Fang stepped up close to Yas.

"I have an idea," the girl continued. "Why don't you help me choose my guardians? Anyone who qualifies will have to fight you. And anyone who survives that fight will get the job."

"What if I don't survive?" Yas asked.

Fang smiled. "That will solve at least one of my choices, won't it?"

Facing down fifty warriors armored for battle on his own was more than Ardeshir thought he could handle. He clenched his jaw, refusing to speak. His hands gripped the reins of his horse, refusing to open in any form of greeting. His legs were like blocks of wood, unable to signal the mount under him.

Across from him, even the horses were shrouded in scale armor. The scarlet helmets of the commanders, with their black plumes and white streamers, demonstrated that this war party was comprised of the elite.

For some reason, his horse stopped in the middle of the road.

"We seek the prince of Persia," the leader of the opposing force shouted as he held up his hand to halt his force.

Ardeshir nodded. The words still wouldn't come.

"We seek to know whether we need to prepare for war or peace," the commander shouted again.

Another nod.

"With the invasion of the Han Empire, we are willing to join forces to defend our own lands," the commander continued.

Ardeshir's jaw finally loosened. "That is wisdom."

"When can we meet with the prince of Persia to negotiate a treaty of peace with the Magi and the Parthians?"

"You are speaking with him."

"We have brought our chief warriors and representatives from each district," the commander said. "We are one in this quest."

"If you are one, I only need to speak with one," Ardeshir said. "I will bring the chief of the Magi and the chief of the Parthians. We four will settle the matter."

"Do you desire a festival of games to show how well our champions can fight?"

"No. There's been enough death and destruction. It's time to unleash our champions on those who rise against us. From this day on, we shall be one people working and warring together."

The commander nodded his head. "Will this treaty include the chance to open trade borders and share our merchants with all of Parthia?"

"Choose your negotiator and we shall work out all the details."

"You truly are a wise prince," the commander said. "I will be representing Elam. My name is Kamnaskires."

"You are welcome to set up your tents among us," Ardeshir said. "I will return when a negotiator for the Magi and Parthians has been chosen."

Three days later, the Parthian council was still arguing about who would represent them and whether they even wanted to join forces with the Elamites.

During a midafternoon session in the council chamber at the palace, a messenger approached Ardeshir.

"Prince, the Elamites have removed their tents and are mounted at the cross-roads," the messenger said. "They are demanding an immediate gathering for peace or they will light the town on fire."

Her reflexes were definitely slower than she remembered, but Yas sparred for a week against volunteer guardians using a wooden sword to get her moves back. Fang watched from the edge of the arena.

"Good enough!" the girl announced when she felt satisfied. "You're already faster than half my guardians, so we'll see if the new ones can do any better. When I told the group I chose that they'd have to fight you to the death, more than half dropped out. I have seven left."

"Are you expecting me to fight all seven at once?" Yas asked. "Your father tried that one."

"Don't speak of my father. We still haven't heard for sure what happened."

"If you're not sure what happened, but you're blaming my father anyway, why are you making me fight to the death?"

Fang frowned. "I don't think I should have you fight them to the death. If you kill them all, I'll have no new guardians." She turned to leave. "The last thing I want is for my future husband to think the Persians are better fighters than the Han. If your brother is now prince of Persia and my husband is emperor of the Han, we should use our relationship to build stronger trade instead of fighting."

Yas lowered her wooden sword. "That is the wisest thing I've heard you say."

Jing bounced up to Yas. "When are you going to be free to teach us horse-riding again?" She glanced at Fang. "And why are you wasting her time with games and boys when she could be teaching us skills that matter?"

Fang clenched her fists and knitted her brow. "I need her to find men who can protect us. If she spends all her time teaching *us* these skills, we'll end up having to protect ourselves. She can teach you horse-riding when I'm done with her... if she survives."

A golden-robed guardian approached with his eyes lowered.

"Eternal flower," he said. "Another survivor of General Ban Chao's elite troops has arrived. He has a message for your mother."

"Send him to me," Fang ordered. "I will decide what my mother needs to hear."

The messenger left. Within a few minutes, a tattered warrior, grubby and weary, approached the arena. He knelt in the sand some distance away.

"May the general's daughter live forever," he said, face down with palms up.

"Speak the truth!" Fang said.

"Of all your father's men, I alone survive. We were ambushed by the Persians and your father could not survive his wounds. I would have thrown myself on their swords if I didn't know you needed someone to bring you news."

"Tell me what happened."

"We set out to travel across the desert and dispense justice to a fugitive of the empire, but he escaped us through the deception of Bedu tribesmen. We pushed hard to catch him at his own fortress, but he ambushed us as we arrived. He had too many men to count. Your father fought bravely, taking many with him, but in the end he was overcome."

Fang placed her hands on her hips. "And why were you not at his side?"

"He divided our band, some to chase the horsemen and others to attack the archers. He faced the archers and I helped take out the horsemen."

Fang motioned to one of the nearby guardians. "Take him, wash him, feed him, and then return him here. He will demonstrate his skills by fighting all seven of my future guardians at once. He was loyal to my father in his death. Now he will be loyal by fighting for his own life."

Yas followed Fang and Jing as they walked away from the arena.

"Stay away." Fang clasped her hands behind her back as she walked. "He confirms the previous messengers' story, but he must have been lying when he called himself the lone survivor. There is no room for a liar in the Han Empire. For you, this is good news—you no longer have to fight my guardians. He will take your place."

Yas released a sigh and shared a hug with Jing.

"Can she teach us horse-riding now?" Jing asked.

"Only until I consider whether there is another way she should die."

Yas clenched her jaw and turned away. Would this dance with death never end?

Eighteen

The confrontation with the Parthians was short.

"The Elamites are getting ready to burn down your family homes," Ardeshir shouted. "Which of you wants to hang on to past grudges and disputes until you're forced to pick the bones of your loved ones from the ashes? Choose one person now who will figure out a way to bring our peoples together."

"Vardanes will serve us," the leader of the Parthian council said.

One figure, looking as large as a bear, rose to his feet. A red beard grew like a bush from ear to ear and down to the man's chest. His piercing eyes and curled lip gave no doubt that he would as soon devour an enemy as negotiate with one.

"Good!" Ardeshir said. "Prepare a horse for him. We leave immediately."

Ardeshir turned to the messenger. "Tell the Elamites to set up their tents again. We're on the way."

Ardeshir and the giant Vardanes rode out side by side to confront the fifty Elamite warriors. Ardeshir found them to be as intimidating the second time as they had been the first. But having a companion like Vardanes stilled his nerves.

The Elamite named Kamnaskires dismounted. He was shorter than Vardanes but also broad-chested and muscular. He held his sword against his chest with confidence, showing no indication of being intimidated by Vardanes.

Ardeshir joined him on the ground in front of the assembled mounts.

Into this triad, a silver-bearded skeleton of a man trotted forward on a bony donkey. He was draped in a blue-coned hat and matching robe embroidered with golden crescent moons and stars.

Ardeshir groaned. This was the representative of the Maji?

Vardanes stood with his mouth open and Kamnaskires suppressed his smile.

"Have we been waiting for this bag of bones or the one riding him?" Kamnaskires asked with a smile on his face.

"I am Bithisarea, agent of the stars," the bag of bones introduced himself, grinning like a hyena.

"So we are all here," Ardeshir said. "The treaty tent is prepared and ready. While the Parthian flag flies above us, there will be no aggression from any of us. We will have a feast prepared to help us focus. You may step out to talk to your advisors at any time, as long as we know that the purpose is to keep the talks moving forward, not to abandon them."

Kamnaskires nodded. "These terms are acceptable to the Elamites."

Vardanes crossed his arms and grunted, his bushy red beard closing over his mouth.

Bithisarea grinned and rubbed the side of his canonical cap. "What if I have to consult the stars?"

"Shall we sit?" Ardeshir said. "The tent is ready."

Kamnaskires rested his sword firmly across his chest. "I'd rather stand."

"I'll sit," Vardanes volunteered. "But I want to sit nearest the roast lamb."

"I will lie down," Bithisarea said. "As long as we're outside where I can see the stars."

Ardeshir sighed to himself. "I can see we're off to a good start…"

When the horses were at full gallop, Fang seemed to release her stress and embrace her girlish ways. Laughter bubbled out of her and she raced against Yas with abandon.

"This is what every girl needs to do," Fang cried out as they came to a halt near a small pond. "If all the girls in the empire could ride, we would show the men how to build a great nation."

She slipped off the horse and led it to the water.

"It's too bad you weren't born among the Han," Fang remarked to Yas. "It would make my decision so much easier. I should have thought harder before I matched you with the best of our teachers."

"Perhaps there is a greater mind at work bringing truth to the people," Yas said.

"Yes, I know your teaching," Fang said. "The Way is the way. Yeshua is the Way. I hear this all the time, yet I know nothing about this all-knowing, all-powerful, all-present ruler."

"Would you like to know more?"

"Only if it doesn't interfere with my decision on what to do with you."

"That, I can't guarantee," Yas said. "You should talk with my brother someday. All I know is that our Creator loved his creation and became one of us after we broke off our relationship with him. He sacrificed his life so our wrongdoings could be covered, so our relationship with him could be restored."

Fang narrowed her eyes. "So he's dead?"

"He was dead, but he was stronger than death and rose again to life. We talk with him each day to gain the wisdom and truth we need for whatever we face."

"So you can talk with him and ask him what you should do about the death I have planned for you?"

"I can talk with him about the life he has planned for me even after the death you have planned for me."

Fang didn't seem able to quite believe what she was hearing. "Are you saying that he will bring you to life again if I kill you?"

"Yes. I don't have to fear death because I will live again."

"Then what is the point in killing you?"

"I guess that's up to you."

"How many times can you live and die and live again?"

"One time."

Fang sat cross-legged on the grass and watched her horse nibble. "The Greek philosophers spoke of immortal souls in rebirth. The teachers in Hindustan speak of reincarnation. Our own teachers teach about a soulless entity that fills us and then pools back like drops of water returning to the ocean." She plucked a blade of grass and chewed on it. "I think you are speaking of something different."

"I am," Yas said.

"This sounds like a wise teaching, maybe even a true truth," Fang said. "Perhaps I should keep you around to learn more."

"I would like that very much," Yas said.

Just then, Jing trotted up on her horse. "Don't look now, but I think we have someone coming fast…"

It was evening before the quartet had agreed to reorganize the space for their negotiating room.

Kamnaskires stood with his back to a tree at the edge of the tented awning. "I don't trust anyone who might be behind me," he said, sword resting against his shoulder. "I'll remain right here."

Vardanes and Ardeshir sat at the table loaded with food, Vardanes far too busy eating to say much. As for Bithisarea, he lay on a mat outside the awning, peering up at the heavens through a scope of some kind; his bony donkey nibbled on a nearby shrub.

"It would be better if we had a pool of water under a canopy," Bithisarea murmured. "There should be a hole in the tent to provide a view of the stars. As it is, I'll have to wait until nightfall before I can decide anything."

"I'm not negotiating all night long to keep your stars happy," Kamnaskires said. "All the Elamites want to know is whether we can move as one nation against our enemy, and whether we can open our borders for trade with you. How many of your warriors can we count on to ride against the Han?"

"What do you have to offer?" Vardanes asked.

"Fifty thousand warriors and more traders than you could count," Kamnaskires answered.

Vardanes didn't seem impressed. "We have four times your number of warriors and enough traders to keep us in poverty forever."

"What do the Magi have to offer?" Ardeshir asked.

"We offer the guidance of the stars," Bithisarea pointed out. "That way, you know the best time to attack and the best time to trade."

Kamnaskires stepped forward from his tree. "We have shamans for that. They dissect goat intestines. Why do we need any more superstitious magic to know when to shed our blood?'

"I don't see the point in my being here." Bithisarea sighed audibly. "My presence and influence aren't appreciated."

"I don't see the point either," Kamnaskires agreed. "The three of us can figure this out without the stars interfering. Or perhaps he would lend us his donkey to fill in for him."

Ardeshir raised his hands into the air to quiet the tent. "Nothing in Parthia happens without the sanction of the Magi. Kings, judges, councilors, bakers, priests, and even gardeners depend on their words of wisdom. If this treaty is going to work, it will work because the Maji and all our peoples support it." He backed to the edge of the awning. "I need to take time with my advisor to strategize where we go from here. Let's meet again when the sun goes fully down."

He withdrew to a small grove of platanus, cedar, and ziziphus trees. Under the broad leaves of the platanus, he knelt in prayer to seek wisdom.

When it was dark, he rose in peace.

The rider coming up on the pond turned out to be Liu.

"Ride!" he called to Yas and the girls. "Ride fast!"

The girls stood in place until he arrived.

"What's going on?" Yas asked.

"That so-called lone survivor of General Ban Chao's army? Well, he'd turned the new potential guardians against you, Fang. He convinced all seven that you sent him to kill them. Even some of the formerly loyal guardians are joining his rebellion."

Fang drew herself to her full height. "So I'll send the other guardians to finish them off."

"They've already thrown your mother in the koi pond to drown," Liu said. "They forced her to tell them where you were and are now trying to find a way to get here. They plan to throw one sister in the pond and the other in the wild things enclosure."

Tears came to Jing's eyes. "Not my mother… she never did anything wrong."

"So I am now an orphan." Fang gently gnawed on her lower lip with her front teeth. "The new emperor will never want me now."

"You are the chosen eternal flower," Liu reminded her. "We must act."

"This is what happens when we don't have a general to keep order," Fang said. "Where can we go until this is sorted out?"

"How about the village of the unwanted?" Yas suggested.

Liu nodded in agreement. "Yes. None of the guardians will know the way, but I can take you there."

"I have none of my things," Fang said. "I need my clothes and food."

"You need your life more," Liu said. "Eternal flower, it's time for us to hide until we know how we can fight back."

The ride took the rest of the day. It was evening before they arrived at the hidden village, exhausted.

Wai Ling, the one-armed sentry with half a nose, met them well outside the limits of the unwanted. He waved them down. After ascertaining their need, he hobbled ahead of them towards the settlement.

"We heard about what happened to Colonel Wei," Wai Ling said. "We've been expecting and preparing for trouble."

Fang looked around with wide eyes as they crept deeper into the forest. "Who are these people and how did they get here?"

"They are the unwanted from the emperor's kingdom," Liu explained. "Humble people who only want to be left alone."

"Why have they been allowed to live here?" Fang asked.

Liu shrugged. "Because they have nowhere else to live."

"I hope we don't bring more trouble your way," Yas said to Wai Ling. "We need to protect the future bride of the new emperor."

As the newcomers crossed under the trees, they looked into the eyes of the lame, the lepers, and other outcasts who crept out of their caves and ravines to watch the small procession.

Wai Ling pointed toward the same grass-thatched hut in which Yas had slept during her first visit. The woman who had no legs below the knees still sat on a bench nearby, and her whistle drew out the same young man with the two canes who had met them before.

The man with the canes pointed them toward the blue forest. "Whole people must proceed beyond the hill," he said.

"But we are unwanted," Fang said.

The young man hobbled closer. "Two feet, two hands, two eyes, everything in place. You will never remain unseen in this place. You don't fit and so you can't stay."

"But we will pay our way and build our own shelter," Yas said.

"We will take the horses in exchange for shelter," the man said.

Fang wouldn't hear of it. "But we need the horses to ride back!"

The man just shrugged. "There's no going back if you live here."

"We *will* go back," Fang insisted. "You are one man. You need only one horse."

"But my mother has no legs." He nodded at the woman on the bench. "One for me and one for her."

"Agreed," Fang said. "Yas and Liu, give him your horses."

"Plus I will need some coin to feed them," the man added.

He extended his hand and kept it there until Yas and Liu had turned over enough coin to satisfy the man.

With the transaction complete, the young man turned on his crutches and disappeared into the thatched hut. The woman without legs nodded and smiled as the four newcomers led their remaining horses on toward the forest.

Bithisarea lay on his back with a canonical tube pressed over one eye. The heavens were in bright array tonight, and he muttered as the other three council members stood over him awaiting his conclusions.

"What was that streak across the heavens?" Vardanes said. "Was it a goddess or a spirit?"

"It was neither," Kamnaskires said. "The celestial lights are only there to guide those who understand their messages."

"You're almost right," Bithisarea told them. "There are dark celestial bodies and light celestial bodies. Some are close and others far. They interact with our world to guide us in terms of the timing of when we should act." He handed the tube to Ardeshir. "Look at the brightest light in the heavens. Long ago, one of the ancients prophesied that a star brighter than that would appear in such a way that the King of Kings would be identified. A Magi named Daniel identified the precise time. A generation ago, my grandfather was among a party that saw such a light and traced it to the land of Judea. They found such a one."

"It was Yeshua," Ardeshir said. "My father's master grew up with Yeshua and knew him as the Messiah. The dream was that this Yeshua would rule the world. But the Romans killed him."

Vardanes looked down. "That's one way to destroy the dream of a people."

"The dream isn't dead," Ardeshir assured him. "He defeated death and rose again. He is still alive."

"The King of Kings is still alive?" Bithisarea asked. "My grandfather never told us this."

"I'm surprised you didn't read that in the stars," Kamnaskires muttered.

"Hush!" Bithisarea said. "Look! The king planet rose as the morning star in the house of Aries… the same as when my grandfather took his journey to Judea. Perhaps another king has been born."

"The Messiah cannot be born again in this life," Ardeshir said. "There must be another meaning. We can't stand here all night waiting for a sign to help you understand whether we should unite our peoples."

Kamnaskires thrust his sword at the ground angrily. "I agree! The three of us can make a decision without him."

"Wait!" Bithisarea held up a hand. "The other planets have not aligned in their ideal houses. The moon isn't lending favor to the relationship."

"I've heard enough," Vardanes said. "Back to the tent."

Bithisarea spun seven times and raised his tube above his head. "Saturnus and Mars have moved together at last."

"What does that even matter?" Kamnaskires demanded.

"Saturnus and Mars are the planets of war," Bithisarea said. "Because they are together in the early summer, that is when they favor us to move forward. The stars remind us that this will not be an easy relationship."

"I could have told you that before we even spoke," Vardanes said. "When else would kings go to war? I've heard enough. I'll give you two full moons to raise your armies before we march toward Hindustan and the empire of the Han."

Ardeshir nodded to himself. "This is in line with what my advisor says. Only one more thing would I add. We will march with warriors, but also with merchants, in case our counselors can enforce peace before we arrive."

"So let it be," Vardanes said.

Yas, Liu, Fang, and Jing stood outside the grass hut they had bargained for at the cost of two horses. Two months had passed and the second full moon was in its ascension when Yas stepped up beside Fang.

"What are you finding out from your messengers?" Yas asked.

Fang crossed her arms, closed her eyes, and sighed. "The new emperor is sending out search parties for me. At least the rebellion has been put down. The wild things are happy."

"Will you let the new emperor find you here?"

"Of course not!" Fang said. "I'll ride to the mountain of the moon and let him find me *there*." She bit her lip and worked it gently. "If he is wise, he will take me to the Weiyang Palace. I'm told that there is no bigger place in the world."

"And what will become of me?" Yas asked.

"I'll give you three days to ride ahead of the assassins who will be sent after you. I'll keep your husband here as my advisor and teacher. You can return to your people and let them defend you when we eventually come."

"But she has served you well," Liu said. "And you've tied our fates together."

Yas frowned. "I thought only the new emperor could decide my fate."

"That is true," Fang agreed. "The problem is simple: he will hear that trouble after trouble has come upon our people since you arrived. He'll also hear that trouble after trouble has come upon his bride-to-be. He'll want to spare his wife and his people and choose mercy for his nation over mercy for a foreigner."

"So I must run," Yas decided.

Fang stiffened her back, tucked in her chin, and clenched her teeth. "If you go now, I can give you four days."

"But you've given our horses away."

"If you're going to take a horse that doesn't belong to you, I would advise that you at least not take mine."

Yas placed a hand on her shoulder. "May you know that the Way is the way one day."

"I will miss you," Liu said.

Once Fang had left them in peace, Yas turned to her husband. "The time has come to either choose love or life…"

Nineteen

Seventy-five thousand men on horseback gathered on a large grassy field at the base of the Zagros mountains. Thousands upon thousands of merchants, support staff, and traders jostled for position in the line that stretched across the plain from horizon to horizon.

On his warhorse, Kamnaskires charged up to Ardeshir and Vardanes.

"This is insanity," the gigantic man said. "Do you see how poorly equipped these traders and merchants are? They'll never be able to ford the rivers or survive the mountain passes."

"Perhaps they'll adapt by finding supplies along the way," Vardanes said. "Caravans have been travelling this route for almost two generations now. The silk and pearls get through somehow."

Ardeshir held up his arm. "I've taken this journey four times now, and I know that we have to make the crossing before the snows come. It'll take us six full moons if all goes well. The traders will only venture so far, but they'll exchange what they have with others who come from the other direction." He turned toward a seething mass of horses being corralled nearby. "My sister took a thousand horses there and almost all of them survived. We've got two thousand this time. If there's one thing the Han want from us, it's our horses."

"Did I hear you're bringing your family?" Kamnaskires asked. "How could you hope to subject them to such a long and difficult journey?"

"My wife wanted to see her homeland, and I fight better when she's happy," Ardeshir said. "My sister's still there and I hope my wife can say something to convince the empire's new rulers to let her go."

Kamnaskires nodded at that, satisfied, and began to look around the assembled caravan.

"Where is the Magi representative?" he demanded. "We are leaving whether he's prepared or not."

As though on cue, Bithisarea appeared in a flash of smoke. "Invisible I was, invisible I'm not. We will end our journey with you on the other side of the Indus River. There is much teaching we wish to share and absorb there."

"That bag of bones you ride will never make it," Vardanes said, looking with disdain at the old man's mount.

"I'm riding in a horse-drawn carriage," Bithisarea told him. "We have enough goods to last us for a year if we need them. Will someone be watching over the trade caravans?"

Ardeshir inclined his head. "We'll send a small force to watch over them. Another force will guard the horses. Those two groups will be much slower… and it's possible they'll meet up with bandits along the way."

"Fine with me," Vardanes said. "I need to keep my men motivated. But how are we even going to put up a fight after such a long time on the road?"

Ardeshir's smile came easily. "When you hear the Han charging at you, drums beating, voices yelling, horse hoofs pounding like thunder, you'll either find a way to survive or you'll die. If you want to stay behind, now is the time to call your men and leave."

"Do we have entertainment for the evening fires?" Kamnaskires asked.

"We have poets, dancers, musicians, and acrobats," Ardeshir assured him. "If you need more than that, you can arrange your own jousting matches." He put his fingers to his mouth and gave a whistle. "Anyway, the trail guides are here. It's time to go. I hope you've said goodbye to your families for a few years."

The wind carried the dry scent of dust and pine resin as Yas clung to Liu's waist, her cheek pressed against his shoulder. The single horse's hooves struck the rocky trail with a steady rhythm, scattering loose stones that clattered into the ravine below. Behind them lay the Han Empire—and Fang's promise that neither of them would live if they dared defy her. Ahead, the mountains of western China rose like jagged teeth into a pale sky streaked with late-afternoon gold.

The trail wound between cliffs draped in scraggly pines, their needles whispering under the wind's restless fingers. Far below, a river coiled in silver loops, flashing in and out of shadow as it threaded through gorges carved by centuries of meltwater. The air was sharper here, scented with wild herbs and the faint musk of distant yaks grazing on unseen slopes.

"You could have stayed," Yas said over the rush of wind. Her voice was steady, but her fingers gripped him tight. "Fang would have rewarded you for betraying me."

Liu didn't look back. "Fang rewards no one. She only spares the useful—until she doesn't. You… are worth more than her approval."

A hawk wheeled high above, its cry lost in the emptiness of the peaks.

Yas's pulse thudded in her ears. "You risk your life for someone you barely know."

"That's not true," Liu said, urging the horse around a sharp bend where the path crumbled into nothingness on one side. "I've watched you since you first stepped into the imperial gardens. You're not like the rest. You see the truth… even when it's dangerous."

The horse snorted, breath steaming in the cooling air. The shadows lengthened, spilling from the cliffs like dark water. In the far distance, the last sunlight crowned the mountains in molten orange and turned the snow caps into peaks of fire.

Yas felt the ache in her legs from hours in the saddle, the raw sting of windburn on her cheeks. But beneath it all, there was a strange, fierce relief. They were no longer under the empire's walls, no longer bound by its silks and whispers. The wilderness smelled of freedom—sharp, wild, untamed.

"Then hold on to me," Liu said quietly. "The hardest part is still ahead."

"We're going to need fresh horses," Yas said. "This one has gone as far as it can with both of us on it."

It was two more days of riding hard before they stopped to purchase some fruit and bargain for fresh mounts. They had ridden Jing's horse together at first. Using two gemstones and a golden bracelet Jing had given them, they succeeded at bartering for two other horses that could take them a lot farther.

"How will we know the way?" Liu asked as they walked away from the vendor.

"I've been down this road three times before." Yas swung up onto her mount. "Your Emperor Wudi had his general, Zhang Qian, set up the first trade missions along this route. That was more than three generations ago. One generation ago, the first silk caravans reached us and started taking our horses in exchange. There are caravan stops along the way, then oases when we reach the desert."

Across the windswept plains of western China, Yas and Liu urged their horses onward, the thundering hooves pounding a frantic rhythm against the earth. If Fang had sent Han assassins, the warriors would be on them soon.

The scent of wild sage mingled with the dust as they plunged into a narrow river, icy water splashing high. Liu's grip faltered; he slid from the back of his horse, vanishing into the current.

Yas wheeled her mount, heart hammering, and seized his arm. She hauled him back up to safety. Gasping, drenched, and trembling, they mounted again, the horizon aflame with sunset as they fled deeper into the untamed wilds.

"The Han assassins are fast horsemen," Liu said. "How long before they catch us?"

"We can only survive through deception. Our pursuers will outnumber and outpower us. And unfortunately, your poor horse-riding skills will only slow us down. Maybe I should have left you behind."

Liu pulled on his reins and halted. "I can head back right now and try to send them on a different route. I could tell them that I've decided to serve the future queen as her advisor. It may work."

"I know that I asked you to choose life or love, but you'll have neither if you go back," Yas assured him. "These are assassins and they have one job to do. At least there's a larger river up ahead, giving us our first chance to deceive them. We can trade our horses for a raft, go downstream as far as we can until nightfall tomorrow, then find someone to exchange clothes with us and let them continue on in our place. We can hope the assassins chase the wrong people."

"Won't that get them killed?" Liu asked.

Yas reluctantly had to accept that he had a point. "Okay. I suppose we can leave our robes on the raft and release it down the river. It'll float with the current and end up far enough downstream to give us time to escape."

"That sounds like a good plan. But once we have no horses and no raft, how will we travel?"

"We'll disguise ourselves as part of a caravan and take a different route to Susa. If we continue to change caravans and make it to Hindustan, there are a hundred routes to reach the mountain passes."

Liu looked unpersuaded. "But there are few places to ford the rivers, few passes through the mountains, and few oases in the desert. They'll have assassins watching for us."

"I should have imagined you would have thought this through," Yas said. "Let's take the raft down to the sea and hire a ship to take us home." She held up both hands before her husband could speak. "I know. We don't have the wealth. Perhaps we'll have to work our way home."

"Perhaps we can circle back to the village of the unwanted," Liu said. "The assassins would never expect us to come this far only to return to the heart of the empire."

Yas stopped, furrowing her brows. "That is actually a good idea. We could tear our robes, make them bloodied somehow, and leave them near enough to a village that someone finds them and reports to the assassins when they're questioned."

"I'll sell my horse to a caravan merchant and buy supplies," Liu said. "From now on, you must never be seen. If we're together, we'll stand out and raise suspicion. We'll also be forced to travel by moonlight, keep our faces covered, and depend on one horse. If we have to, we'll sell the last horse for supplies and survive off what we can find along the way."

Yas nodded, smiling. "Fang made a good match for us. I never thought it could work… but with our two minds, I think we might actually survive long enough for someone to rescue us."

They'd lost two carts and a horse while crossing the Indus River, and then one camel to an ambush by bandits on the far side, but Ardeshir was satisfied with the trek thus far.

Bithisarea arrived at the latest rendezvous point, holding his canonical cap as the carriage bounced around beneath him.

"We part ways at the crossroads ahead," said the Maji. "We will head south to study. The way ahead is favorable if you move swiftly."

"At least everyone survived the mountain passes," Vardanes commented. The big man had lost some of his considerable bulk over the journey, but his bushy red beard still exploded all over his face from ear to ear.

Dozens of merchants approached with their mobile carts. Copper and bronze axes, chisels, knives, spears, saws, and razors seemed to be the most common fare. One cart held gold and silver pendants while another held shells and beads fashioned into combs, bracelets, and other decorative ornaments. A brisk exchange of goods kept the energy up during these brief stops.

Kamnaskires dismounted and strolled over to Ardeshir. "I spoke with our guides and they say there are four different routes we can take to intersect with the caravans bringing silk west. They want to know which is the best for us."

Ardeshir pulled out the scroll with a rough sketch of the routes and took a few moments to study it.

"If we take any of the northern routes, we'll have to backtrack," he said. "We may not get east before the snows shut down the passes. If we stay on the southern route, we'll likely be hit with fevers… but the deserts are less harsh and the people more welcoming. There are better grains for our horses up north, but we should have adequate feed until we reach the outskirts of the Han Empire."

"To the south it is," Kamnaskires said, who turned and motioned for the attention of the guides.

Lu Hou dismounted from her carriage and stretched.

"The boys are traveling well so far, but it's too muddy to let them out here," she said to her husband. "I don't remember the journey being this long when we were running from my father. But did I just overhear you choosing the riskier southern route?" Lu Hou wiped the sweat from her brow with the back of her arm. "I fear the boys falling victim to fevers. If your sister were to come west, which route do you think she would take? What if we bring all these men for battle and it turns out she's already escaped?"

"I know you don't want us to battle your people," Ardeshir said. "I hope this ends in a trade negotiation. I hear there's a new emperor, chosen to replace your father. We should arrive around the time of his coronation."

"Do you think we can rest for a few days here?" Lu Hou asked.

Ardeshir drew her close. "A trader told me that the heavy rains will be coming soon. Our wagons and horses will bog down if we wait much longer. We're already behind schedule for the best weather conditions. Perhaps we can rest up ahead where it's drier."

One of the guides walked up to the couple and Lu Hou turned to check on the boys.

"We call this place Naggaruda, or the city of cut stones," the guide said to Ardeshir. "The Buddha's teachings have much influence here and there's a large place of study. According to rumors, a serpent race dwells here… a creature that changes its appearance and mingles with humans." He pulled out his own scroll. "The place of learning teaches mathematics, sciences, philosophy, astronomy, medicine, and other disciplines. This is where Parthian rule ends. The Kushans from the Yue-Chi tribe have been raiding here lately and the new Han emperor will be in coalition with them."

"Are we safe to press on?" Ardeshir asked.

"We've paid the right chiefs and road bandits for the next leg of the journey," the guide affirmed. "The rains are coming soon and we need to be on the road by tomorrow morning at the latest."

Ardeshir nodded. "Why don't you get the horses moving on? The traders will come at first light?"

Lu Hou was still waiting as he trudged back through the mud.

"The sun in your hair is like a chrysanthemum at the peak of its glory," he said as he ran his fingers through her locks. "Your beauty outshines the finest of flowers. A crown on your brow would look dim compared to the radiance of your smile."

"You know how to speak to my heart," Lu Hou said. "Now what do you want?"

"We leave at first light."

"Then that gives us tonight."

In the time Yas and Liu had been gone, the Han had found the site of the unwanted village and destroyed many of its buildings. So there was no one to greet them when they arrived. Dark stains, like dried pools of blood, had congealed on the exposed floorboards. Whoever had lived in this home had either been forcibly removed or else vacated on their own volition.

Scrounging salvageable boards and bricks, the couple cobbled together a shelter hidden in the trees. In the nearby bushes they found an abandoned crossbow, and a spear and dagger were discovered under a partially destroyed floor.

Within a week of their decision to turn around, Yas and Liu curled up in the shelter they had rebuilt, fully equipped to defend themselves.

"I'm sure they forced Jing to show them were we hid," Yas said. "I hope they've been easy on her now that she's an orphan."

"Orphans aren't always looked on well here," Liu said. "They are a burden for the emperor to bear."

"Doesn't it matter that she's Fang's sister? Surely Fang would defend her rights."

Liu ran his fingers through his hair. "Each of us is born into our own fate. Fang is the eternal flower, as recognized by the former emperor's wife. Jing is only a child with no father or mother."

"How will we know when it's safe to reappear?" Yas asked.

"It may never be safe again. The decrees issued against the enemies of the empire never fade away. They are pearls of truth, not flowers of truth. We may never again have a chance to see the emperor's garden."

"Before I got you into this, I didn't realize what I was asking of you."

"We accept our fate, just as we accept that Yeshua is still the Way," Liu said. "I noticed that the wheat fields are ripe and the rice paddies are ready for harvest. I'll harvest the grains if you can find some ripe pears, plums, or peaches. Later I'll collect bamboo shoots and mustard greens so we can prepare something to eat."

Yas pulled back the blankets and sat up, stretching. "Maybe I'll catch us a wild boar or snatch a lamb from a farmer. Maybe I'll bring back a bear… or a camel… or a chicken…"

"I love your imagination. At least you won't have to hunt on the other side of the wall where the wild things live. Maybe you can even find a monkey! I'll make you some arrows for the crossbow when I get back."

During her hunt, Yas found traces of human activity in the area. She tracked a fresh set of footprints along a trail until it ended outside a cave entrance.

Crouching in the bush, she waited for half a day before movement caught her attention. It was Wai Ling, still one-armed, now limping badly. A bit of rag had been stuffed into the cavity where half his nose was missing.

The former sentry dropped a bundle of twigs and branches in a pile at the cave entrance. He rubbed some dried bark against his leg and carefully arranged the smaller bits among the pyramid he'd created. He sat on a stump as if waiting for someone or something. No one came.

Eventually, he stood and looked in her direction. "If you come out soon, we can get this fire going and get warmed up."

Yas stood, frowning. "How did you know I was here?"

"Survival instincts," he said. "It's easier to start a fire with two hands. Do you know what to do from here?"

"I'll get Liu. He needs to know we're not alone."

"Tell him to bring the beans he was digging up by the stream," Wai Ling said. "They'll go well with the taro roots I've been collecting."

Yas turned in a slow circle. "If you know we're here, is there anyone else who might know?"

"Just one. But don't worry. She's not talking."

The marketplace boomed as traders from east and west met with traders from north and south. Parthian and Elamite warriors oversaw the exchange of goods, often at high volumes.

Into the midst of this peaceful melee rose a contingent of ominous-looking soldiers from the east one afternoon.

Vardanes cantered straight for them and hailed their leader. The exchange was vigorous but short.

Ardeshir kept himself secluded until the newcomers had left, observing them from inside his wife's carriage.

"Who was that?" Ardeshir asked when the Parthian representative had arrived to give him a full report.

"The emperor's assassins," Vardanes said. "I saw their kind near Susa before you returned with your father. They say they're looking for a runaway criminal, someone who has kidnapped the tutor of the eternal flower. It has nothing to do with us."

"Did you tell them why we're here?"

"I told them we're here to protect the horses, which we're taking as a gift for the new Han emperor." He smiled. "I'm sure they didn't believe me, and I'm sure they'll return home only to raise up an army before we get to the borders of their territory. Whoever this runaway criminal is, he should thank us for chasing these parasites away."

"I think that criminal might be my sister," Ardeshir said. "The eternal flower is the wife of the next emperor… and the only tutor I know is a likely friend of mine. This means Yas is probably alive, but where could she be? I hope she didn't take one of the other roads west."

Vardanes turned his horse away. "No matter what, we have a mission to conclude. If we're successful, our peoples can unite under your leadership. If we fail, the Elamites will return home and raise up their own leader. Then we'll have a costly war."

Lu Hou was waiting as Ardeshir turned back.

"I think my sister is alive and on the run," he told her.

"Where is she?" Lu Hou asked.

"You just missed a contingent of the emperor's assassins, hired to track down criminals and fugitives. They know we're coming now, if they didn't already know."

Lu Hou lowered her face. "Don't look now, but I recognize a face near the vegetable stand. He used to be a guardian when my father was the emperor. I'm sure he recognized me."

"You better hide in place and keep the boys inside," Ardeshir said. "What did he look like?"

"It doesn't matter," Lu Hou said. "You'll never see him coming. And if these assassins are coming for me, they won't stop until I'm dead."

Ardeshir alerted Vardanes of the threat to Lu Hou, after which the Parthian warrior assigned six men to guard the carriage wherein his wife and the boys rested.

"These are my best men," Vardanes assured him. "I have a dozen others searching the crowd for anyone who looks like they could be with the Han."

Nightfall came without incident and Ardeshir set himself among the security forces. As the campfires died down, his eyes grew heavy.

A scream changed that. His eyes flashed open to see flames licking at the roof and sides of the carriage.

Ardeshir jumped through the doors and scooped up his crying sons.

"Hurry!" he said to Lu Hou. "We have to go!"

As they ran out of the fire, they were hit with splashes of water that doused the flames. Ardeshir saw that the soldiers were lined up with brimming pails.

"Get under the carriage," Ardeshir ordered Lu Hou. "If they're after us, they'll try to flush us out into the open. They're probably using a crossbow."

"Why did you bring us on this trip?" Lu Hou asked with a groan.

The security forces pressed in close. Ardeshir watched as they fanned out. Then, exactly as he had predicted, he saw an arrow pierce one of the Parthians' arms. Another arrow sliced through the robe of a second protector and thudded into the carriage.

"Get them!" Ardeshir ordered.

Four of the Parthians slipped off into the night.

Ardeshir and the rest of his family crawled away from a burning carriage in the mud, aiming for a patch of dark bushes. This wasn't the way he'd envisioned spending the night, but he had to admit this was the perfect place to lay an ambush.

Lu Hou held baby Farshid while he tried to calm the screaming Artabanas. With all this racket, there was no way to disguise their location.

"Take me home," Lu Hou said. "Take me home…"

"I can't," Ardeshir said. "I'm just trying to keep us alive."

That's when Kamnaskires raced into view, screaming and brandishing his sword high. Ardeshir tucked Artabanas into his chest and reached out for Lu Hou. His ears filled with the piercing scream of his terrified son.

Twenty

Wai Ling slipped into the cave and returned with one of the twin girls who spoke with their hands. The sunken eyes with dark circles under them, the pouty lips, the sagging posture, the stained clothing hanging crooked… it all spoke of deep loss.

"These are our friends," Wai Ling said to the girl. Turning to Yas, he nodded to the girl. "This is Liang Na."

Yas knelt before her. "Peace to you, Liang Na."

The girl focused on her own feet.

"She's not doing so well with the death of her sister," Wai Ling said.

"None of us would. Being in a cold, wet cave can't be good for you." Yas looked for traces of rats, remembering her own encounter in a cave even smaller than this one. "Let's build an extra room so we can start our own little family. We can build two spaces and share our food, our fire."

When Liu arrived, looking cautious, watching, and scanning the brush, Liang buried her face into Wai Ling's chest.

"Don't worry, there's only us," Yas told her, then turned to her husband to explain. "She's lost her sister. The guardians came and destroyed everything they saw."

Liang Na began to sob and Wai Ling put his arm around her. Yas watched as the pair walked a short distance away.

"I told them we could build some extra space onto our shelter," Yas said to Liu. "There's still more wood around here."

"How long are we planning to stay?" Liu asked. "It's going to be hard to feed four of us."

"Remember, that also means we have four people to look for food. We can divide up the tasks."

When Liang Na and Wai Ling joined Yas and Liu at the new shelter, they brought a few handfuls of wood Wai Ling had collected. Liu worked with them to start a fire.

"At the cave, we didn't have to worry about smoke giving us away," Wai Ling noted. "I guess out here in the bush the smoke should filter away."

"No one will notice unless they come by and smell it," Liu said. "Once I get the fire started, why don't I work with Wai Ling to collect some wood for the shelters?" He nodded to Yas. "You and Liang Na can collect more food and prepare it."

Yas looked at the young twin girl. "I'm a much better hunter than a chef, and Liu is a much better chef than a builder. Let's distribute the work so we get to do the things we're best at."

The girl shrugged and watched the men fan a small flame to life. Wai Ling added small twigs and some larger pieces of wood that had been broken by the rampaging guardians.

"What's your favorite food?" Yas asked the group, trying to make conversation.

"Do we have to have eaten it?" Liu asked.

"Any food."

Wai Ling smiled as he dreamed. "I would choose turtle soup, bear paws, and monkey brains. During the time of the great wars, the Han leader and Manchu leader shared these things. If it's good for leaders, it's good for me."

"They ate over one hundred different kinds of food over a three-day meal," Liu said, laughing. "I think the motto of our people is, 'If it's alive, then kill it and eat it.' Our people think we can absorb the properties of the food we eat. So even the liver, brains, and blood can help us grow strong and healthy."

"When we eat wild meat, we increase the yang in our system," Wai Ling said. "This yang gives heat to our inner being and helps us stay strong and virile."

Yas nodded. "When I ate with the former emperor, I'm sure I saw foxes, camels, ostriches, snakes, snails, bat soup, porcupines, and other things on the menu. Even insects and bugs."

"We once had pangolin when you were gone," Liu said to Yas. "Your chef friend had no idea how to prepare it."

At the mention of Orotes, Yas clenched her teeth and furrowed her brows. She wrapped her arms around her legs and lay her chin on her knees. Where would she be now and what would her life have been like had she been matched with the chef?

"I think we better gather some wood and get our shelter built," Liu said. "If we don't, I can see that I'll be sleeping in the cave."

Yas rose, brushed off the back of her tunic, and set out into the woods. Liang Na followed.

"I'm going to check our rabbit snare," Yas called over her shoulder. "We set traps to catch our dinner."

After checking the third snare, she and Liang Na heard the sound of thrashing in the bush. Sure enough, a rabbit had been caught. It was a good start!

The shelter didn't get completed that night, so Liu and Wai Ling slept under some boards slanted against the side of the refuge. Banana leaves covered the ground to keep them dry, though they had a clear need for blankets.

Once the extra rooms were done on the fourth day, Liu was assigned the task of finding blankets or at least an animal whose skin could serve as one.

By stealth, over a three-day period, he walked toward the emperor's garden, then crept into his old family home at night and borrowed some. There was no evidence of any members of his family in residence; it seemed as though whoever had been there had evacuated in a hurry. Either that or they had been forced out.

He added cooking pots, spices, and his uncle's secret black powder to his supplies.

By traveling along the road that night, he was never questioned.

The quartet survived off pigeons, a quail, ducks, and a dozen rabbits over the next phase of the moon.

A week before the full moon, Yas felt nauseated after a meal of yarrow root and rabbit.

"I haven't been feeling well," she said. "I think we need to cook the meat better. I hope I'm not catching any of these night fevers."

She continued to feel queasy and achy over the next weeks but kept it to herself. She was a warrior and these minor inconveniences wouldn't slow her down.

At one particularly satisfying meal, Liu stood up and addressed the group.

"At the full moon festival in ten days, the emperor will be enthroned and Fang will become his wife," he began. "All the residents of the kingdom will be there. This is the time for us to leave. The assassins will all be on duty to protect the new ruler and no one will be out looking for us. By now, they have given up their search."

"What about us?" Wai Ling asked.

Liu gave the question some careful thought. "You can come or you can stay."

"We will stay," Wai Ling decided. "We'll start our own family here."

"Don't we get a say?" Yas asked.

Liu sighed. "Do you have a better plan?"

Despite Kamnaskires's slashing run into the face of the enemy, it was Vardanes and his crossbow that cut the assassin down an arm's length behind Lu Hou. Of course, the Elamite later claimed that his sword had finished the work Vardanes started. Lu Hou was too traumatized to care who had done the job; she cuddled her boys in the back of a new carriage and refused to emerge.

"I don't care anymore about seeing the Emperor's garden," Lu Hou said. "Those assassins tried to kill my sons."

"I think they were trying to kill you," Ardeshir said. "Yeshua protected us."

"Yeshua!" she erupted. "It was those two killers of yours who saved us. I can see they want one thing: to kill as many of my people as they can."

Ardeshir sat on the edge of their carriage. "They are proud of their homeland and know I'm supposed to lead them." He rubbed his chin. "They're hoping a good fight will unite us as one nation. They also want to open up trade for their merchants, and they know the Han Empire represents their best hope of growing wealth as goods start moving toward Rome."

"You know they're not going to stop." Lu Hou suckled baby Farshid to quiet him. With her free hand, she stroked the head of Artabanas as the boy wiggled in his sleep. "By now they know that General Ban Chao is dead. One of those soldiers who escaped will have told them by now what happened. No doubt they're now training to destroy us all."

"They may be disorganized and unprepared," Ardeshir said. "Without a general or emperor, they don't have clear leadership. If we arrive at the palace with a gift of horses to celebrate the coronation of the new emperor, it may make them hesitant to attack. Someone in a position of influence may open the way for us."

"And then what?" Lu Hou asked. "We kill the new emperor and the new general and everyone else we can reach?"

"We have to meet power with power."

"Have you learned nothing about the martial arts from your time with us? If you come with power, that same power will be used against you. You will still lose."

"What can I do then?"

"Send the horses ahead with a smaller force," she said. "Go with your two comrades and offer to share four noble truths in honor of the emperor. They will be challenged more by a contest of truths than a contest of force."

Ardeshir slipped to the ground from the edge of the carriage. "We'll see if the others agree. It seems a long way to come if none of the soldiers get to prove themselves."

"Do you even know this new emperor you're going to face?"

"No. How can I know someone I haven't met?"

"Oh, you met him at a banquet," Lu Hou said. "You didn't realize who he was. He's the fourth son of the emperor through his favorite consort. This is what took the succession so long. He is wise and compassionate, the traits of his father." She swaddled the sleeping babe and laid him to rest. "Everyone in this family is named Liu, like your gardener. The emperor was named Liu Yang but had to have his name changed to Liu Zhuang because Yang is such a common name. It is forbidden to name a child with the same name as the emperor, or to even speak this name out loud."

"How old is this new emperor?"

"He's twenty-eight, but to the people he is eternal."

Ardeshir smiled. "I shall appeal to him ruler to ruler. We're both young and eager to lead well."

"I'm glad you think that way," Lu Hou said. "Just be careful of the snakes and dragons slithering all around him, whispering in his ear."

The unusual silence among the birds alerted Yas that something wasn't right. She reached across the mat for her husband as the faintest whisper of dawn probed the cracks in the hut's wooden siding. Liu was breathing rhythmically.

What could be wrong? Wai Ling should have woken her by now for the next watch.

She set aside the blankets and slipped on the crude pair of deerskin slippers Liang Na had sewn for her.

An involuntary shiver crept up her spine. There it was—a twig cracking. The swish of a branch where leaves rubbed against leaves. Ever so slowly.

Too slowly.

She curled her fingers around the sword next to the mat. It was cool to the touch as she gripped its shaft.

Liu stirred. He needed to be still, quiet, so she could focus.

She knelt by his side and pressed her hand over his mouth. "Be still."

He attempted to roll over onto his back, but she held him in place.

"Be still!" she whispered. "Someone is here."

Moving quickly to the door, she raised the sword and waited.

"Yas, they know you're awake." Wai Ling's voice carried to her. "The place is surrounded. I didn't hear them coming, but now they have a dagger at my throat... and Liang Na's throat."

"You might as well drop your weapon and come out," Fang called loudly through the morning stillness. "Did you not believe that I know you by now? When the men found your robes by the road, with no one having seen you, I knew exactly where you would hide. It was my life for yours. A gift to my new husband."

Yas wrapped herself in a robe and ducked out through the door. Dozens of heavily armed guardians stood around Fang, who wore a wide smile.

"My life for my husband and my friends," Yas offered.

"Too late!" Fang shook her head. "I've turned your life over to the emperor so you can serve as the entertainment at his coronation. I hope you haven't forgotten how to fight. As for your husband, I've turned him over to the emperor so he can serve as my tutor and advisor."

Liu stepped out of the hut behind her. "I won't be advising you on anything," he said. "I've made my choice. By linking us together in marriage, you sealed my fate to my wife's. If she dies, I will die."

Fang stepped toward Liu. "I'm taking you to the grand council so we can break this marriage tie. There's no need to waste the life of such a wise man." She stepped back and spoke to her guardians. "Take them both!"

"We belong to the Way and can never be separated by the decree of a man," Liu shouted.

"The emperor will be like a god when he is crowned," Fang said. "What he declares will be."

Yas struggled as the men tried to bind her. "This burden of choosing life or death for others is too much for you," she said to Fang.

Fang clenched her teeth. "I know. Don't make it harder by dying in the arena."

She was fastened belly-down onto the back of a horse with her hands tied to her feet under the animal. A sack was tightened around her head.

"I've told them to beat you lightly if you struggle," Fang said. "They wanted to feed you to the wild animals, but I saved your life again by promising you to the emperor. Can you breathe okay?"

Yas ignored the question. "What will you do with my husband?"

"Such a strange man. I offer him life and he would rather die with you. What is this strange love teaching by Yeshua? I will hear more from your husband before I set him in the arena with you."

"What if I win in the arena?"

"Then you can meet your brother," Fang said. "Our scouts say your brother is coming with two thousand horses as a gift for the emperor. He also has a hundred thousand warriors ready for battle. But we have a special surprise for him when he comes within our borders."

"My brother is here?"

"He will be soon."

Yas tried lifting her head. "Let me speak with him before I die."

"Your life is in the hands of the emperor. This would be a good time to discover the most noble truths your people have ever discovered. He'll want to know them before you have your day in the arena."

The long journey had exacted a far greater impact on the herd than Ardeshir had initially estimated. Halfway through fording a major river, a flash flood had taken the lives of a dozen stallions. The growth of fresh grass along the trail had been sparser than anticipated, leading hundreds of horses to grow weak. The distance from one watering hole to the next while in the desert had been very long as well, costing them another six of the warhorses.

"We're not going to make it in time," Vardanes said as the three members of the council stood around a fire. "Many of these animals aren't going to make good gifts for a people like the Han who pride themselves on the quality of their horses."

It was only a few nights before the full moon, which would mark the coronation of the new emperor. The whole party was growing restless.

Ardeshir threw a stick into the fire and the sparks jumped up like startled rabbits. "I say, let's gather a dozen of our best men and ride into the heart of the emperor's garden. They already know we're coming. When we promise them two thousand horses, they will already have seen the herd for themselves. And my wife says that this new emperor will be more impressed if we bring four noble truths. So if your people have any special wisdom to offer, now is a good time for it."

"Special wisdom?" Vardanes asked. "I'll show them some special wisdom with my sword. But your plan is a good one. I'll find twelve men and ride out with them at first light. We'll each take an extra mount so we can keep moving no matter what."

Ardeshir nodded. "I'll need to inform my wife that I'll be going with you."

Lou Hou was less than happy at Ardeshir's surprise departure. "Who's going to protect me and your sons?" she asked. "You haven't taken the time to come up with four noble truths, and such a small group of you will easily be defeated."

"I need your prayers, not your anxiety," he said. "If my sister is there, I need to find a way to rescue her. The full moon festival will be starting soon."

"So you're choosing your Persian family over me again?"

Ardeshir shook his head in frustration. "I'm doing what I have to do. I can't be in two places at once. If I go on ahead, perhaps I can make sure that the situation is safe enough for you when you arrive."

"Don't let your arrogance overcome your humility," Lu Hou warned. "And don't do anything stupid that's going to get you killed."

Ardeshir hesitated. "Perhaps Vardanes could do a little advance scouting before I get involved."

It wasn't hard to see where the boundaries of the Han Empire began. There were thousands of slaves out in the field, marking out fresh farms for the empire's senior warriors. The slaves were working under the supervision of blue-robed men brandishing whips.

Twice Ardeshir, Kamnaskires, and a group of elite troops riding out from the caravan came across scouts who were a little too slow to get ahead of the newcomers. Kamnaskires took them down with a crossbow and the group rode on. Ardeshir then rode back to accompany his wife for a few hours.

Horses were normally switched out for fresh mounts every two hours, but these Persian warhorses had special stamina and could go four hours. Their rest stops were short, including naps, refreshments, and time for riders and animals alike to stretch.

They passed dozens of caravans on their way to the coronation and took solace in the fact that they weren't the only ones who might be late.

"The new moon will be the start of the celebration, not the end," a cart driver noted in Cantonese to Lu Hou. "We'll have feasting and fighting and recitations of truths to entertain us all month."

Ardeshir negotiated with Lu Hou and raced after Vardanes. The small war party was still a two-day ride away when the full moon crested over the hills.

"I wonder what we're missing," Ardeshir said.

Kamnaskires just shook his head. "It's nothing you can do anything about."

Ardeshir and Kamnaskires caught up to Vardanes and his scouts at a village as the advance group negotiated with a former Han security officer who had settled in the area. Vardanes wanted the man's services in exchange for the lives of his wife and sons. The man said that he would guide them the rest of the way in exchange for four horses. Ardeshir offered two horses plus the life of the man's family. The deal was agreed to with a nod.

One night before engaging with the Han, they all stopped for a rest and to stretch their legs. Ardeshir and Kamnaskires huddled with Vardanes and the guide to discern the best way forward.

"Remember that the emperor is at the top of the Han society," the guide said. "He shares power with the nobility through ministers who oversee areas called commanderies and kingdoms. Confucianism is the official belief system for education and court politics."

He waited a minute for this to sink in.

"The main idea of Confucianism focuses on people having a good moral character, which puts them in harmony with the world around them," he continued. "If the emperor has perfect moral character, his rule will be peaceful and benevolent. The way you approach Emperor Ming at the beginning of his reign will make all the difference."

Twenty-One

The humiliation continued as two guardians carried Yas into the huge open-air arena with thousands of cheering spectators looking on. They took her before the new emperor with her hands and feet suspended from a pole they rested on their shoulders. The ropes dug into her wrists as her weight threatened to cut off her blood circulation. It was like being swung like a monkey from a tree branch.

As she glanced around the arena, she found that she was one of ten captives suspended on such poles, but she was the only woman.

It was the third day of the coronation celebration. The crowning had taken place on day one, with the wedding following on day two. It was now the third day of festivities and Yas listened in as the chief of the grand council gave a running commentary of the events. This red-robed giant with the silver beard seemed to smirk from under his red canonical cap embroidered with golden dragons.

"The chief warrior from Persia," he announced as Yas was paraded into position. He continued to announce the others. "The general of the Xiyu territories. The commander of the Xiongnu region. The rebel leader of Lelang commanderie…"

Without ceremony, all ten captives were dumped into a corner and left tied up.

While lying on the ground wriggling to release her bonds, she felt a strange sensation in her abdomen. She turned her head to the side and wretched.

Now was not the time to be sick!

The next to enter the arena was a parade of wild things—many of them in wheeled cages, drawn by slaves—tigers, lions, bears, gorillas, pandas, leopards, and hyenas. Five elephants plodded by in single file. These were followed by cages containing monkeys, birds, various reptiles, and antelope. At last came dozens of horses ridden in intricate patterns. Dancers in colorful costumes flitted in like butterflies, deploying fans, while acrobats, musicians, wrestlers, and martial artists offered displays of strength and agility.

The festivities slowed to a halt as the young emperor left his seat during the heat of the day. Still, Yas and the others remained tied to their poles. The only time she was given attention was when she attempted to gnaw at the ropes around her wrist. The guardian nearest her jammed a stick into her ribs and twisted. The pain ensured that she would avoid trying that again.

When Emperor Ming returned, he called out to his grand council and the chief gestured toward the gates. Hundreds of men were herded into the arena like cattle, their faces confused, angry, and bereft of hope.

Yas braced herself. Something ominous was about to happen.

Again the strange sensation nudged at her belly. She pressed hard to suppress the feeling and was sure that she felt a response from inside.

The emperor began to speak to the crowd, promoting honesty and integrity as the basis of both society and government. Corruption and dishonesty of any form would not be tolerated.

The speech was short and to the point.

When he sat again, guardians throughout the arena squatted and lifted the captives by the poles from which they were suspended. At the same time, a machete slashed the ropes on Yas's hands and she tumbled backward, almost landing on her head. Her legs thudded to the ground.

"Join them," one of the guardians said, pointing toward the hundreds of condemned.

Yas and the other ten stumbled slowly into the middle of the arena, where it became clear that they were about to face judgment.

Twenty mounted warriors armed with lances and swords rode into the arena and the crowd roared its pleasure. They raised their lances and charged into the condemned, spearing anyone not quick enough to dodge these long messengers of death.

Everyone moved with lightning speed and Yas could only look out for herself.

By the time the horses regathered on the perimeter, herding the survivors back into the middle of the arena, it seemed to Yas that at least forty of them had fallen.

The doomed men and women huddled closer, but Yas managed to spare a glance toward the emperor. Beside him, dressed in the robes of the empress, stood Fang. She held her fists tight against her chest.

In that moment, the two made eye contact.

And at that moment, another movement in her belly brought her to the truth: another life was at risk in the arena.

The horses charged again and Yas set herself low amidst the scrambling mob. She waited for the rider closest to her, then sprang from his blind side and knocked him off his mount. The warrior lay stunned for a moment, and that's all it took for Yas to break his neck. Without its rider, the horse stopped charging.

She grabbed the dead man's lance and sword and immediately drew the attention of the other nineteen horsemen.

Another of the condemned leaders, who had started the melee suspended upside-down like Yas, jumped onto the back of the riderless horse and charged for the exit. Four of the other horsemen charged in hot pursuit.

The crowd noise rose to a crescendo at the surprise turn of events.

Yas tried to lose herself in the crowd and handed off her sword to the rebel leader of the Lelang commanderie. He nodded in appreciation and the two set themselves in anticipation of another charge.

The mob of the condemned clustered together, making it difficult for the horsemen, but more of them fell nonetheless. Two riders were dragged from their mounts and beaten by the mob; those horses were snatched by escaping prisoners, who galloped for the exits.

By now, the guardians were starting to close off the arena's escapes.

Six of the condemned now wielded weapons and three more horsemen fell from attacks by lance and sword. The frenzy of the crowd grew thunderous as blood flowed on both sides of the melee.

As the horsemen gathered to plan their next moves, the mob turned and began to charge at the guardians protecting the exits.

Yas stepped aside as a horseman swung his sword at a large man who was too slow to get away. She jabbed her lance into the gap in his armor and propelled him off his horse. She stole the man's sword and quickly finished him off. But before she could get onto the horse, a straggler launched himself onto it and tried to escape, only to be tracked down and killed.

The horsemen were hunting her now.

"Turn this inside-out and crouch low," said the general of the Xiyu territories as he handed her his cape. "Give me your lance. What you need is a horse."

The warriors were wary now as they herded the condemned away from the exits, chopping here and spearing there to pick off the survivors one by one. By Yas's estimation, fewer than fifty of the original group were left standing.

Ten horsemen remained to carry out the emperor's judgment, and they were working together to separate Yas from the others.

There wasn't a person in sight as Ardeshir, Vardanes, and Kamnaskires rode toward the coronation grounds. Their chosen guide had met a villager earlier who'd directed them to the location for the coronation and the games that accompanied it.

A sound like a crashing waterfall drew them toward the arena. As they neared, a horseman flew by, galloping at full speed with two others in pursuit.

Ardeshir reined in his mount. Turning to Kamnaskires, he said, "The pursuers are the emperor's assassins. The games must be near."

Kamnaskires drew his crossbow and took out the two pursuers in a few brief movements. They tumbled to the ground and lay still.

"It might be useful to put their uniforms on," Vardanes said. "If we disguise ourselves as soldiers, we might see something useful before the emperor and his officials know we're here." He turned to Ardeshir and Kamnaskires. "Why don't you two wear these robes and pretend that I'm your prisoner?"

The fugitive had already disappeared in a cloud of dust, but he circled back after a few moments as Ardeshir and Kamnaskires began to change their clothing. Vardanes held his sword warily.

"What's happening in there?" Ardeshir asked the fugitive in passable Cantonese. "Why were you trying to get away?"

"The new emperor is reaping his first judgment," the man said. "He ordered twenty horsemen to kill hundreds of us. A Persian woman fought back… and they're hunting her down now."

Ardeshir leaped back into his saddle, uniform still askew. Kamnaskires was right behind him. With capes flying and their hearts racing as fast as their horses galloped, they charged toward the arena with Vardanes following behind.

The arena loomed like a beast carved into the earth, its high timber palisades crowned with banners that snapped in the hot wind. Crimson silk and black lacquered poles marked the imperial stand at the northern end where the new Han emperor sat enthroned beneath a canopy the color of spilled wine.

Even from a distance, Ardeshir could see the sun glinting off the gilded dragons curling along the armrests, their jeweled eyes catching the light like sparks of flame.

The air was thick, hot with dust, and the coppery tang of blood carried on the breeze. Beneath it all was the restless, almost symphonic vibration of the crowd—thousands of voices rising in one ragged, hungry chant. It rolled over the wooden stands like the roar of a storm tide, shaking the ribs of the place.

They aren't here to witness honor, Ardeshir thought. *They're here to feed on death.*

From his vantage in the shadow of the eastern gate, his gaze swept over the arena floor. The ground was hard-packed earth, baked to a pale ochre under the morning sun, already scuffed with footprints and splattered with dark stains that told their own story. Beyond, the prisoner pens were little more than crude stockades, their captives spilling out under the lash of handlers toward the open killing ground.

A sudden metallic shriek, armor striking armor, was followed by the thunder of hooves. Ten horsemen charged into the huddled mob from the opposite side, their spears upright for now, their mounts snorting plumes of steam into the sunlit air.

The crowd's roar swelled into a frenzy and Ardeshir felt his throat tighten. There in front of him, Yas was crouching low near the edge of the group.

Somewhere beyond the walls, he heard the low, pulsing drumbeat of ceremonial war drums, a rhythm older than the empire itself, meant to quicken the heart and drown out mercy. The banners along the walls rippled in unison as if bowing to the violence to come.

His eyes moved to the imperial stand again, lingering on the empress, her lips curved in a smile that didn't touch her eyes. She leaned toward the emperor, whispered something, and the young ruler's expression shifted into one of calculated amusement.

Ardeshir felt that old, familiar heat coil in his gut—the same rage that had driven him across deserts and mountains.

The first entrance to the arena was surging with fighting men and women, so Ardeshir led Vardanes and Kamnaskires towards another opening. A dozen guardians stood watching from this point, their eyes fixed on something in the middle of the arena.

The three horsemen flew by these guardians, knocking several over as they rode.

It didn't take long for Ardeshir to see what was happening. Yas and four others had been backed into a corner with ten horsemen walking their mounts forward, lances extended.

The pounding of the hooves of these new arrivals alerted some of the officials, but their disguises seemed to dull everyone's reactions.

In moments, Ardeshir and his compatriots were skewering, slashing, and smashing their way into the arena long before any of their victims could raise a defensive weapon. And even when the defence began, they were assailed on the other side by Yas and the fighters at her side.

Confusion reigned, with the emperor's horsemen no longer able to distinguish who was with them and who was against them. They began slashing at each other.

Ardeshir broke away and set himself next to Yas. "Jump on," he called to his sister. "We came to rescue you!"

One of the riders charged toward them, lance extended, but Vardanes unleashed an arrow from his crossbow that knocked the man off his horse. Within moments, eight other horsemen lay writhing on the ground, their mounts skittering nervously off to the side.

The last two horsemen looked at each other, examined the invaders, and charged. They soon joined their comrades in the dirt.

Ardeshir, Vardanes, and Kamnaskires galloped out of the arena. The crowd had transformed into a frenzied mob, surging down onto the sand to encircle the condemned as the guardians proceeded to put the wounded out of their misery.

"What took you so long?" Yas said as she hung onto her brother's waist.

The frenzy behind them dissipated like an outgoing tide. They slowed momentarily for Yas to leap off Ardeshir's horse and onto one of the abandoned mounts.

"I hope you can keep up," Ardeshir yelled.

The four riders pushed their warhorses hard for two more hours, taking lesser roads until finally the mounts could go no more.

Vardanes's mount stumbled first and he pulled up quick. "We need to stop!" he yelled.

They were all breathing hard, chests pounding, pulses racing.

"We have to go back," Yas said.

The urgency pressed in on Yas as strongly as the terror she'd felt at facing ten horsemen with their lances pointed at her. But there was no denying the essential truth: she had to go back for Liu, no matter what.

She knew Liu would be fine, that Fang would advocate for him as her tutor. He lived in the culture of his people as comfortably as a fish in water. Pulling him away into a foreign land might even be cruel.

And yet something had happened between them. A bond had formed. A union.

And she knew. She had to be with him.

"We're not going back," Vardanes insisted. "Did you see what those people wanted to do to you? And now they'll want to do it to us!"

"And who are you to say what we'll do?" Yas demanded.

"Vardanes is the leader of the Elamites," Ardeshir said, leaping off his horse. "He's working to unite our peoples into one nation." He gestured toward the hulk of a man with the massive red beard. "And this is Kamnaskires, representing the Parthian council. There is one more, representing the Magi, but he stayed back. Together we have seventy-five thousand men ready to meet the Han."

"If we're going back, let's at least wait until our soldiers join us," Kamnaskires said. "We can let them know that we brought horses as a peace offering. And if that doesn't make the emperor happy, we can roll over him like a boulder. Their warriors didn't seem that skilled."

Yas raised both her hands and stepped forward. "Those warriors were little more than boys being trained to obey a new master. I've fought with some of their trained assassins and they're as deadly as any in Persia. We only need to go back for one."

Ardeshir grasped her by the wrist. "Who is the one we need to go back for? Who is worth risking your life for?"

Yas felt the heat rise in her neck and cheeks, an unfamiliar feeling. "You know him well," she said. "He was your friend. Liu."

"Liu will be fine without us," Ardeshir said. "He's a distant relative of the emperor's family and knows how to survive. We don't need to worry about him."

"But I want him to come with us," Yas said. "I *need* him to come with us."

Ardeshir narrowed his eyes in confusion. "If you need a tutor or an advisor, Lu Hou can help you. She knows everything about the Han dynasty."

Yas looked him in the eye. "Liu is my husband."

Her brother's smile started in his eyes, then spread to his mouth. "Are you serious? That's why we have to go back? You're in love with Liu? How did that happen?"

"Fang, the emperor's new wife, put us together to save my life. We've been on the run ever since, but they caught us. Liu is being held to become the empress's advisor. I was expendable as entertainment for the coronation ceremonies."

Seeing Yas blush took Ardeshir by surprise. Hearing her express her union and love for his friend tested his belief. And understanding that she'd been no more than a mob toy lit a fuse to his rage.

"If this is the level of moral uprightness demonstrated by the new emperor, these people can rot in their ignorance and weakness," he spat.

Yas lowered her hand on his shoulder. "They're neither ignorant nor weak. The last emperor brought many groups together, as I can see you are doing." She nodded at Vardanes and Kamnaskires. "The Persian warhorses have given them an edge, so your gift will be valued. Every new leader needs to establish himself. Before you act, consider what you'll be facing in trying to bring all our peoples together."

Ardeshir pursed his lips and took a deep breath. "Lu Hou and our sons are here with me. She wanted to see her old home. Now that her half-brother is the new emperor, perhaps she can help us find peace." He leaned into her embrace. "Such a strange thing to consider that we've both married into relatives of the Han emperor."

"And don't forget that they've married into the royal family of the Persian Empire."

Vardanes stepped forward. "Okay, give this up before I stop believing you're brother and sister. The rest of the men and horses will be less than a day down the road. We better find and warn them before the Han army mobilizes."

"We'll go back for Liu once we sort out how the emperor is going to respond to our gift, and our army," Ardeshir assured Yas. "Since he's a distant relative and trusted advisor, his life should be safe for now."

"I heard that Father killed General Ban Chao… and that the general also killed him," Yas said. "Is any of that true?"

Ardeshir nodded. "They ambushed us at the farm. I saved Father from the death squads in Rome. He was near the end, but the thought of seeing you and returning to the farm kept him going. He rallied with enough strength to kill the general but died in the effort."

"So we're orphans," Yas said.

"We're orphans. Why don't you stay with Lu Hou until everything is safe?"

Yas let out a sigh. "I need to tell Liu something."

"What is it? I can tell him."

"This is something I need to handle personally." She hesitated. "You see, he's going to be a father. I want him to be with me to raise our child."

"He doesn't know?"

"I just realized it myself while I was in the arena. That's one reason I fought so hard to live. I was fighting for two. Or maybe three."

Saying the words reinforced the reality and brought sense to the questions she'd been asking herself. About the nausea. The cravings. The tenderness in her breasts. The fatigue.

She was going to be a mother. Liu would be a father.

But how was she going to get him out of the emperor's grasp? Even more, how was she going to take him from Fang?

Ardeshir was jabbering away, so she decided to give him her attention.

"And that's another reason why you need to stay with Lu Hou," he was saying. "There are enough of us to fight this out. If anyone can convince Liu to come with us, it will be me." He turned away as if his arguments were enough to settle the issue. "Yas, come with us. Just let us know if you need to stop along the way. I know from dealing with Lu Hou how pregnancy can change a woman's body."

As if a man knew anything about a woman's body!

"I'll be fine," she said. "If I fall behind, I'll catch up. I know how to get back to the main road from here."

Yas swung into the saddle and rode along at an easier pace as the four of them tested the trail ahead.

"Their scouts are going to know where our men and horses are by now," Kamnaskires said. "If they're going to come after us, I say they'll aim for the horses."

"I agree," Vardanes said. "I've talked with the guides and they think the Han will try to distract our army from one direction and steal our horses from another."

"Do our commanders understand this?" Ardeshir asked.

"I've alerted the Persians to keep alert and maintain forces around the horses," Kamnaskires assured him. "But we should pick up our pace. We'll be in trouble if they catch us divided from the rest of the group."

As if having announced a prediction, a thundering vibration of horse hooves suddenly filled the forest around them.

Vardanes slipped off his horse. "Sounds like they're already here."

Yas peered into the forest as she and the three men stepped into the bush. If they had travelled any faster, she feared the Han army would have devoured them as they came up the main road. The Persian warriors were on their own now.

Twenty-Two

Feeling the ground vibrate beneath his feet sent a shiver of fear up Ardeshir's spine. How would his men respond to an ambush of such magnitude without leadership?

"We need to ride ahead and convince the emperor to save the horses and call off his troops," Vardanes said. "This is going to be a bloodbath."

"I've got to get Lu Hou out of there," Ardeshir said. "The Han will wipe everyone out without exception. My sons are the future of the Persian Empire. We need to save them."

Kamnaskires held up his hand to make a point. "But if we lose you, we lose the nation. You and your sister need to wait here while we go into battle. Ride back to the emperor, if you wish. Maybe you can prevent this from ending badly."

Was this the test of kings? To forsake your own flesh and blood to save those who would undermine you the moment they had the opportunity?

Yas donned the spare Han robe to serve as a disguise, then flung herself into her saddle and started pushing east along a trail parallel to the main road.

Ardeshir fell in behind her.

The sound of thunder from the road continued long enough to leave a sense of dread in his mind. Hopefully those Persian scouts would be alert enough to warn the entire army. The smart move would be to scatter the horses in the face of an enemy ambush. Such plans had been worked out along the trail. But the visionaries of that plan were now far from the point of attack.

"The last of the Han are past now," he yelled ahead to Yas. "Let's take the main road and gain some time."

"They'll have their support wagons and supply trains coming behind them," Yas reminded him. "It's better to keep out of sight."

That made good sense. But how in the world could he expect to be the King of Kings, to direct an entire nation, when he couldn't even direct his own sister?

He pulled up the scarf across his face, loosened his reins, and charged ahead.

It didn't take long before they heard the rumble of chariots, carriages, and carts on the road. Yas had been right.

Better to stay humble and keep pressing on, he told himself.

The weariness sapped him of energy, though. How was Yas dealing with the demands on her body after all she'd been through? This couldn't be good for the baby.

Their horses had been pushed enough for one day and they could only travel so fast. They had to stop for two extra rests before coming back into sight of the arena. By this time, the crowds had dispersed and the sun was sliding back toward the horizon.

Alighting from their horses, they crept up behind a hedge outside the structure. On the field ahead, they saw a long queue of donkey carts rolling in to collect the corpses, which had been lined up like fish at the market. Vultures flew overhead and peasants swung brooms and sticks to keep the birds away from the remains.

But there was no sign of Emperor Ming, Fang, or Liu.

"They will have gone back to the palace by now," Yas said. "Maybe Liu would have stopped by his home to pick up a few things. I'm sure they'll find him a room in the palace from now on."

Ardeshir pulled her back behind a tree to keep out of sight of the workers. "Do you know anyone on the inside?"

"What do you mean?"

"Someone besides Liu. Someone you could trust to deliver a message. Someone who knows you and won't be regarded with suspicion."

"I know Jing. She's the empress's sister."

"How can you reach her?"

"There's a maid who cleans rooms in the palace. She could carry a note to Jing. I'll keep it simple in case she's found out."

What kind of a plan was this? Handing a note to a maid, who would hand it to a girl, who would hand it to her sister, who would hand it to the very advisor she wouldn't let go of yet needed to?

"It'll never work," Ardeshir pointed out.

"There are no other options," Yas said. "Unless you plan on the two of us storming the palace and taking out dozens of guardians and sentries."

"If it weren't for your baby, I might consider it." He smirked. "Where can you meet the girl?"

"She'll be finishing her day at the palace soon. I can meet her near the maze, but we'll have to go the long way around. We can cut through a farmer's field, through a hedge near the wild things, then enter the maze and meet her by the servant residences."

"And you're going to do this in the dark?"

"We'll have to if we wait any longer," she said. "Come! These outfits will have to help us get past anyone who's curious. We'll keep our faces covered."

The ploy worked. Although hundreds of workers streamed back into the empire's unseen villages after the day's activities, none of them looked twice in their direction. In fact, every single individual averted their gaze and stayed focused on the ground.

"Makes you think these guardians carry a lot of power," Ardeshir said.

"More like they carry a lot of death," Yas replied.

They abandoned their horses near the farmer's field and Yas led them through the split in the hedge and into the maze. Darkness had almost enveloped the landscape here.

"If this is a maze, how are you going to get us through it?" Ardeshir asked.

"Jing and I tried to memorize it, going through its passages as though we were blind. We have it memorized both ways now. We knew we could hide in here forever if we had to."

"That's what I'm afraid of," Ardeshir said. "I don't want to be in here forever."

"You'll have to trust me. Grab hold of my robe and don't let go."

They were halfway through when it became impossible to distinguish one bush from another. Yas kept her hand extended out front, feeling for openings. She knew her brother could hear her mumbling, but she didn't care; she spouted off numbers and counted steps and did anything she could to keep herself focused on the task at hand.

After a while she stumbled and she felt him grab hold of her robe and pull her back.

"What's happening?" he asked. "Are we almost there? Don't do this if you're going to hurt the baby."

"Will you hush! I tripped over a root. We're almost there."

Ages later, she pushed through an opening in the hedge and felt the cool night air on her face. In the distance, she saw a pair of torches flickering as the bearers moved in their direction.

"That might be her," Yas breathed. "Stay here."

"I'm not letting you get caught."

"Fine! There's another bush you can hide behind, but don't show yourself and don't say a word. She's probably got a guardian walking her to her room. I wouldn't want you to kill him for no reason."

This plan had too many flaws. Every beat of his heart could make a difference and all he got was cramps from crouching so long. By now the Persians and the Han ambushers would have finished their first clashes and were reorganizing for the first light of dawn. How many casualties might there be? Had Vardanes and Kamnaskires made it to their encampment in time to save Lu Hou and the boys?

The wait was agonizing as the two torches got close enough for Ardeshir to finally view their carriers' faces. Yes! It was a young maid and a guardian.

"The empress will see you in the morning," the guardian was saying.

Ardeshir turned away to keep his face obscured.

The maid continued to her door, then hesitated midway through opening it. The guardian stiffened. Something was wrong. If the guardian got suspicious and came back for a closer look… Ardeshir would have no option but to kill him. He wrapped his fingers around the hilt of his dagger.

The door closed with the maid inside—and at last the guardian continued on.

Where was Yas? More cramping.

Wait! Don't panic. Trust her.

The door opened again and a hand touched his shoulder. He swung the dagger hard. In a moment, he found himself landing face-first in the dirt with a knee digging into his back.

"It's me," Yas said. "Are you sure you still want to be an uncle?"

"Where did you come from?" he asked. "Why didn't you warn me? I could have killed you."

"But you didn't. We both know who was meant to be the warrior and who was meant to be the king." She released him and stood freely. "There's going to be enough moonlight soon for us to find our way back. I've passed the note to the maid. Now it's up to Yeshua to let us know whether this is part of the Way."

"I'm not sure if this has anything to do with the Way."

"If the Way is the way, then everything has to do with the Way," she said.

Now she was the warrior *and* the philosopher? If this kept up, there wouldn't be any room for him. Of course, he could make his own space.

"Do we wait here all night?" he asked. "How will we know when the plan is working?"

"We'll wait where we left the horses," she said. "Didn't you learn anything from living here for two years? We flow with the streams, we drift with the wind, we sink ourselves deep into the earth like the flowers. Life happens around you if you don't learn to live with it."

"You're scaring me, sister."

"I already did that, remember?"

"How much further?"

"Flow with the streams…"

It felt good to be a little more in control.

Yas felt invigorated from standing with the horses in the open pasture under the moonlight. She had done it, leading her brother through that crazy maze. Still, she couldn't help but think of the battle they had left behind. The Persians and Han had likely wounded each other significantly in their first clash. They would do it again in the morning.

Everyone who lived in this part of the country would be reeling from the first judgment day under Emperor Ming and would be evaluating their loyalty to the empire. Word had probably also spread about the Persian invasion. No doubt every farmer had his pike ready to defend every step of earth.

"I never feel so close to the Creator or to Persia as I do when standing under a moon like this," Ardeshir said, looking up at the heavens. "I'm praying hard that Yeshua has protected Lu Hou and the boys. I'll add my prayers for your own baby now."

"This is a side of you I'm not used to seeing," Yas said. "It's hard to believe that the years have gone by so fast. We should get a short nap so we'll be ready when the sun rises. The note we left could be having an impact before we realize it."

"What did you say in the note?" he asked.

"I said, 'I love horses.'"

"That's it?"

"It's enough."

"How is anyone supposed to understand anything from that?"

"We'll find out soon enough."

Ardeshir tried to warm Yas up by rubbing her shoulders, but she was shivering hard from the night air.

"I should have brought an extra blanket," he said.

"Right now, every moment I get is a gift. Yesterday I faced the end and prayed like I'd never prayed before. The next moment I was thinking, 'What's the point. I might as well lie down and get this over with.' Now I have you and my baby… and I want to live more than anything."

She was suddenly struck by how much she had changed. One minute, a warrior relishing the chance to go out in a flash of fury and glory. The next, a woman desiring nothing more than to nurture and care for a helpless little one. What would she do if they had to fight their way to freedom again? Could Ardeshir depend on her?

When the sun launched in the morning, Yas spotted movement near the opening to the hedge of the emperor's garden.

"Someone's coming," she said.

Ardeshir pushed off from the tree he'd been resting against. "Can you tell who it is?"

"There are two of them. It's Jing and Liu. They must have gotten the message."

"Is there anyone else behind them?"

"Not that I can see." She began to move. "Let me talk with them. Stay here in case I need to be rescued."

Yas walked out into the open and stood waiting as Jing and Liu made their way to her. They greeted each other with enthusiastic embraces.

Jing held up the note, clearly proud of herself for understanding it. "Horses! I remembered."

"What are you still doing here?" Liu asked. "I was told you were all the way to Hindustan by now."

"My brother rescued me yesterday from the arena, and I came back for you." Yas hesitated a moment before dropping her big news. "You're going to be a father and I need you to help me raise our baby."

The man's mouth dropped open and he gave her a vacant stare. The expression said it all.

That's when Ardeshir stepped out from behind the tree he'd been hiding behind. Liu's eyes grew even wider at the sight of his friend.

"You're going to be a mother?" Jing flung herself into another embrace. "I didn't give the note to Fang because she would have sent the guardians to collect you. Liu says that the emperor tried to kill you yesterday!"

"He didn't get his way," Yas said.

Liu still seemed a little confused. "How do you know you're going to have a baby?"

"I'm a woman," Yas said. "I know how my body works."

"Are you sure you can't have it here?" Liu asked. "The empress wants me to be her advisor."

Yas backed away a step. "As you saw yesterday, the emperor wants me dead."

"Don't you think the empress could change her husband's mind?"

"If she could have, don't you think she would have?"

"So I need to choose whether to stay as a royal advisor or come with you to a land where I have no standing whatsoever?"

Yas backed off another few steps. "You need to decide whether to raise this child together with me or remain under the thumb of a girl who treats you like her personal slave."

"When do you need to know my answer?" Liu asked.

"They're trying to kill me right now!" Yas said. "My people are fighting for their lives against a Han army down the road, and you're hesitating? What happened to the man who pledged his life to me? Remember when we decided that our fates would be bound together as one?"

Liu nodded. "Yes, sorry. I haven't had time to process this. Of course I'll come. But everything I own is now at the palace. How am I going to get my things without arousing suspicion?" He looked toward Jing. "Your sister is expecting me to tutor her on court protocols in the midafternoon."

Ardeshir placed a hand on Liu's shoulder and smiled. "Tell her that the Persians have come with a gift of two thousand horses for the emperor but the assassins are trying to destroy them outside the gates. There's nothing like the truth to motivate an emperor."

Liu embraced Ardeshir with a bear hug. "I was sure I would never see you again. When I heard that General Ban Chao killed your father, I was sure he must have killed you as well. When did you arrive?"

"You saw my arrival in the arena," Ardeshir answered. "Once you learn Persian, I can make you my ambassador of trade. By marrying my sister, you already have royal status. Your first task will be to work out a trade agreement with the Han emperor."

"Please take me with you when you go west," Jing pleaded.

Ardeshir sighed. "A kidnapping? That's all we need."

It sure didn't seem like life could get any more complicated. Ardeshir's army was being ambushed by the Han without him. His pregnant sister, being hunted by the Emperor, had a husband who was hesitating about joining them. And now the empress's sister wanted to come along for a journey that would put a double price on their heads?

Ardeshir took Liu by the forearm and pulled him aside. "Work out how you're going to get from the palace and meet Yas back here tomorrow. You can tutor the empress today as if nothing's wrong… but then get out while you can." He pivoted to connect with his sister. "You can explain all this to Jing. In the meantime, I'm heading back to the battle. I need to make sure that Lu Hou and the boys are okay. If we can get those horses to the emperor, it could solve all these other problems."

"I've only just had the chance to see you," Yas protested. "What if you get yourself killed?"

"I don't know how you've managed to survive this long, but I aim to finish this mission and hear every part of your story." Ardeshir smiled at his sister, then at Jing. "While you're talking this young woman out of her dreams to come with us, maybe you can think of four noble truths to tell the emperor. Something that will convince him to let us all live and enter into a trade deal with Persia. And maybe to give real consideration to the Way."

"If I can figure out even one of those things, I'll be happy," she said.

It took most of the remaining daylight hours for Ardeshir to ride to the scene of battle. Taking the trail parallel to the main road made it easier to avoid detection and all the foot travelers he encountered quickly stepped out of his path at the sight of the uniform.

From time to time he checked on the main road, which was still packed with wagons, carts, and horses moving to support the Han army.

As he neared the conflict, Han sentries began to appear at intervals, monitoring new arrivals. His uniform kept him from having to stop and explain himself.

In the shadows of evening, he continued to ride until the camps of the Han filled the fields ahead.

Every hundred paces or so, a bonfire rose up to defy the darkness. Hundreds of warriors milled about in the spaces between. Every individual seemed preoccupied with either getting something to eat or someplace to rest.

The energy around these fires and food tables was undeniable.

He dismounted and led his horse further south and around the Han encampment. Only when the last light of day had winked out did he shed his uniform and tied his horse.

Within a few hundred steps, Ardeshir heard the first smatterings of Persian drifting toward him on the breeze. He then encountered Parthian sentries reinforcing their barricades and calling for support.

"There's a trail here that needs to be watched," he heard a man shout. "Bring others and set up a barrier!"

"How are we supposed to see the Hun in the dark?" another called back.

"Use your crossbow and shoot at anything that moves!"

Ardeshir crouched and waited.

Behind him, the bushes rustled. He lay flat on the ground as a pair of scouts crept along the trail toward the Persian lines.

"We've reached the frontlines," a Han warrior whispered in Cantonese. "Should we kill a scout to show them how easily we're able to penetrate their defences?"

"Maybe one," said another. "They've stampeded their horses into our ambush and dug themselves into hiding. It won't be easy to surround them now. They're too spread out."

"Let's finish off one at least."

Ardeshir waited a few moments longer, then spoke up in Cantonese: "Fall back, hurry!"

The two scouts scurried past him in retreat without a word, trusting that he was a Han commander.

Crawling forward, Ardeshir approached the position where the scouts had just occupied. He soon came upon two young Parthians hunched over a flickering clay lamp; they were whittling, oblivious to how close they had come to forfeiting their lives.

"Secure the perimeter!" Ardeshir commanded in Persian.

The two scouts rolled for cover and knelt on one knee, daggers drawn.

"Who's there?" one man said. "Speak or lose your life."

"I am Ardeshir of Nabonidus, prince and commander of the forces of Persia." He rose up and walked into the small circle of light. "You men are fortunate.

A moment ago, two Han scouts were crouching five steps away from you with their daggers ready to slice your throats."

The first sentry peered into the bushes. "Where are they?"

"I ordered them back," Ardeshir said. "Now, where are the rest of our troops? Where are Vardanes of the Parthians and Kamnaskires of the Elamites?"

"If you mean the red-haired bear, he's recovering from an arrow in his shoulder," a sentry said. "When our scouts galloped into camp warning that the Han army was attacking, we unleashed the horses, as we had been told. The horses were like a river and stopped the enemy advance. That Parthian came charging out of the bush screaming like a Wildman, but he took an arrow."

The second man jumped in. "Our archers rode beside the flank of the horses and unleashed arrows on the first group of attackers. Some fell and were trampled. The Han unleashed their arrows on our infantry... some were lost."

"Was there hand-to-hand combat"? Ardeshir asked.

"You'll need to ask the commanders," the first man said. "We were sent to secure the perimeter and watch for infiltrators."

"You'll have to do better," Ardeshir said. "You were about to be trophies of Han assassins."

Twenty-Three

Yas wedged herself into an alcove on the roof of the servants' quarters. A tree growing nearby, with an overhanging branch, had provided the perfect access route to the top. Jing had been agile in joining her.

Perhaps this wasn't the best way to protect a baby or a young girl.

Regardless, this didn't feel comfortable at all. She had her knees pressed against her chin and her arms tucked tight across her chest. Not exactly her preferred form of relaxation! The board pressing up against her spine didn't help either. How long was it going to take for Liu to slip out of the palace with his things?

Twisting her neck for a better glimpse of the koi pond was a strain. She should have chosen a better refuge while she waited. It had started comfortably enough, looking over the top of the roof while on her tiptoes. That had been midmorning. By noon she'd changed her hiding place and wedged herself against a tree. Now she had nowhere left to maneuver.

"He'll be back," Jing whispered from her prone position along the wall. "My sister will always find ways to get more from a person than they expect to give."

"If we wait until night, it could be impossible to get away," Yas asserted. "The grand council and the guardians will want to protect the emperor from the Persians. I should have gone with Ardeshir."

"Do you honestly think your brother is going to be killed?" Jing asked. "I can try one more time with my sister. Maybe she can open up the way for your people."

"Your sister isn't going to go against the emperor now," Yas said. "My brother and his men somehow got through all his security and stole me away from justice. There is no chance for their trade mission to prevent an all-out war. Too many people are going to die unless we find a way to stop this."

"Challenge the emperor to the four noble truths." Jing pushed herself up on one elbow. "Fang always said that the four noble truths are the key."

"We've tried over and over and failed. Persians think about truth and the world differently. It's like we're trying to sing a love song, but both the words and the tunes are so different that we can't hear each other. Not only are the words different, but they're not even in the same language."

"Do they have to be?" Jing asked. "Do you need the same words or the same tune if you understand the underlying meaning? Can't one singer see what the other means in another way?"

"What do you mean?" Yas asked.

"Think about how our people and your people ride horses." The girl sat upright. "You train your warhorses to feel the thrill of battle. We train our horses to dance with the world around them. We are servants to our horses and worship them as otherworldly. You make them your earthly servants and hope they worship you."

"That's not how I see it," Yas said, turning sideways to escape her discomfort. "But I can appreciate that we see things differently. Perhaps we can have a festival where our two peoples show the other what can be done with horses. We can do it to honor the emperor."

Jing rose her feet. "Yes! This is a good idea, one my sister can appreciate. I will tell her and we can stop this war."

Before Yas could say anything, Jing ran toward the palace.

Ardeshir found his family huddled in a shelter well behind the front lines. It was well past midnight when he rapped on the door. When he whispered his wife's name, Lu Hou flung open the door and threw herself into his arms.

"This is a nightmare, but you're alive," she sobbed. "What's gone wrong? Our boys are terrified. Artabanas finally cried himself to sleep, but the little one won't eat properly."

"I'm here now," Ardeshir said. "I'm here now."

"Don't leave us," Lu Hou begged, stepping back. "Take us back home. I don't need to see the palace or the gardens. I don't belong here anymore."

"We can talk about all that in the morning. You and the boys need to rest. It's going to be okay."

"Don't make promises you can't keep," she said. "We are not okay."

"I'm going to need you to come to the emperor's palace with me," Ardeshir said. "I need you to remember everything you know about the right protocols to restore honor and peace. I found my sister, but the emperor was trying to kill her and I had to rescue her from his security forces. We need to find a way for our nations to overcome their fear of each other."

Lu Hou glared. "And why do you think there is fear? You've brought seventy-five thousand warriors across the world to march into a new emperor's homeland. What did you think they would feel?" She turned away. "I know you don't need me to be weak right now. I need to be the courageous partner of a sovereign, but I haven't slept for days, the boys are scared, and I didn't know what had happened with you."

He placed his arms under her elbows and pulled her close. "I know this is hard. I'll go meet the commanders so we have a plan for tomorrow. If I go anywhere after that meeting, you'll go with me. This road has been hard, but it's been far better having you along."

A watchman escorted Ardeshir to the central command tent. When he arrived, Vardanes had just pulled an arrow out of his own arm while an assistant staunched the flow of blood with cabbage and rags. He lounged on a stool, but fire burned in his eyes.

"So our commander decided to return, did he?" the Parthian said. "My men released the horses as planned, but where were the Elamites?"

Kamnaskires stepped into the tent from behind Ardeshir. He brandished his sword.

"We did exactly as we agreed," the Elamite man reported. "We rode to the perimeters of our camp and set up a security cordon. Our archers launched an attack at the heart of the enemy riders. If you had pressed the attack, Vardanes, instead of using the horses to protect yourselves, we could have finished this war by now."

Ardeshir raised his hands to prevent an argument. "None of us was in position to guide our men. Remember, our own actions caused this ambush. Our commanders did the best they could based on their training, and stampeding the horses did stifle the Han charge."

He began to pace back and forth through the confined tent, his thoughts running.

"We have to change our strategy now," he continued. "They have lost men and we have lost men. We'll send a delegation for peace."

"My men have hardly seen any action," Kamnaskires pointed out.

Vardanes favored him with a withering glare. "And whose problem is that?"

"Listen!" Ardeshir interrupted. "We came together to forge a nation and establish the biggest trade agreement our nation has ever seen. We can't expand west because of the Romans, so we need to push our influence east. It's the only way for us to be prosperous again. We must control these trade routes. The world needs them more than ever."

"But how are we going to stop the Han when the sun rises?" Vardanes asked. "We've already released the horses. For all we know, those assassins are already crawling through the bush, surrounding us with daggers, ready to slash our throats."

Ardeshir moved aside the tent flap and peered into the darkness. How many of the Han scouts crawled through the bush, hoping for one Persian throat to slit? How would a king act when the life of his people stood like a flower under the heel of a giant?

Yas watched as the two sisters marched across the koi bridge, speaking animatedly to one another, and headed straight toward her. Slightly behind them, a pair of guardians hurried to keep up. Fang was dressed as elegantly as she'd been at the emperor's side in the arena.

Jing ran ahead and motioned for Yas to emerge from her hiding place. Meanwhile, Fang stood her ground with her arms crossed.

Before stepping out into the open, Yas questioned herself. Was this insane? Would it make any difference to try one more time to reach the heart of this young empress?

She inhaled deeply, slowly released the air, and then stepped out of hiding. She bowed slightly.

"You have embarrassed our nation and humiliated the emperor," Fang began. "You aren't even good enough to be ground up for koi food. Why are you not on your face begging for mercy?"

Yas focused on the ground at her feet. "Thank you for coming to see me."

"What is this nonsense my sister tells me about horses dancing and fighting?"

Yas held her hands out, palms up.

"Yes! Speak! Why do you follow protocols only when it suits you?"

"My brother has come with two thousand of his best Persian horses," Yas explained. "It is a gift for the emperor. But your army has attacked us and the horses have now scattered. We're concerned that your husband won't receive his gift, especially if more of my brother's men are killed before they can gather the horses again. We would be happy to put on a showcase for the emperor to demonstrate what our horses can do. And of course we would be pleased to see what your own horses can do."

Fang merely grunted. "Why did your people need to bring so many men?"

"It is a long journey, passing through many warring nations who would love to take the horses for themselves," Yas said. "My brother had to protect them. He would also like to negotiate a trade agreement between our two empires, to take advantage of the open road between us."

"Bring your brother and we will talk."

"He's with his wife and sons, trying to keep them from being killed."

"Is he not married to the former emperor's daughter? Is she not the half-sister of my husband?"

Yas bobbed her head, keeping her eyes trained on the ground. "Yes! It is the same woman."

"Didn't the emperor condemn her to the lions and delete her as his daughter?"

"Things are complicated," Yas said. "Perhaps if she can talk with the new emperor, they can reach a new understanding."

"My husband is a merciful and just ruler of his people," Fang said. "I will ask him what he is willing to do with a rebel like you and a traitor like his sister." She turned to the two guardians nearby. "Hold her until I get back. If she gets away, you will exchange your own lives for hers."

Yas bowed as Fang pivoted and left.

Ardeshir sat in his saddle as the dawn broke over a wide field. Next to them, Vardanes and Kamnaskires looked out over the two combatant armies. Sixty-two Persian men formed a V-formation behind them, their weapons so far remaining sheathed.

He nodded first to Vardanes, then to Kamnaskires, signaling the start of a slow march toward the Han camp.

At the edge of the field, among the trees and shrubs, the Han assassins await-ed the Persian advance. A long line of archers, hundreds of them, emerged from the foliage with bows drawn.

"Peace!" Ardeshir called out in Cantonese as he and his fellow commanders approached the Han front line.

"Peace," the Han general called back.

When Ardeshir knew he and his men were within reach of the Han archers, he dismounted and stood his ground.

Now it was the Han general's turn to order an advance.

"Why have you desecrated the lands of the emperor?" the general asked when they drew close enough to speak without yelling.

"We bring a gift for the new emperor," Ardeshir said. "The horses you met yesterday are his."

"You bring a gift yet scatter it into the wind? How can we hope to regather what is lost?"

"We will help you. If our armies can spread out and work together, we can herd them back together in this very field."

"More than two hundred of my best warriors breathe no more because of your assault on our empire," the general said. "What am I to do for their families?"

"We will compensate the families for their loss. We've also lost many men, at least a hundred. What can you do for *their* families?"

In response, the general huddled briefly with two of the men mounted near him. After a short conference, the general turned back to Ardeshir.

"We will ask our emperor what can be done," he called. "We will allow the rest of you to live, for now, assuming there are no further hostilities."

"We will give you one day to return with an answer from the emperor," Ardeshir said. "Now, let's work together to collect the horses. If not, we'll finish what we started. All the extra graves you're forced to dig will turn your time of celebration into one of mourning."

"What good can there be if our two nations are made up entirely of widows?" the Han asked. "Give us two days so we may give the emperor time to choose the truth by which we need to live."

Ardeshir nodded curtly. "Two days."

The stone felt cold on Yas's nose and forehead as she prostrated herself before the chrysanthemum throne. The slate was smooth apart from the smallest grit of sand indenting the palm of her left hand. There was no mercy if protocols were violated at this level. The tip of the guardian's sword next to her was visible in her peripheral vision.

The rustle of garments and the faint slither of a sandal echoed across the floor. Somewhere a dove cooed. A collective sigh from the audience resonated in the breeze.

"The ray from the rising sun has come," a voice announced. "The guardian of truth and life has risen. By his mercy, we live. Let all be silent before him."

Another figure arrived and prostrated himself beside her, but it was the first voice that spoke again.

"Who dares seek the council of the Han emperor?"

Yas turned her palms up for permission to speak. The side of the sword beside her hit her strongly enough that she turned her palms down onto the floor again. What was happening?

"Speak, General," the emperor said. "What news do you have of the battle?"

Now the time had come for the figure beside her to make his report.

"The Persian prince claims to bring two thousand horses to honor your coronation," the general said. "When we attacked, they released the horses into the countryside. Both sides have delayed battle to seek your guidance. Do you accept these horses as your gift or do you wish us to continue to fight for the honor of the empire?"

"Persian horses are the gifts of heaven," the emperor replied. "What else does this prince say?"

"He wants to establish trade between our two empires and believes both nations will increase their wealth and influence by working together."

"Delay the battle one more day, until I can speak to this prince. Bring him to this court tomorrow."

There was a pause.

"Who else would see the face of truth itself?"

The sword whacked her again. Yas turned her palms up.

"Who dares to speak for this recipient of the black stones?" the emperor asked.

Yas waited as the throne room fell silent.

"I will speak for her." This belonged to Fang.

"What would you say on her behalf?"

"She escaped judgment through the sword of her brother, who is the prince of Persia," Fang said. "She has humbly returned to seek your mercy. She has also proposed another way to honor you in your coronation."

"And how will she honor me?"

"She proposes that we hold a festival of horses. The Persians will show you what their horses can do in battle and our people can show what we can do with ours. Together we will celebrate this gift of the gods that will make you and the Han the greatest nation of all."

The emperor seemed to hesitate. "Can we trust these invaders to do what they say?"

"It is my life for hers," Fang said.

Yas shook her head. Was this the little empress, the eternal flower, pledging to give her life for Yas?

"I will give her the white stone," the emperor said. "You both may live. Bring the horses. Stop the battle."

Yas gulped for air and sobbed in place. Could this really be happening? The emperor had given a white stone? She would live. There would be no war?

"One more thing," the emperor said. "The condition of the white stone is that Liu will remain as tutor to the eternal flower, and the Persian will remain to oversee the training of my horses…"

A Han messenger galloped across the field, ignoring the Persian crossbows he must have known were aimed at his heart.

"Come!" he called to Ardeshir. "The emperor will see you now. He will accept the horses. The battle will not be."

"What is he talking about?" Vardanes asked in a quiet voice. "We haven't even collected the horses yet. Every farmer in the countryside must have claimed one by now."

Ardeshir mounted his warhorse. "You and Kamnaskires work with our captains to form a net and herd the horses into this field. We must trust the Han to do the same from their side. If you have to confiscate horses from farmers, do what needs to be done. The emperor is summoning me and I had better go."

"Remember, you are the King of Kings of Persia," Vardanes reminded him. "You are master of the greatest nation on earth. You should bow to neither the Romans nor the Han."

"I will hold my head high," Ardeshir said. "We will win the day. I trust Yeshua to give me the four noble truths I need to win the favor of this man. I just hope I don't have to save my sister again."

Vardanes nodded. "You should take your wife and sons. If this is her half-brother, you may need all her help."

Of course he had already decided to bring his family.

"Try not to let the men cause too much damage while I'm gone," Ardeshir said as he turned his horse and began riding towards the carriage.

When he entered through the door, he found Lu Hou napping with the boys. He woke her gently.

"Your brother, the emperor, has invited us to come for a talk," he whispered into her ear. "We can bring the boys. When do you think you might be ready?"

"My brother? At the palace?" She shook her head slowly, then reached for Artabanas. "We will be ready soon. I don't even have a gift to take to him."

"Don't worry. I've brought him two thousand horses. I think that's enough."

While Lu Hou roused and readied the boys, Ardeshir cleaned the carriage with the help of two of his aides. They couldn't go meet the emperor looking as though they'd been travelling for the past six months.

He also decided to take some time to wash himself and put on his royal robes.

"Lu Hou," he called to his wife. "Don't forget to wear some of your special robes."

A short time later, Ardeshir had advanced the carriage to the guardians stationed along the front line. The guardians were insistent that none of the men with Ardeshir should accompany him and his family to the palace. This didn't seem wise or safe, but they eventually negotiated an agreement: six generals would ride alongside the carriage and stand guard during the palace visit.

Ardeshir returned to the carriage where the family awaited him. Lu Hou held the baby while Ardeshir hoisted Artabanas into his arms.

"We're going to see a king," he said as the carriage lurched into motion.

Twenty-Four

The shock of the emperor's ruling still hadn't worn off as Yas sat at Liu's feet and wept. "There must be something we can do," she said. "The emperor cannot mean this. How can he do it to us? All I want is to leave this place and take my rightful standing in Persia with my brother."

Liu stroked his wife's hair, gently massaging her scalp. "It's the emperor's decision to make. We must both remain. It's the only way to raise our child together. If either of us leaves, the other will forfeit their life."

"How can your people cherish such beauty and grace in your arts but practice such cruelty in your relationships?" Yas asked. "Why am I the one who has to sacrifice? What did I do?"

"The mind of an emperor operates at a different level. He brings order and justice even when we don't understand how."

"What good could possibly come from my staying here?"

"Perhaps we will be able to share what we know about the Way."

"And who will listen?"

"It seems you already have a willing follower in Jing. And there is that maid, you know."

Yas sighed loudly. "Something still isn't right. This empire is supposed to be about truth-telling, but I have to stand in front of my brother and tell him that I want to stay. How can I be expected to tell such a lie?"

Liu took her by the hands. "You must make it true. You have two days to change your heart and make it true."

"I think I'm going to be sick." Lu Hou halted, closed her eyes, and took a deep breath. "I promised the boys they could see the swans. Did you see the swans as we passed the koi pond?"

Ardeshir glanced over his shoulder. "I didn't even look for them. We can see the swans on our way out."

"Assuming there will be a way out," Lu Hou whispered. "Have you got any other plans if this doesn't go so well?'

A dozen golden-robed guardians stepped into formation in front of the family and marched them into the palace. They soon came to the entrance to the throne room—a wall of gold embedded with rubies, emeralds, and blue sapphires.

Two red-robed members of the grand council stood just inside the doors.

"How shall I announce you?" one of the council members asked.

"Ardeshir, son of Nabonidus, Prince of Persia, King of Kings, and commander of Parthians, Magi and Elamites."

The guardian nodded in deference. "Follow me. The emperor will not need you to bow for permission to speak."

As Ardeshir neared the chrysanthemum throne, Lu Hou fell on her face with her palms down. Ardeshir immediately knelt beside her.

"Are you okay?" he asked. "Your brother isn't even here yet."

A swish of red robes alerted him to rise and face the throne. The emperor, dressed in a large-sleeved embroidered black wrap secured by a belt, shuffled through a curtained doorway and sat on his throne. As he sat, Ardeshir noticed his yellow baggy trousers.

The emperor stared down at the two supplicants. "What is wrong with the woman?"

"This is your sister," Ardeshir said. "She is my wife. She understands the protocols of the empire."

"But she is dead to the Han," Emperor Ming said. "She belongs to Persia now. You may ask her to rise."

Ardeshir touched Lu Hou at her elbow and she rose slowly with her eyes lowered.

"So your people address you as the King of Kings?" the emperor continued. "How do your people distinguish the common people from those of status? We wear clothing according to seasons but need something stronger to distinguish us at a glance."

Ardeshir nodded. "Yes, blue or green in the spring, red for summer, yellow for autumn, and black for winter. You distinguish the emperor, the councilor, the duke, the prince, the minister, and other officials by the symbols sewn on your garments... and by the style of those garments. You also have decorative headgear and ribbons to help determine your status."

"Ah, but I am changing the use of these symbols. Only the emperor and his family may now wear all twelve symbols on their ritual robes. Do you know what the symbols are?"

Ardeshir nodded again. "The sun with the three-legged crow; the moon with the rabbit; the three stars for happiness, prosperity, and longevity; and the sacred mountains, showing stability and inner peace. Then there is the dragon for strength and adaptability, the pheasant for refinement, and the two cups with a tiger and a monkey to show faithfulness and respect. You have pondscum to represent purity. Fire symbolizes brightness. Rice grains represent agriculture and wealth. An axe over two animals shows courage, justice, and the resolve to distinguish between right and wrong."

"You have studied well." Emperor Ming motioned to a council member, at which point the curtain parted. Fang stepped through and took her place beside her husband. "Now what is the significance of the dragon on my robe and the phoenix on the robe of the empress?"

"A dragon is the male and the yang of your philosophy," Ardeshir said. "The phoenix is the female and yin of your philosophy."

Emperor Ming stood. "From now on, it is declared that only the emperor will wear all twelve ornaments. Councilors, dukes, and princes may wear nine and others may wear seven. So it is decreed."

"You are indeed a wise and just emperor to help your people see truth and help them avoid confusion."

"What brings you to my kingdom?" Emperor Ming asked.

"I bring horses to honor and strengthen you," Ardeshir said. "Many in the west once thought that the kingdoms of the Wei, the Chu, the Zhao, the Qi, the Qin, and the Yan were stronger than you while your territories were at war. Your leaders have proved themselves, but this world only respects those who remain strong. The Wei continue to be known for their military skill and strong fortifications. The Chu are rich in resources and population. The Zhao are famous for their cavalry and military. The Qi are known for their commerce, sea trade, and learning. The legacy of the Qin is still vibrant and their warlords dangerous. The Yan's warriors guard your frontiers. If you can keep them all united, your legacy will be powerful. Our horses will help you guard your borders, enforce your justice, and administer your territories."

"And what benefit will there be for you?"

"Your strength will develop your mines, your silk, and your pottery. Many westerners want what you're making and Persia is right on the road to Rome. Our caravans can deliver the items you love from the west, and in return we can take your items back."

"In this way, you hope to empty the pockets of Rome." The emperor glowered. "And us."

"I hope to protect all that you wish to offer the rest of the world," Ardeshir said. "I too must keep a strong army to stop Rome from marching in our direction."

"Tell me again what the west would desire of ours and what we might want from the west."

Ardeshir unrolled a strip of vellum he had carried here in the confines of his robe. "You have teas, dyes, spices, porcelains, paper, medicines, and black fire powder that will be greatly desired. From us, you may welcome vessels made from glass. You may want textiles, animal furs, fruits, honey, live animals, rugs, blankets, armor, and better saddles for your horses."

Emperor Ming stood, signaling the end of the meeting.

"Our ministers will confer," the emperor announced. He then turned to Lu Hou. "You look like your mother."

Having said that, he walked back through the curtain.

The horse exhibition went better than Yas could have imagined. The most powerful leaders of two nations had come together to demonstrate the beauty of the majestic animals on display.

"They are heavenly indeed," Yas remarked from the side of the dais as she watched the horses parade through the arena.

Ardeshir nodded with an absent look in his eye. "Yes, but I can't wait to get home. Lu Hou will finally have her chance to talk with her brother tomorrow. Then, as soon as our ministers finish the trade talks, we can get on the road." He smiled at her. "I'm sure you'll be so glad to get out of this place, too."

"I'm not going," Yas announced, not daring to look at him. She kept her eyes trained on the horses.

"What do you mean?" Ardeshir asked, his eyes wide with surprise. "They brought you here like an animal. They gave you a death sentence! Not to mention, you're giving birth to a future prince of Persia."

"I'll be giving birth to a son of the Han. Liu is going to stay here as the advisor to the empress and I'll be in charge of the training and care of the emperor's horses. You see how beautiful they all are. It would be a shame to leave them here without anyone nearby who knows how to work with them."

"But there are others we could send," Ardeshir protested. "You belong with me. In Persia."

"Lu Hou belongs with you," Yas said. "Don't you see? Part of the Han dynasty will sit on the throne in Persia and part of the Persian dynasty will influence the throne here. By having you there, and me here, we'll link the arms of our nations and ensure a lasting peace and prosperity."

Ardeshir momentarily seemed at a loss for words. "Once I'm enthroned in Persia, I won't be able to travel back and forth with the caravans. If I leave without you, we may never see each other again."

Tears streamed down her face as she finally turned and reached for her brother. "It is the sacrifice we must make. For us and for our children."

"We'll delay our departure," Ardeshir decided. "I'll send the others back and keep a small force to accompany me in a small trade caravan. My boys need to know you, the greatest warrior Persia has ever produced. They must know that their aunt is a champion like their grandfather."

"I only wish my child could know his uncle," Yas said. "You are a righteous and loyal leader, a wise ruler, a brother any sister would love to die for."

"I only want you to live," Ardeshir said.

"You came for me," Yas said, her tears streaming faster. "You came for me."

Ardeshir cried for the first time. Releasing his mother had demanded stoicism. His father's death in battle beside him had left him numb and in shock. But waving goodbye to Yas tore his heart in two. He knew there was more to her story than she was willing to share, but he also knew he was helpless to change anything. The hug of desperation they exchanged signaled a choice of will, not desire.

As he sat in his saddle, following the carriage that carried Lu Hou and the boys, he looked back towards the palace. The sight of Yas grew smaller and smaller until she was little more than a speck among the trees and foliage.

Still, he looked.

His parting hug with Liu had been one of long friendship and the shared knowledge that they may never have another moment like it. He knew he couldn't blame his friend for his separation from his sister. He also knew that his friend had sacrificed his sister to save himself.

Vardanes charged up to him with a smile. "You have done it, King of Kings. You've united our people, worked out a trade deal with the Han, and are leading us back to take your rightful place on the throne."

There was no smile in his own heart. "I'm going to need someone to lead my armies, and I can see no better warrior than you. Lead us home."

Kamnaskires rode by with a wave. "You are truly the one our nation needs," he called.

"If that's true," Ardeshir replied, "I'll need someone to protect the throne and organize our nation into one people. I am calling on you to do that."

"What about Bithisarea and the Magi?" Kamnaskires asked.

"The Magi are the Magi," Ardeshir said. "They'll show up and do what they do. We can only be who we are where we are."

"Then today we are Persians opening up the world," Kamnaskires shouted. "What we're doing will change people all over the earth in ways we can't even understand yet."

"May it be so," Ardeshir said quietly, almost to himself. "May it be so."

About the Author

J ack A. Taylor (PhD) grounds his novels in solid historical research and real-life characters. His eighteen years in Kenya, current work in Rwanda, and twenty-five years in cross-cultural ministry keep him globally aware and connected. He and his wife Gayle live outside Vancouver, Canada and have been married for forty-seven years. They have four children and eleven grandchildren. Jack is an award-winning author with Faithwriters and writes monthly for Light Magazine and other publications (www.jackataylor.com). He has helped found nine organizations, including the New Hope Community Services Society, which has provided housing for more than eight hundred fifty refugees from sixty countries. He is a credentialed marriage coach and focuses on helping leadership couples when he isn't writing (www.1heartcoaching.com). He has master's degrees in leadership, counseling, and theology, plus his PhD in counseling. Jack's hobbies include raising tropical fish and reading.

One Last Wave

Katrina [Katie] Joy Delancey has staked her life on keeping the past and future away from her heart. But she is no master of fate or captain of her own journey. A near fatal race with a wild stallion, an unexpected discovery of lost African journals, and a chance encounter with a tae kwon do master, leads Katie through love, grief, faith and terror like she's never known it.

One Last Wave is a story about being discovered by faith and love no matter where you are, no matter where you've been, and no matter what you think may lie ahead.

No Place to Run

Pushed to her limits, Katie Delancey stands at the pinnacle of a bridge. Growing up as a missionary kid changes nothing now. Witness protection has failed her. The determined human trafficking ring has tracked her down. A continent away from her fiancé, she is wooed by a 'wolf in sheep's clothing' and trapped. Weary and vulnerable from losing her mother to cancer, the upcoming wedding of her sister, the loss of her horse, the needs of the refugees she loves, and the constant surveillance of the police, she has no place to run. When you haven't got a prayer where do you turn? Katie is about to find out.

No Place to Run is the second novel in an adventure about rediscovering faith, hope and love when the maze of life seems to close all exits. It is a story about how the whispers of the past can be keys to our future. It is a tale about how the illusions of the obvious may be sinister traps designed to destroy us.

Stretching for Home

A blissful love nest amidst a brutal Minnesota winter turns into a fiery ordeal of grief and terror as Katie is caught up in the never-ending pursuit of human traffickers who want to eliminate her from their deadly game. Isolated and forced to go undercover with the RCMP, the gambit almost backfires. Escaping to Africa doesn't release her from the trail of death relentlessly pursuing her.

Stretching for Home is an education into the heart of missionary kids searching for healing as life tumbles in around them. Their quest for home can be as elusive as a rainbow's pot of gold. Finding old roots and spreading new wings can be a challenge.

The Cross Maker

First-century Palestine is a hotbed of political, cultural, and religious intrigue. Caleb ben Samson, a carpenter from Nazareth, and Sestus Aurelius, a Roman centurion, both want peace. Can this unlikely partnership accomplish what nothing else has accomplished before? Can they bring about peace through the power of the cross? And what role will Caleb's childhood friend Yeshi play in a land that longs for hope?

In *The Cross Maker*, Jack Taylor weaves a tapestry of creative history, powerful characters, and dynamic dialogue to bring to life a shadowy world. In a land where tragedy is as common as dust, triumph is about to make itself known.

The Cross Maker's Guardian

Roman legions thunder across first-century Palestine, seeking to use the power of the cross to crush the lightning strikes of the zealots led by Barabbas. Behind the scenes, a secret squad of thespian assassins are being trained—and Titius Marcus Julianus is caught up in this silent whirlwind, conscripted to be the new guardian of the cross maker, Caleb ben Samson.

Titius is fuelled by vengeance and love as he seeks to regain his stolen Roman estate and the young Jewish slave who once captured his heart. Meanwhile, voices from his past and present wrestle for control of his heart and mind.

In *The Cross Maker's Guardian*, Jack A. Taylor unveils the clash between the Roman and Jewish civilizations as they battle for life in a world suffused with international intrigue. Descriptive narrative, biblical history, and powerful characters all come alive in this thrilling read where death and love are only a blink away.

The Cross Maker's Champion

Persian slaves who fight for their lives in gladiator arenas rarely rise to be anyone's champion. But the wounded Nabonidus is soon wooed by two women—a priestess at the Temple of Artemis and a humble follower of Yeshua, Daphne. Soon he must learn the truth about himself—is he a missing Persian prince or simply an unwanted orphan?

The arena claims whatever soul may venture there, and Demetrius, a silversmith, joins forces with a giant German giant gladiator, Selsus, to confront the followers of the Way.

Meanwhile, Caleb, Suzanna, Titius, and Abigail fight through their own life-threatening challenges to join the apostle John and Nabonidus in time. Soon the arena will be packed with chanting patrons. Who will still remain standing when the final blood is spilt?

Jack A. Taylor weaves his readers through a maze of Ephesian mysticism and terror as Roman and pagan powers combine to destroy the infant movement of the Way before it takes its first steps out of its birthplace.

Honest Conversations on Thriving through Conflict

When Ministry and Marriage Collide

Over twenty-five percent of marriages among today's ministry leaders face significant struggle and strain. The demands and temptations of our public and private worlds often create a tension that pushes our love relationships to the breaking point. Through honest conversations with seven couples, Jack A. Taylor reveals five quagmires that can capture the souls of dedicated leaders.

Areas like Identity, Attachment, Calling, Family, and Intimacy can seem straightforward until you're stuck in the challenges they present. *When Ministry and Marriage Collide* provides over fifty practical tools to help strugglers move from striving to thriving. Ideally, this work is designed to be paired with a relationship coach (see 1heartcoaching.com), but it is sufficient on its own to produce significant conversations with anyone willing to delve into the roots of their challenges.

Based on crucial training from the Thriving Relationship Center, readers will discover the five stages of thriving relationship growth and six foundational pillars for healthy intimacy and communication. After the vows—in the middle of real life—investing in your most important earthly relationship is vital to avoid becoming another statistic. While the couples described here are fictional composites, the issues they deal with are anything but imaginary.

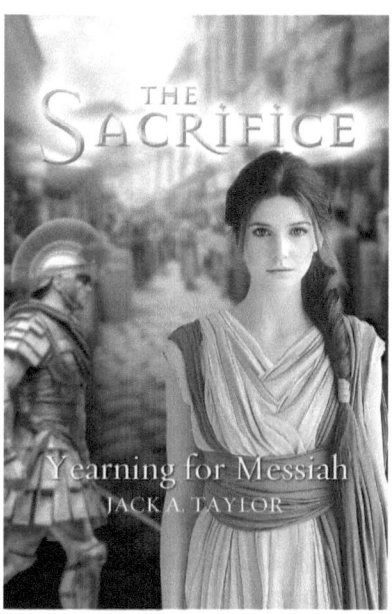

The Sacrifice

The Temple of Jerusalem was recognized as one of the seven wonders of the ancient world, but how did it rise out of the rubble of social chaos, international intrigue, family mutiny, and a passionate quest for the Messiah?

How did two simple servants of Yahweh linger through bloodshed and traumatic leadership changes to remain standing when the day of the Messiah's arrival finally came?

In a place dedicated to sacrifice, there was one sacrifice no one expected. This is the untold story of the years before the event that forever changed the course of world history.

The Persian Prince and the Han Princess

Ardeshir ben Nabonidus lives in the shadow of his father, an accomplished gladiator—indeed, the Roman emperor's champion—who accomplished thirty kills to secure his freedom and release him to pursue his identity as the Prince of Persia. Struggling to find his identity in a world that overlooks him, young Ardeshir finds himself exiled on a trade mission to the far east, fueled by a single mantra that pushes him forward: "The Way is the way."

At the palace of the Han emperor, Ardeshir seems to have nothing but a common gardener for a friend. But when he saves the life of the emperor's daughter, everything goes topsy-turvy. His love for the princess soon escalates into an intense conflict with a diabolical general, and his man-eating leopard, who is intent on securing the princess's affections for himself.

www.ingramcontent.com/pod-product-compliance
Lightning Source LLC
Chambersburg PA
CBHW031223260626
47169CB00007B/2167